DON'T ASK IF I'M OKAY

JESSICA KARA

PAGE STREET YA

NOT ALL THOSE WHO WANDER ARE LOST
. . . BUT SOME OF THEM ARE.
THIS BOOK IS FOR YOU.
I HOPE YOU KEEP WALKING.

IT'S NOT EASY TO MARRY condiments when you're also monitoring a potential thief, but I've been doing both for so long, it's mostly muscle memory.

I angle one ketchup bottle into the open mouth of another and squeeze while I watch the kid, Colby. I'm anxious to leave and technically we're still open, but if he weren't here, I could've locked up by now.

He pokes around the chocolate bars and magazines at the far end of the diner, keeping me in the corner of his vision. I try to summon patience. He's thirteen or so and I graduated last spring, so I don't know him well, but I know him well enough. I knew one of his older brothers from school until he dropped out. I know of his family's reputation. His dad, in particular.

That's how it is in a small town: you know people, even if you don't *know* them. You notice things. I only remember his name because it's a kind of cheese.

His mess of loose brown curls is mostly stuffed under a beanie and his clothes are my old classmate's clothes, so they're too big and they're worn out and they don't suit him. Those things aren't his fault. It's why I haven't busted him or even accused him of anything yet even though he puts something in his pocket every time he comes into Nan's Newsstand. I just try to get in his way.

I'm protective of the diner. I've worked here since I was practically Colby's age, sweeping, stocking, busing, washing dishes, until grumpy old Andy finally trusted me with cooking.

So I watch everything, including the Snickers bar Colby's been carrying around for five minutes, waiting for me to get distracted. I want to tell him to get lost and not come back. But it's hard to be an authoritative dick over candy bars when you know someone's life sucks.

It's ten minutes to close and we're the only ones in here, so he's running out of excuses to hang around and I'm sure he can tell I'm ready to leave. I twist the cap back on the ketchup, wipe both bottles clean, and move on to the mustard.

The quaint old-town lamppost outside illuminates flakes of falling snow, fat and soft in the amber light. The other restaurants and bars are just getting warmed up. A couple of skiers down from the hill peer into the diner, check their watches, the sign, then me, hopefully. Nan's is one of the best places to come downtown, an old-school burger joint with magazines along one wall, bins of candy for sale by the pound, milkshakes, malts. Travel bloggers have written about our burgers—at least, they have for the last couple of years, since I've been on the grill. But we're really more of a lunch and early-bird spot.

I shake my head at the tourists, tap my wrist as if I actually wear a watch, and they walk on, pointing out other dinner options to each other.

Colby flips through a *Car and Driver* magazine. His foot taps the floor to the current song, and the sound wakes a familiar rhythmic clicking in the back of my brain. *Tck tck. Tck tck.* I shove it away, focusing on the mustard.

His foot taps.

The soft flicker of frustration and impatience in my chest warms to anger. "Can you stop that?"

He looks at me. "What?"

I glare at him. "Tapping your foot, can you stop please?"

"Uh. Sure." He stops. Flips the magazine one-handed. Still holding the Snickers bar.

My gaze drifts to the clock: 6:55 p.m. Usually I'd wait him out, but I have someplace to be.

I wish Hunter were here.

The thought shoots like an arrow out of nowhere, pierces my chest and seizes my breath. My fist spasms, clenches, mustard splatters all over the condiment caddies and table, and I bark a word Mom would not approve of.

Colby startles and looks at me. I suck in a quick breath. Hunter would think of a brilliant way to kick Colby out but make it nice. Like throwing gummy bears at him, one at a time, until he took the hint.

Or Hunter would buy the candy for him, because Hunter was the best person I knew, better than anyone, better than me. Merlin to my Arthur, Obi-Wan to my Anakin. Aragorn to my Boromir. Especially that. My brother, my captain.

Heat and moisture swarm my eyes and I press my thumb and forefinger against them, heart pounding. It'll be a year, next week. A year without my best friend. We should've been born twins, but we were born cousins instead, a day apart, and grew up next door to each other. Hunter and Gage forever.

Our friends called us *Gunter*, like a celebrity couple. Hunter loved it. We watched too many of our friends grow apart after middle school, competing for everything, and we vowed that wouldn't be us. We kept each other's secrets and stayed tight and stayed honest, honoring our blood and our history.

I don't know anyone else with a friend like that.

Not even me, anymore.

I stare at the mustard mess, breathing hard, skin buzzing, and press my palms against the cool red tabletop, letting my head hang while I compose myself.

Colby busts up laughing like a little donkey. "Nice."

Rage blazes across my whole body and it's all I can do not to flip the table, to roar at him to get out and never come back, to ask how many candy bars he's stolen and if he knows how many people are nice to him when they don't have to be. To ask why he can't sort himself out or steal from people in his own town. The miserable little punk.

But I don't. My own anger shocks me and I take a deep breath. This isn't right.

My hurt isn't his fault. I don't care about a worthless candy bar. I know real loss now, and how it feels and how it changes who you are, and how it sets everything in your life into its proper place. *Priorities*, as my stepdad, Jack, would say.

My priorities are strictly ordered now, knowing every day could be the last day I see someone. Or the last day they see me.

I don't know what Colby's priorities are, but that Snickers is worth something to him, and it's meaningless to me. Stealing isn't. The principle of the thing is a big deal. But knowing about Colby's meth-addicted dad is bigger, and seeing him wear clothes that aren't his, and knowing people stare, waiting for him to do something bad because his family is bad—that's a big deal.

I stand tall and square my shoulders—which gets his attention because I'm a big guy and my mom's distant Italian heritage gave me dark eyes and hair so I can give a hard, stern look when I need to. I stare him down until the grin leaves his face and his gaze darts between me and the door. His sweaty, spindly pale hand is probably melting the Snickers bar.

"Are you hungry?" My voice catches and I swallow, but I raise my eyebrows inquiringly.

Colby jerks as if I threw something at him. "What?"

Any remnants of the anger drain from my body, leaving me tired and raw. As I return to this moment, the shadow of Hunter shrinks back in approval and I can act okay again.

It's time for me to be okay. I just don't know how. But I can try by not making my problem Colby's problem.

"Do you want a burger?" I flip my cleaning towel over my shoulder and lean forward to grip the back of the diner chair so he doesn't see my hands shaking. Sam Cooke serenades us from the speakers tucked into the corners of the diner. It's been the same music here for as long as I've been alive, and we aren't allowed to change it lest we face Andy's wrath. I imagine it's the same music since Nan's opened, when those songs topped the charts and chrome trim was the hot new thing. Every song that was popular from 1950 to 1967 is woven into the fabric of my brain for all eternity.

"A burger?" he asks, as if he doesn't know what that is.

"Yeah, a cheeseburger? Do you want one? I've got to go soon, but I can make you something."

His face screws up in suspicion. I look at the candy bar, then his face, and he flushes red. "I don't have any money."

I shrug. "That's okay. I got it."

He looks weirded out, but I'm not worried about his opinion of me. "Why?"

I feel like he's not going to pocket the Snickers now, so I tug the towel from my shoulder and focus on cleaning up the mustard. "I have leftover meat I have to cook, and I want to use a new cheese Andy won't let me try on the regulars." The first half is a lie, the second is not. He doesn't answer. I shrug, finish cleaning, walk to the door to flip the sign to Closed, and tug the chain that turns off the neon Open in the window. "If you want something, sit down. If you don't, you have to go." I tap the door.

He looks at the falling snow and wipes his free hand on his pants. He doesn't live here in Clark, but a few miles away in an unincorporated map dot called Spruce Falls. There's a lot of jokes about Spruce Falls and the people who live and work there, and I feel rotten for even letting them come to mind, looking at this kid now. We're not any better than them just because Clark is closer to the ski hill. We just have more money in the town.

The dislike is mutual. They think we're yuppies, we think they're hicks, and in some ways we're both right. But we all live and work together and a single bus connects us, which is amazing. It's not typical in northern Idaho. Not enough people for real public transit. But it bridges the gap.

The funny thing is *Spruce Falls* sounds like a prettier town, and tourists always ask if there's anything to do there, and about the waterfall, which doesn't exist.

Sure, we say. Plenty to do. If you like the smell of a paper mill. Or watching weeds grow.

I'm sure the things they say about us are worse. What snobs we are, with our steak houses and "expresso" shops and a real bookstore.

Maybe I am a yuppie and I don't know it.

During his silence after my ultimatum, I realize Colby's been waiting for that bus in the one place that will let him sit around inside at this hour and not buy something.

Finally he tosses the Snickers on top of the bin of peach gummy rings as if he never wanted it, and slouches to the counter to sit on one of the round red stools.

"Sure, I guess."

"Cool."

He spins idly on the stool while I head behind the counter to the grill—my solace, my altar to all that is good and true in this world—but pause to text my friend Imogen.

Me: I'm going to be twenty minutes late to the meeting. Start without me.

Imogenesis: :(Everything okay? Want a ride?

A wry smile stretches my mouth and I shake my head.

Me: I'm okay. Just a late customer. And I'll walk, but thanks.

Imogenesis: You sure?

Me: It's only a mile. It's a beautiful night :))

Imogenesis: :/ I had to try.

Dicing onions, selecting crisp leaves of lettuce, and peeling two fresh, pockmarked slices of Havarti from the stack I picked up at the deli brings me level again.

Food is a miracle. Cooking for people is a true pleasure, a powerful alchemy, and the best act of service I can think of. I have loved everything about making food since Mom let me play with the measuring spoons when I was still in diapers. Maybe filling Colby's ungrateful stomach will help us both for a few minutes. I can't believe I almost cried in front of him.

The snow falls in a dizzying curtain outside. Winter is my time. Dark, cold, muffled, shrouded. It suits my mood.

I nudge the onions around in a pat of butter on the flat-top grill, then let them sit while I form the patty, smash it thin, and spread a layer of mustard on top. Efficient, but unhurried. You can't hurry good food, and my friends already know I'll be late.

I wasn't lying to Imogen. I will enjoy the walk. She'll keep trying anyway, even though she knows I don't drive. She knows I don't ride in cars. Everyone knows I haven't gotten inside a car since last winter when a drunk driver drove Hunter and me off the road.

I slap the meat on the grill with an immediate, satisfying sizzle.

The savory scent of cooking beef, sharp tangy onions, and frying mustard almost clouds the memory of headlights coming our way, Hunter jerking the wheel, the stomach-swallowing spin on the ice. Almost.

Outside of Nan's, a car turns the corner and headlights crawl over our front picture windows. I close my eyes. Too late. The shadow lunges around me—the shriek of studded tires against ice, the horrifying spin, the Honda smashing into a tree. The sharp shock of my head hitting glass.

A metallic, rhythmic ticking brought me awake to stare at the trickle of blood on Hunter's temple. It took a minute to understand what had happened, to shout at him, shout his name, and when I realized he wasn't going to wake up, to start screaming like an animal. Staring into the lifeless eyes of my best friend, incoherent when I finally managed to dial 911, screaming. Screaming until my throat was raw. His turn signal was jammed on the whole time. *Tck tck. Tck tck.*

I stare hard at the grill, flip the patty, claw my brain back to the diner. Carefully, I layer two slices of the beautiful Havarti cheese on top, then the onions, to melt the cheese and let the flavor soak in. Focusing on making the burger perfect keeps me present, and I have to be present, here, now.

The only other option is to crumple to the floor and start screaming all over again, and that doesn't do anyone any good, not even me.

I MANAGE TO WAIT UNTIL COLBY has picked off my perfectly grilled onions and stuffed half the cheeseburger in his face before asking, "Well?"

His eyes lift to mine. He swallows, glancing side to side. "Uh. Thank you?"

"You're welcome, but do you like it?" I've boxed the shadow of Hunter back to his corner in my brain. *Not here. Not now.* Not ever. He's gone and I cannot have another breakdown, not a year later. There's a time limit on grief no one talks about. People say to take as long as you need, but they don't mean it. After a few months, I could tell people were weary of me being sad, or thinking about it, or letting it run my life.

"Yeah, it's good." Colby wipes his mouth on his sleeve. I drop a stack of napkins by his plate and draw him a Sprite from the fountain.

"I meant the cheese, specifically."

"It's good," he says again, and I withhold a sigh. Apparently, I'll have to try it on a different critic for a more in-depth review. I guess I could do worse than "it's good." My favorite chef, Michael Andrus—who's traveled the world, has five cookbooks on my shelf, and owns a dozen restaurants in six countries—says you shouldn't worry about what people say about your food, but how they eat it. That's their real opinion.

Aside from the onions, Colby digs into the burger with gusto. So I'll take that as a win.

"Well, thanks. Hang tight. I have to clean up, then we're both leaving, okay?"

He nods and eats while I shut down things in the diner. I leave a note for Andy to count the cash in the morning because I don't want to do it in front of Colby. One last wipe-down of the tables, turn off the music, the lights, the various neon signs on the walls. I have a route around the diner that's in my bones. I could do it eyes closed.

Now it's lighter outside than in here and for a second I enjoy the scene. The glittery white lights in the trees, the streetlamps, the snow that catches the light and makes everything brighter, the shuffle of people along the powdery sidewalks. Hunter used to hang out with me until close some nights, and we'd walk home together.

I try to remember what it was like to look at things without thinking about him, but I can't.

Colby follows me obediently to the door and out. I rarely leave through the front, but I'm not taking him out the back. The scent of frost and cooking food permeates the air—steak, pizza, fish. Laughter and the soft crunch of cars rolling in fresh snow fill the avenue.

"Bus will be here in a few minutes." I lock the door, then tug on my gloves. "Are you okay to wait?"

Colby shoves his bare hands into his pockets, looking up the street. "Yeah."

"Unless you want to come with me to this meeting."

He looks up, eyes narrow. "What meeting?"

I point, although the bowling alley is a mile away and he can't see it. "Just some friends and I who meet up a couple of times a month and talk about stuff."

His mouth screws up tight. "What, like church?"

Surprise and his expression make me laugh, and he startles again, like a skittish cat. "Not really. Just a group we made a few years ago." I don't go into details. He's already on edge and I don't even know why I invited him. Except that's the purpose of the group. For people who feel alone. I'm supposed to be leading it and I'm late, but it's important to get Colby's attention, to let him know he's seen. It's what Hunter would do. Hunter would stay right there and talk to him for an hour until he saw new possibilities for his life.

"What is it then?"

I pull out my wallet and one of the stickers we printed, a cool logo Imogen drew of silver wolves tucked around a star. Worked into the design are the letters *LWDA*.

Colby steps close to see the sticker in the lamplight, and I can tell he wants it. Who doesn't want a badass sticker with wolves on it? But he's sharp, and wary.

"What's LWDA?"

"You should check it out. We meet every other Tuesday at seven thirty, at the bowling alley." Strawberry Lanes is the only bowling alley from here to Coeur d'Alene, so it's not like he won't know where to go.

He shuffles his feet and shrugs as snowflakes coat us. "I have to go home. Maybe next week."

"Week after next." I gesture a rolling motion. "Every other Tuesday."

"Okay." He finally takes the sticker and turns it over in his fingers. "What's it stand for? LWDA?"

I meet his gaze, man-to-man, and smile in challenge. "Come sometime and find out."

MOUNTAIN MUGS IS ONE OF HALF A DOZEN PLACES TO GET coffee downtown, but the only one that stays open until nine, and it's on the way to the bowling alley.

I'm late, but I need some energy so I can keep it together around my friends. Almost losing it in front of Colby was bad enough.

A bell jingles over the door to announce my entry, there's a line, and every table is stuffed with people. I stomp snow from my boots and take my place behind the last person, head low, arms crossed, glancing around. Mostly couples, skiers, tourists. It's good to not see too many people I know. They often get this wary look around me, around my family. Not as much now, but when Hunter first died, as if they didn't know what to do or say. I guess they didn't. None of us did. I still don't.

The line inches forward and the clatter of dishes and the hiss and whining grind of the espresso machine beats back my mood. I brace for an interaction with Aiden, who's usually working Tuesdays. He's a couple years older and always asks more questions than I want to answer, cheerfully probing, as if his parents always tell him to ask about my family.

I'm thinking about Aiden and about how I'm not sure about using Havarti on the burgers after all because we like to keep it classic and simple, how I wish Colby had given me an actual opinion, and how I'm going to stop almost melting down in public.

So when I get to the counter, I'm startled to discover it's not Aiden standing there.

It's a girl. A stranger with a sweet, bright smile, warm rosy skin, sparkly pink lip gloss, and bright brown eyes. A knitted white beanie is tucked over brown curls that fall just below her ears. She's wearing a Mountain Mugs apron over a fuzzy pink sweater and leggings, and everything about her looks round and soft and welcoming.

I've never seen her before in my life. I glance over my shoulder, then back to her bright customer-service smile.

"Hi!" She twirls her pen. "What can we get you?"

I can't even remember the coffee I wanted.

"Where's Aiden?" Immediately I realize how rude and gruff the question is, but she's caught me off guard. It's too late to take it back, though.

She tucks a curl under her hat. "You know, you're the third person to ask that tonight, but I think he slipped his tracking collar, so I couldn't say."

It takes me a second, then I want to laugh, but my eyes have now informed the rest of my body about her loveliness, the curves in her sweater and leggings and her curious little smile.

My brain is busy with all that, so I skip the laugh even after I've gotten the joke. "Sorry, I, uh . . . I meant, it's nice to see a nice face. A new face." I motion to her while my brain explodes with profanity. What am I even saying? It's like I've never seen a pretty girl before. "Someone prettier than Aiden, I mean."

She laughs, checking me up and down. I can't tell if she likes what she sees. "Thanks. It's hard to be prettier than Aiden, so I'll take that as a compliment." Now that she's spoken more, it's clear she's my age, or near it, which makes sense. Teens run the downtown after hours, for the most part. The souvenir shops that stay open late, the waitstaff, this place. Taking the hours old people don't want.

"Um." I forget why I'm standing there.

She leans forward conspiratorially and lowers her voice. "What can I get you?"

Her cheeks are soft and pink with the warmth of the coffee shop and my heart crawls up to my throat. I was not prepared to meet someone like this tonight and I almost turn and walk right out. She's so fresh and new and she doesn't know any of the sad things and she's looking at me like I'm intriguing. Or maybe annoying.

I'm holding up the line.

"Uh." I rub my forehead and manage a smile I hope makes me look less random. This is not me. "Sorry. Large Americano with four shots. Please."

"Wow. Big plans tonight?" She plucks a cup from the stack and checks the boxes.

"I don't really sleep." I remember to dig out my wallet.

"Huh." She rings in the order, looking me over again. Warmth creeps up my neck and face. "Wonder why."

Her mouth purses and she cocks her head, batting her eyes, teasing.

A smile whispers over my mouth and fades. I can't exactly tell her that when I sleep, I get to relive the accident that killed my best friend in warped, explicit detail. "I just have a lot to do."

"Guess so," she says. Intrigued? Annoyed? I still can't tell. I just try not to stare as she continues. "It's four twenty-five. What name should we call for the order?"

"Gage."

She takes my money, then writes *Gabe* on the cup. I almost let it go because there's three impatient people behind me.

But I want her to know my name. "It's, uh . . ."—I point at the cup—"it's Gage."

She looks at the cup, then at me, with her brown eyes. "Gage?"

"Yeah, with a *g*."

"I'm so sorry." She grins and turns the whole incorrect name into an artful collection of swirls and flowers in five seconds like it's nothing, before writing my actual name on the cup.

I form another smile. "And . . . you?"

"I'm Olivia. With an *O*." She traces a circle in the air, then brushes curls from her cheek. A spark of amusement pops colorfully in my brain. Is she flirting? Am I? I had one girlfriend in high school and we'd known each other growing up, so it was never a question, just happened for a while until we figured out we were better off as friends. It wasn't this feeling of uncertainty and thrill.

"Olivia." I nod, rolling my shoulders, trying to be

something other than an inarticulate lump dripping melting snow on the floor. She's smiling at me, at least. "Nice to meet you. So . . . have a nice night."

"You too, thanks." Her gaze lifts meaningfully to the line behind me.

I have nothing charming to add, and retreat. The chatter and steam and noise cluster close, more over-whelming than comforting now.

My brain babbles. *She's pretty, she's so pretty and nice and I don't know who she is*—then it's Hunter's voice, not mine. *Go for it, oh my God, find out who she is, Ranger mode, man, come on.* My throat locks. *Olivia. With an* O. And what a smile, dimples and everything.

A woman edges around me to get to the straws while I stare at the sugar packets and lids.

Fist clenched in my coat pocket, I crack two knuckles to ground myself, and glance over my shoulder. Olivia is sparkly and chatty with all the customers. Not just me. Of course she is. She's working.

Never hit on a woman who's working for tips or trapped behind a counter.

Jack's advice, given years ago when he noticed my new preoccupation with girls, decides it for me. My bio dad's advice amounted to "If you do anything, use a condom," which I guess is true, but less helpful. But Jack's advice is solid and Imogen has confirmed it after working at Nan's together. And I'm clearly in no shape to be talking to anyone tonight, much less a sweet girl whom I have a chance to give a better first impression to. Someone who doesn't know the sad things.

"Gage." The guy making coffee pushes my cup over;

I dump two sugars in it, tuck the lid back on, and leave, not looking back. Brisk air and snow swirl around my hot face. I realize I didn't tip. Crap. It would be an excuse to go back in, but maybe weird. Maybe I'm assuming too much. I'm not special. She was in customer-service mode. I have that mode too.

When I raise the cup to take a sip, there's a teeny smiley face inside the second *g* of my name. A unique thrill flutters in my chest—and my very first urge is to yank out my phone and tell Hunter about the encounter and send him a picture of the cup.

An ache hooks my chest so hard, I gasp in the cold air. The butterflies dissolve.

Clenching my teeth against the exhausting sorrow and aimless anger, I shoulder my way along the crowded sidewalk and finally turn off the main street, into the darker air and snow.

THE CLATTER OF TUMBLING PINS and the rumble of balls down the lanes are a comfort. The oily scent of fried food from the bar next door and the stale ghost of cigarette smoke fills the space, even though smoking's been banned indoors pretty much my whole life. Bowling shoes, cheap nacho cheese, and popcorn—the smell of my childhood and late Saturday night study sessions, and now, in the last few years, our LWDA meetings.

Olivia. With an O.

She crowds against my mood. Like a bright cloud above a dreary world. I know she's not—I know she's a person and has her own stuff going on and nobody's perfect, but I wonder if she'll ever know what that smiley face in the *g* meant to me tonight.

I keep my eyes forward to avoid the shadow of Hunter in every corner—the snack bar, the arcade, the glass door where we'd peer into the forbidden casino.

Imogen spies me and waves me over to the lane by the far wall. There's only one other group, a kid's birthday party, shrieking and running around their own corner.

I shrug out of my coat and shake the snow from it, stomp my boots, and head over to Imogen. Looks like there's only four of us tonight, and they started bowling without me. Sometimes the group is big, but as we've grown up and scattered to schools, jobs, or other priorities, the numbers have fluctuated.

Imogen trots forward for a hug and I hold my coffee wide to keep it from spilling. She's almost my height and looks like the daughter of old Norse fairies, statuesque and fair-skinned with a splash of peachy freckles, pale blue eyes, and pale hair, short and straight. Although I think she dyes it that frosty gold. I seem to remember it was reddish brown in middle school. She's engulfed in an oversized Washington State hoodie.

I wrap her in a protective bear hug. I think people were constantly surprised we never dated until she finally came out last summer, which was only a surprise to people who weren't paying attention. She, Hunter, and I read all the same books and ran around the woods together wielding sticks like swords even when we were way too old. Our shield maiden—the fearless Éowyn to our hopelessly dorky Rangers. There's a hollow space in our friendship since Hunter died, more since she left for college, but nothing will ever take away our history.

"Tourists, huh?" she asks, and after my silent trek through the snowy town, swirling in my own thoughts, I come back to reality and her asking why I'm a half hour late.

She eyes the coffee cup and I grin, shrug, and have a sip.

"No. Colby Harting was hanging around."

Her lips purse. "Did you call my dad?" Imogen's dad is a sheriff's deputy.

I glance past her to Bryson and Mia, who are looking at something on his phone, and back to Imogen. "I made him a burger."

"Of course you did." She pushes my chest. "We got nachos and we haven't done any official business since there's only us. Mia's been bowling for you."

"Oh good." I smile to keep Imogen from staring at me. She lost Hunter too, but she is doing so well, crushing it at the veterinary program at school, happy, flourishing. The last thing I want to do is make her worry or let her see me struggling.

I am the guy you lean on, figuratively and literally. Jack's veteran buddies call me a "steel marshmallow"; physically, at least. I'm solid, with the kind of husky mass I can sort of shape by running and doing push-ups, but never quite shed or shred. Reliable, resilient Gage. The guy you lean on, the guy who has it together. That's who I want to be, who I'm supposed to be. Not the guy who breaks down over hamburger patties anytime he thinks of his dead friend.

I just thought I might feel better by now.

I pass Imogen's evaluation and she releases me to head back to her seat.

Mia flicks a hand to summon me. Her family is one of only about seven Black families in Clark. She's a year younger, at eighteen, but already off to college for theater, more focused than I am. Or maybe she just needed to get out of Clark. I'm beginning to understand the feeling.

Short, wavy black hair and dangly gold earrings frame her face, and she is plump and gorgeous in a sweater dress and denim jacket, adorned in stylish, artistic accessories— all gold bracelets and patches and buttons.

One of the theater kids, Mia bonded with Imogen in junior high over cosplay and fantasy books and they have been inseparable since. When I asked Imogen if they were actually dating, she only laughed and rolled her eyes and informed me Mia is straight, but she seemed happy that I had considered the possibility. Clark can still be small-town Idaho that way.

Mia stands to hug me too, the delicate bangles on her wrists tinkling as she moves. "Time for you to come ruin my perfect score." She points to the board, where she's been rolling strikes, except just now, when she left me with a 7–10 split. I think she did it on purpose, for being late.

I put my coffee down and wrap her in a hug too, hoisting her off the ground while she laughs. I try to give comfort, not take it or cling too long, but the hugs are good and filling and as much as I try not to need them too much, I do.

Bryson watches the hug from his seat, and I tip my chin up in acknowledgment. He smiles, but then his gaze settles back on Mia with an admiration I haven't noticed before. I wonder how long he's been looking at her like that.

I set her down and she peers at me closely, too discerning. "Long day?"

"Yeah," I say, instead of telling her about almost crying at work. "I like your jacket." It's a weak dodge, but I suspect she made the jacket herself, so it's a good subject change.

She looks unimpressed, but goes along. "Thanks. It was a project in class." She pushes me gently while Bryson finally stands, and he gets a hug too.

It's mandatory, even for big former high school running backs like him—especially like him. I'm not sure what happened to half the guys in my life when we all turned thirteen and stopped hugging each other, but I never bought it. Everybody needs hugs. Especially most of the guys I know. Especially Bryson.

That's why Hunter and I made the group.

"Hey, man." I clap him on the back. "Good to see you."

"Hey, bro." His hug is tight, if brief. He was born and bred in Clark like the rest of us, but looks like he belongs on Laguna Beach or somewhere similar, golden and blond with a relaxed surfer's ease to his voice. "Thought maybe you weren't coming."

"Nope, just slow." We shove apart and he punches my arm.

"Time to call the meeting to order," Imogen says, clapping her hands. "Now that our fearless leader of the pack is here and meeting time is almost over."

I toss my coat onto the back of the bench and claim it with a sprawl. "I think if anyone's the fearless leader of the pack, it's Mia, because she always has snacks and Band-Aids."

Imogen snickers but nods sagely. Mia rolls her eyes even as she is, at that very moment, opening a bag of peanuts in the shell. "I didn't think we were that literal about the wolf thing."

Bryson flashes a grin at her and tips his head back to howl. A couple of moms from the kids' party shoot us annoyed looks, like their kids aren't all howling and screaming already.

Mia makes a scandalized scoff and smacks his leg with the bag of peanuts. Imogen laughs and drops cozily next to me, while Bryson steals the peanuts and sits again.

This is a good number, for tonight. Sometimes we have as many as ten, sometimes only a couple of us, but these three are the people I needed tonight, my core group.

Now they're looking at me. I lean forward and rub my hands together. Onward. I've got this. "Okay, okay, I call the meeting to order. Good news, bad news?"

"Good news, good news!" Mia says, as if she's been dying to start, to share. We all lean in. She sits up and presses her hand to her chest. "I got that summer position with the Idaho Shakespeare Festival."

"Oh, Mia!" Imogen leaps up and Mia hops up with her, both of them shrieking, while Bryson leans back, bewildered, and looks at me for guidance, blue eyes wide. I shrug and grin. Imogen pelts Mia with questions at a speed and octave that I don't bother trying to follow. I'll catch up later. Bryson and I gather enough to know Mia will be working as a stitcher in the costume shop, they're doing some of her favorite shows, and it's what she's wanted forever.

When the girls settle down, we all enjoy the glow of Mia's success for a minute. I have a sip of coffee and allow the thought of Olivia's smile to brush by before Bryson clears his throat.

"Good news," he says quietly. He's the kind of guy in high school you assume has everything. Tall, athletic, polite, good-looking, good grades, nice house.

Hunter saw under it, not me. Hunter paid more attention to people. Hunter started this group after we lost a classmate named Ethan four years ago.

"My dad's parole was denied," Bryson says, eyes on the floor, rubbing his knuckles. "I went to the hearing because Mom was afraid to. She didn't want to see him. But they say it helps if you go. Like, to remind everyone of the—the offense." He clears his throat.

Mia rests a hand on his back, and I lean over, offering him a fist. He bumps it with a smile and drops his gaze again.

"Good job," I say firmly.

"Hear, hear," Imogen says, raising a nacho. Her eyes are fierce and sad, but we're all proud of him. You can only take the hits for so long, before enough people start asking questions. Before the need to survive outweighs the shame and fear. Before slowly, surely, someone like Hunter gets you to admit that things are not okay.

Mia drops a peanut into Bryson's anxious hands and he looks at her gratefully, then ducks his head, fiddling with the shell without cracking it. "That's all," he says.

Once the moment settles out, Imogen says, "Not good or bad news, but I was thinking about Hunter." I close my eyes and take a drink of coffee, and the others nod. Imogen slips her hands inside the sleeves of her hoodie and hugs her arms. "It'll be a year since the crash, next week."

Mia reaches over to squeeze her arm, while memories burst through my brain and I stare hard at the golden wood of the bowling lane. Imogen talks softly, but the words don't come through as my heart rate picks up.

Over at the kids' party, a boy laughs and shrieks and I lift my gaze to that group.

We came to this dank, old, beloved bowling alley for

Hunter's thirteenth birthday. The older I got, the more I appreciated that Mom and Aunt Gina always gave us each a birthday celebration instead of lumping them together, although we probably wouldn't have cared. Hunter almost got us kicked out for running up the lanes and knocking pins over.

I've been doing my best *not* to think about Hunter, but I can see that's going to be impossible here. Maybe anywhere. And it's not fair to the others.

I fight the urge to double over and cry. But Imogen is already teary-eyed, and I need Bryson to know I have it together if he needs something, and Mia to see I'm strong enough to lead the group. People have comforted me enough.

"Gage?" Mia crosses the booth to sit close on my other side. "Should we do something?"

I force myself to sit up. "Do something?" Bryson stays where he is, watching me with a frown.

"Get together or something? A memorial?"

My throat cinches shut and I rub my eyes, then clap my hands together to startle myself and them out of the shadow clumping around me. "Yeah. Let me think about it."

Mia watches me closely. "We don't have to."

"No, we should. You guys are going back to school soon and it'll be the last year of firsts." First birthdays without Hunter. First summer without him to camp, swim, or hike with; first Halloween, first Christmas, first everything with the empty space where he was. All those dates, and now this.

Imogen rests her head on my shoulder. "Are you okay?"

Words stampede across my mind and out again, unspoken. *No. I miss him. I love him. I'm not okay.*

26

"Yeah," I manage. "Just thinking about it. I miss him."
I share that scrap, and Bryson makes a quiet, supportive sound. I segue roughly. "Good news, though. I invited Colby Harting to a meeting and he didn't run screaming."

They stare at me a second for that randomness, and I shrug, stretching an arm around Imogen's shoulders. I don't know what else they want me to say. Mia squeezes my arm before going back to her seat and toying with her bangles.

Imogen tucks a knee to her chest. "And you fed him."

"Someone needs to," Bryson mutters. "Is he going to come?"

"I don't know." I try not to sound too relieved they've willingly switched to talking about Colby. "But he'll probably try to get another free burger out of me."

"I think it's so cool you cook," Mia says. I'm eternally grateful for her managing to make my awkward subject changes relevant. "That you really like it. Any word on jobs?"

I smile with a shrug. I stopped applying for schools and jobs when Hunter died, when my life stopped. "Nah," I fib. I've had word. A stack of responses. She frowns in sympathy and I shake my head. "It's okay."

Bryson's eyes flick to Mia's admiring face. "You like that? When dudes cook?"

"I like it when people have basic life skills, yes." Her mouth quirks and she pops a peanut into her mouth, gaze sliding away mischievously. Bryson frowns, sorting his way through that.

"I find it ironic," Imogen says, "that some people still consider cooking a woman's job when it's really hard for women to break into the industry, and most of the top chefs in the world are men."

Red touches Bryson's cheeks. He looks to me, so I nod. She's right, but Bryson isn't always prepared to hear about things outside his realm of experience. Sometimes the cost of being heard and seen is cracking open your own worldview to see and hear everyone else, too. "I didn't say it was a woman's job. Just that——"

"Hey, man." I punch his knee again, playfully. "You think my food is girly?"

"What's wrong with being girly?" Mia inquires, and I get a peanut to the side of the head.

"Nothing, ow." I grab the peanut and throw it right back at her.

"I like girly!" Bryson says quickly, glancing between us to gauge where the teasing ends and the listening begins. "I was just asking. I think it's awesome."

His bewilderment makes me laugh. He's trying so hard. But he's a good guy, trying to break a generational curse of abuse. He's here, and that's good. Hunter invited him, and I was amazed he came—we weren't exactly in the same social circles. But sometimes it only takes one person reaching out. Asking if you're okay. Seeing you. No one saw Ethan until it was too late. We weren't close, but we wanted to try to keep anyone else from going down that road.

"Gage?" Imogen nudges me. "Any more good news, bad news?"

I think of mentioning Olivia, but I don't know if she's news yet and I can't handle a lot of questions, so I shake my head. "Things are good."

We all look at each other. I look at them, trying to

make sure they're *really* okay, because we naturally wrap ourselves around our weaknesses and pain so we don't stand out in the pack. Even here we do. People were shocked when Ethan took his own life. But when you look at all the pieces together, it wasn't shocking at all. So I'm always on the lookout for the weakest member of the pack. Whoever needs the most help. It fluctuates between us. Everyone seems good tonight, even with the mention of Hunter.

I sit forward and stretch my hand out, into the center of the circle of us. "Then I declare this meeting done, and time for some bowling."

Imogen rests her hand on mine, Mia presses hers over Imogen's, and Bryson's big hand tops us off.

"Thanks for coming." I make a point of meeting their eyes. "For sharing."

"And caring," Mia says with a wry grin. The rhyme is cheesy, but the truth of it binds us. Hunter made it silly so we would always smile.

"And why do we come together?" I ask firmly. Our hands flex against each other's and Imogen leads us off as we all say:

"Because lone wolves die alone."

THEY KICK US OUT OF THE BOWLING ALLEY AT TEN, EVEN though the bar next door is still open. There's another round of hugs from Mia and Imogen before they take off in Mia's Outback. I trek into the snow, but Bryson jogs up to me.

"Hey, man, do you want a ride? It's freezing."

The temperature dropped in the hour and a half since I walked here. My heart skips in warning at the thought of a car ride, but it is cold. I know he's a safe driver and it's not even far. I haven't tried again in a while. Maybe I should. It will probably be fine.

"Sure. Thanks."

He looks surprised. "Cool." He turns to walk with me to his truck.

The parking lot is quiet and two inches of fresh snow blanket the ground. There will be a line of cars up to the mountain in the morning for powder and I try to think about that instead of my pulse, amping up as we approach Bryson's truck.

I'm proud of myself for accepting the ride—until I grip the handle of the door and pull. The metallic click and release washes my veins with adrenaline, and the dirt and vanilla scent of the truck is so like Hunter's car, it leaves me breathless. Bryson's climbing inside, but I shove the door shut again, shaking as if I'm facing an armed murderer instead of a blue Toyota Tacoma.

Bryson leans over to open the door for me. "Hey, it's unlocked. . . ." He frowns.

A heat like hives crawls up my neck and I back away, gulping air. Not this. Not here, not again. It's been a *year*. I lean forward, staring hard at my own footprints in the snow while headlights flash over us from other people leaving the parking lot.

"Gage?"

I swallow nausea, straighten, and shove my hands into my pockets, eyes squeezed shut. "I changed my mind.

I'm going to walk. Thanks, though."

I pivot and stride a couple hundred feet away from him, sucking cold air. I'm not in the car. Not crashing. My own two feet are on the ground. I crouch, scoop snow, and press it to the back of my neck to soothe the rising panic.

Bryson grabs my shoulder and I lurch to my feet with a growl. I didn't realize he'd followed me.

He backs off a step, palms out. "Hey?"

I grunt a response, avoiding his eyes as icy melted snow slithers down my back.

"I was calling you." He points at his truck. "Didn't you hear me? Are you okay?"

The rage that isn't directed at him swells like lava up my chest. *Do I seem okay?* I want to scream. I want to deck him. *My best friend is dead, ask me again.* But it's not his fault.

I step back, putting space between us. "Yeah. All good."

"Yeah, right." He's grimacing as if I threw up in front of him. I love making a spectacle of myself. "Look. I know you don't want to like . . ." He stops, starts again. "I know you're putting up a front for the girls, but you can tell me what's going on. We're friends, right? You know everything about me, so . . . "

I tug my wool hat off and scrub a hand against my hair, then yank it back on, staring away at the sidewalks and the streetlights that turn the snowy air violet all around us. "Yeah."

I want to talk to him even less than I wanted to talk to Imogen. Hunter died and left me with our wolf pack. I can't break down again when they're counting on me, and I definitely don't want to break down in front of Bryson.

With his dad in prison and him taking care of his mom, he doesn't need one more person to worry about. Especially the guy who's supposed to be there to support him.

It's not his fault the one person in the world I want to talk to isn't here.

"So?" he prompts.

I clear my throat roughly, since I do see the irony of insisting everyone share their feelings while I'm not. "I just miss him. The anniversary thing is . . . It sucks. I'm just thinking about him a lot and how if we hadn't gone out that night . . . ." The words clot in my throat.

No, no, no.

Bryson shifts his weight. I wonder if he's uncomfortable with me even sharing that much. People ask, but I don't know if they really mean it.

"I get it," he says quietly. "Isn't that what LWDA's about? I talk about my stuff. You talk about not being a lone wolf and you've seen us pour our hearts out sometimes—"

"I told you what was wrong." I look up at him, scraping myself together, straightening, realizing I've hunched as if I'm curling around an injury. A phantom ache pulses at the spot just above my temple where my head hit the glass. I just want to go.

It's funny to see that he looks angry with me. Angry I won't talk, angry I'm not sharing. Angry at nothing, like I am. But it's for the best. It's too much. It's been a year, I should be further along and I'm not, and I'm not going to make everyone else deal with that. It's concern, and pity, but it turns his face angry.

Maybe that's what I look like. Lost and angry.

A stiff wind blows snow against us, cooling, soothing.

"Thanks for the offer," I say. "I just want to chill out at home, and I want to walk."

He looks slightly mollified. "Sure. Just don't . . . you know. Don't go off in the woods alone."

I crack a smile as he stretches the wolf metaphor. But that's what it's for. "I won't," I promise. I offer him my hand to seal it. "I've got this."

The first time someone called Ethan a "lone wolf" was what gave Hunter the idea for the name of LWDA. Whether it's dragging a friend off Reddit for a few hours or telling someone they really need some deodorant or standing up for someone who needs it, or just knowing you have somewhere to go—friends at the bowling alley, that's what we're for. We're pack animals too, and lone wolves die alone.

LWDA is about helping people, but there's nothing they can do to help me.

Bryson sizes me up, like he might ask again, or challenge me. If anybody could, it's him. He's taller, broad-shouldered and strong, but he's hidden pain before. So he *knows*. He knows what it's like to try and get people to ignore your pain. After Ethan, so many of us learned that ignoring people and looking the other way can get them killed, and my friends, at least, have been trying to tighten the ranks. The adults do stuff. Start groups, encourage sharing, counseling, not isolating. Walking for suicide awareness.

But at the end of the day, we have to join the fight too.

Bryson surprises me by taking my offered hand and pulling me into a quick hug. I laugh, fighting not to collapse to the ground in gratitude.

"Thanks." I know he's doing the thing Hunter and I did for him. Seeing me. But there's only so much I want him or anyone else to see.

"No problem." He smiles faintly, but when I turn to leave, he speaks again. "Wait. Could—uh, can I ask you a favor?"

The cold is seeping through my coat and I want to walk again, but even as my brain scrambles, knowing I have no room for favors, I nod. I'm the leader. If he needs something, I'm there. "Sure."

He ducks his head, glancing to the bowling alley. A few people stumble out of the bar, talking loudly. "I want to ask Mia out, but—"

My sharp laugh stops him. The relief that it's something like that, something good and light, makes me laugh, and he glares at me. "Sorry." I grip his shoulder. "I'm sorry—I'm not laughing at you. That's just not what I was expecting. What do you need?"

He's suddenly blushing, nervous at the idea of Mia and whatever he's going to ask me, and he runs a hand through his messy blond hair. "I was thinking, like, I could . . . cook her something, but I could use some help." He grins lop-sidedly when he reveals his ulterior motive for offering me a ride. "Is that weird?"

I draw myself up, head clearing. "You want me to help you cook something?"

The red flush from the cold is filling the rest of his face. "I don't know where to start."

"Me?" I'm still on that. When he's got cookbooks and YouTube and a million online recipes, he wants my help?

"Yeah. If you have time."

Another laugh holds in my chest and I keep it there, not wanting him to mistake why I'm laughing. Relief and confidence push everything else away. "Sure, I can help. I'd love to. I'm honored. I think she would love it."

He grins. "Awesome. I want to make something cool, not just like meatloaf or whatever."

"Meatloaf can be cool," I counter.

He shrugs one shoulder. The temperature sinks further with an icy wind, and the snow lightens, frozen somewhere high in the atmosphere. "I don't know. Something fancy. She's been in Boise all fall."

"Boise's fancy?" I grin, latching onto this new quest.

He rolls his eyes. "You know what I mean."

"I know, I know. I've got you. I'll check out some recipes tonight."

He looks panicked at the word *recipes*. "Something easy, though."

"Easy and fancy." I back away, clapping my hands together. "You got it."

"Thanks, Gage." Relief and determination replace the panic on his face and he lifts a hand to wave bye.

I turn on my heel and am productively distracted the whole walk home, away from downtown and into the neighborhood, pondering something that would be easy for him to cook but would look impressive. My stepdad helps people, and he says that was part of his own healing. Maybe it will be part of mine.

Restaurants and shops give way to houses still sparkling with festive lights. It's tradition to leave Christmas decorations up almost through Valentine's Day to brighten up the long winter, so cheery light and fresh snow gives everything a cozy postcard feel.

Then I reach my house, and the unexpected sight of my

dad's old silver Ram truck parked out front stops me cold. A familiar, complex blend of happiness and anxiety tightens my chest and I consider sneaking in the back and up to my room. But then people would worry.

With a sigh, I pull myself together and head inside.

H EAT SWAMPS ME INSIDE THE mudroom and I shed my layers—coat, hat, sweater, boots, and even my socks—before I sweat more than I already am.

Adult voices float from the living room, but that's not who greets me. I'm down to a T-shirt when my cousin Justine, ten years old going on forty, flies into the kitchen and smacks into me for a hug.

She's a typical Clark kid—wiry as a reed and perpetually tan from summers outside, cheeks ruddy from skiing and windburn, sun-washed brown hair and huge hazel eyes, currently wearing one of Hunter's old Minecraft T-shirts like a dress over purple leggings. Hunter was her brother and her hero. Now she only has me.

I fake-stumble upon impact and hoist her up in one arm. "Shouldn't you be in bed?"

"Shouldn't you be in bed?" she mimics, deepening her

voice. She wriggles free of my arm and sets her hands on her hips. "Your dad's here." It's an accusation, as if I have anything to do with it. "He's been here *forever.*"

Forever probably means about an hour.

"I saw the truck. Is your mom here?"

"No, she's in the studio."

They live next door, and we go in and out of each other's houses as if they are one big house and all spaces are communal. Mom used to come home from work and find Hunter and me both in the living room, or just him if he was bored of his own house. Or vice versa. Aunt Gina and Mom borrow utensils and books and eat each other's leftovers. They probably should've been born twins, but Mom's a couple years older.

Hunter and I joked about keeping the houses when we grew up and keeping up the tradition, and I don't think he ever knew I was serious about it.

Or maybe he did.

Justine takes my wrist and hauls me toward the living room, where they have a fire going and it smells like Jack's favorite apple cinnamon candle, and the cozy space is full—my mom, Jack, and my bio dad, who stands when I come in, grinning at me. I haven't seen him in a month, but that's just the nature of long-haul trucking.

He offers me his hand while Justine retreats to the couch, where there's some paper and pencils, and she resumes carefully following a video on Mom's phone about drawing some birds.

With my hand freed up, I take Dad's offered handshake. He is not a hugger. I look nothing like him, more like Mom: full-bodied, dark hair, dark eyes, all Mom, except for my height. That's from Dad.

He is a tall, hard, rail of a man, clean-cut, like a rugged sixties movie star. He squeezes my hand harder than he needs to, a quick crush until I tug it free. "Hey, bud. I'm home for a few days and thought I'd stop by, see how you're doing." When I was a kid, he called me "buddy," but somewhere between age sixteen and hitting my final height of five eleven, I graduated to "bud."

"Thanks, I'm doing okay." I look to Jack, who raises his eyebrows in silent question. I shake my head slightly to indicate I'm okay with the visit and manage a smile for my dad. Probably rolled in, left his rig, and came right over to see me. I try to be polite even though I wish he'd given me a heads-up. Tonight it would've been especially nice. "Happy New Year."

He laughs. "Happy New Year. You put on some weight?" He pats my stomach with the back of his hand.

I smirk and cock my head, punching his arm in return. "Probably, I'm working out."

"Just watch that cholesterol, bud, runs in the family." He taps his own chest. He used to remark that he could never put on weight himself. I guess it's either too much, or not enough for him.

"Never trust a skinny cook," Mom says. She appears to be reading one of her nursing journals, but it's a cover so I don't feel stared at. She sees everything, and that was a warning for Dad to check his comments.

Meanwhile, Jack leans forward from his spot on the couch, near the fire. He is unassuming, not what I ever would have pictured for "retired Marine" until I met him. Solid dad bod, mostly bald with dark hair shaved short, glasses. He rests his arms on his knees and folds his hands together. "How long are you in town?"

Dad glances at Jack, then at me. "A bit. I came to see if this guy wants to ride with me for a couple of weeks." He cuffs my hair, then drops a big hand to my shoulder. Mom closes her journal, staring at him in disbelief. All of us do, for a second, and the only sound is Justine's pencil on paper and the crackle of the fire. He's never invited me to ride along in his truck before. I wonder if he's doing it on purpose in front of everyone, to challenge me. "Thought you might like a change of scenery."

I imagine trying to climb into his rig. My throat tightens and I can't meet his hard but jovial gaze. "Thanks, but I don't think so. I'm working full-time at the diner. I can't leave Andy in the middle of ski season."

"Oh, come on, he'll live."

"Let him keep his promises," Mom says, frowning over her journal. "He doesn't want to walk away from the job without notice."

"Why don't you let him decide that?"

"He just did."

I duck my head, wondering how my dad always has such abysmal timing and where he gets his ideas. I don't think I've ever, in my life, expressed an interest in trucking. I guess it's more about quality time. I know he's trying to connect, but I don't know why he can't pick something he knows I like to do.

Or at the very least, something he knows wouldn't make me physically ill to do.

"I cook for him, Dad. It's busy."

"Lots of nice restaurants on my route," he offers.

"We could try some of those fancy upscale places you like."

I twist my mouth against a smirk, thinking of Bryson calling Boise food fancy. But I don't want to have to explain the joke or laugh at my dad when he's trying to connect. Usually it's fine, fun even.

After Uncle Tyler left Aunt Gina when she was pregnant with Justine—one kid too many, I guess—my dad stepped in even though he and Mom had split when I was a baby. I vividly remember the day. Dad arguing with Uncle Tyler to make him stay, then Tyler driving off. Hunter crying. I was so shocked and confused, I just hugged him. Dad was so proud of me for taking care of my cousin. *Come on, Hunter, big boys don't cry. Look at Gage. You guys want to go fishing?*

He was there for us. He took Hunter and me fishing, camping, let us ride in the back of his truck—did all the dad stuff when he was in town a couple times a month. Our hero.

Then came Jack. And Jack is . . . more like me. More into books and gaming, mellower. I don't feel like I have to prove myself around Jack all the time. We get along, and maybe that's why Dad's gotten pushier over the years. But I feel like that's his problem, not mine.

"It's not good timing," I tell Dad. "Maybe the shoulder season, like April, before summer."

"April?" Dad asks incredulously.

I shrug against my irritation. "March, whatever— I just don't want to go right now."

"Gage doesn't like riding in cars," Justine reminds the room, casting an exasperated look at my dad, then goes back to her drawing, satisfied she's done her part.

Horrified heat washes up my neck and I flick my gaze back to Dad.

His heavy eyebrows draw together. "Still?"

"It's okay," Mom says, but I can't even look at her for support.

"Is it?" Dad frowns at her, then at me.

My jaw works and clenches and I lift my shoulders, and they stay there, hunched.

After a second of heated silence, Jack pats his knees and stands up, crosses the room, and claps Dad on the shoulder. "Well, we don't want to keep you, Barrett. I'm sure it was a long drive today. Nice of you to stop by."

Dad looks at him, frowning at the blatant dismissal and still gripping my shoulder until I shrug him off. "Sure thing, Sarge." He touches his brow in a faux salute and Jack's eyebrows lift a fraction, mouth tightening, but he only tips his head up while Dad backs out of his space. "I just wanted to say hi, and offer." He looks at me and jerks his thumb toward the kitchen. "Can I talk to you for a second?"

Jack frowns, but I nod at him, then at Dad. "Yeah, sure."

Dad lifts a hand to Mom and Jack. "Have a good night."

"Night," Mom says coolly, dark eyes narrow.

I follow Dad back through the kitchen to the mudroom. "You holding up okay?" he asks quietly.

"Yeah. I guess." I pick at the stickers on my skis, which are propped optimistically against the wall even though I haven't gone skiing all season. It requires getting in a car and driving on winding, snowy roads. "It'll be a year since the crash, next week. I'm just thinking a lot—"

"Right. A year, bud." He tips his head close to meet my eyes sternly. "You have to get back in a car someday. You can't do this your whole life. You know that, right?"

My brow furrows and I study the stickers, their faded edges. My favorite: *Not all those who wander are lost.* "I know. It's not my whole life. I'm working on it."

"I'm surprised Major Dad in there hasn't talked to you about it."

Anger and defensiveness coils in my throat. "Jack's great. Don't call him that."

He lays his head back as if I'm too much to deal with. "Relax, it's a joke. I don't like getting kicked out when I'm just trying to see my kid."

I square my shoulders, forcing my gaze to his. "Well, sorry. If you let me know you're coming, we can meet somewhere else."

His eyebrows shoot up, then he lifts his hands with a wry grin. "All right, all right, I'm sorry about that." He considers me. He does make the effort to be in my life, and I respect how hard he works, and how he included Hunter in all our dad-son stuff. It meant everything. I know he cares. We're just not the same.

Finally he speaks again, voice low. "You just remember what we talked about. Especially now."

My breath shortens, heat curling into a soft buzz all over my skin when I understand why he brought me out here. "I know."

"You need to keep it together." He grips my shoulder again and I close my eyes against the swelling anger and mortification. If only Justine had stayed quiet. He would've bought the work excuse. "You can't do that meltdown shit you did to me. Your mom couldn't handle seeing you like that." He aims a finger in my face and I tip my head down and away. "You've got a good life, bud. I know it hurts, but you need to move forward. You've been coasting and moping for a year. Your mom and aunt and that little girl in there need you to man up. They lost Hunter too, and they need to know you're okay."

"I know." I stare at his work boots as the familiar ache lances through my temple, a scream inching its way up my throat until I swallow it. "I've got it."

"Good man." He gives me a fond, rough shake as if that'll snap me out of it or loosen me up. It does the opposite, lashing tension across my shoulders. "We'll have dinner or something while I'm here. Or bowling. You still bowl?"

"Yeah." He's not always weird and gruff like this, but obviously he's embarrassed by me not riding in cars, or hurt I don't want to go with him, or mad at Jack. Or something. "Sounds good, Dad."

Another shake. "You're okay?"

Heat and nausea and the desire to punch something tighten my arms from shoulder to wrist, but there's only one correct answer when he asks that. I look up, raise my chin, meet his eyes levelly. "Yeah. See you soon."

"Maybe I'll come by the diner. You can make me one of those famous burgers."

"Sure," I say, because he won't. He pats my shoulder again and leaves. Staying just long enough to spin me up, put me in my place, and head out again, feeling like he's being a good dad, I guess. I'm pretty sure he liked me better when I was a kid, rough-and-tumble and full of potential, and the more I grow into myself, the more disappointed he gets. Or maybe it's the last year. Everything after the accident has been a mess, including me. Mostly me.

The big engine on his Ram rumbles and he guns it down the street, marring the peaceful snowy scene, leaving the scent of diesel in the air. I stand there until his taillights blend into the Christmas lights and he turns the corner up the street.

Justine marches into the kitchen. "Auntie Liz said you should walk me home."

"All twenty feet?" I shake my head. "Put your shoes on."

She flops against me dramatically. "You put *your* shoes on."

"Okay, fine, I'll carry you." I duck in to scoop her up and throw her over my shoulder. She shrieks and squeals and I grab her boots off the floor while she's laughing, and carry her back to the living room. Mom is still there, Jack is not. Maybe he retreated to his man cave now that my dad left.

I pat Justine's head as she squirms in my arm. "I'm taking this monkey home."

"Thank you, sweetie." Mom looks me over, eyes glassy, and she's probably thinking of Hunter too.

"I want to sleep here!" Justine's small hands patter against my back and I set her gently on the floor. "I want to make a pillow fort in the living room and do marshmallows."

"Another time," Mom says. Storm clouds gather in Justine's face, but having a tantrum at my mom is likely to end with you cleaning baseboards, not getting your way.

"Not after you gave me a heart attack by disappearing today."

Justine scoffs as she plops onto the floor to pull on her boots. I crouch to help. "I didn't disappear, I went into the trees and I took the next lift by myself." She looks at me proudly until she sees I'm tying her bootlaces together, and smacks my hand away.

Mom looks at her over the journal. "You have to tell people where you're going."

Justine looks at me pointedly with those hazel eyes that are too old and sharp for her face, as if she can't believe what she has to put up with.

"You really do," I say. "That's not cool. There's tree wells and stuff, and if Mom didn't know where you were . . ." I don't finish.

Justine ducks her head with a pout, outnumbered. "Hunter let me ski in the trees."

I close my eyes.

"Be that as it may," Mom says, "you were skiing with me today, and I would like to know the general vicinity you'll be in."

Justine humphs. Mom and I watch her, then our gazes lift at the same time to look at each other. I don't know what she sees in my face, but she closes her journal. Before she can ask the broken record "Are you okay?" that everyone asks and no one really wants the answer to, Jack leans in from the hall, pushing his glasses up his nose.

"Gage? When you have a minute, I want to show you something." He tips his head toward the hall. "I'll be in my cave."

The energy my dad stirred up settles when no one

brings up the car thing, but I still wonder if they agree with him. I wonder if everyone does. I think of Imogen and Bryson offering rides. What if everyone is wishing I'd get over it?

My heart rate climbs. "Okay."

Justine and I take the side door and walk under the breezeway our families built between the houses. After wrangling Justine, I forgot to put my shoes on at all, remembering only when my feet hit the ice-cold gravel of the breezeway. Justine shudders and huddles against me. It's stopped snowing entirely, dark and windy.

A dim light glows from their garage and I glance that way as I herd Justine inside the house. The slow *click, click, click* of Cassidy's claws on the linoleum greets us, and her soulful black-Lab-mix eyes are hopeful in her graying face. I rub her ears. "In the morning, Cassie girl."

Justine pats Cassidy's rump, then she turns and leans against me. "I want to stay with you," she whispers. "Mom's been sad all day."

Ice clamps my throat and I kneel to give her a squeeze, unable to tell her I've been sad most of the day too. "I'll meet you after dance tomorrow and I'll make you a milkshake at Nan's. Whipped cream and sprinkles and everything."

"But I want to stay now," she whines, and I want to build her that blanket fort and let her stay there, with marshmallows and books and drawing paper, where everything is quiet and safe and warm, and nobody dies.

"I'll see you tomorrow," I say instead. "We're all right next door."

Her arms loop around my neck and she's silent, so I stay there, arms around her, until she feels safe to let go.

Cassidy looks at me, huffs a disappointed sigh, and turns to follow Justine. I wait until she goes all the way inside and I can close the door behind her.

For a second I stand still, enjoying the cold and dark.

In the garage, glass shatters.

A jolt skips down my spine. More shattering and tinkling, a chorus of breaking glass.

I trot off the breezeway, snow numbing my feet, to peer through the dusty windows, but I can't see much through the dirty pane. My heart throbs in my throat. It's probably fine. I shouldn't interrupt. I have nothing left after today.

And yet.

Your aunt needs you.

Mom's been sad all day.

The painful cold on my feet and the brisk wind keep me grounded. I knock on the door. When there's no answer, I ease it open and lean in. The garage has never been a garage in my lifetime, but a glass studio filled with fire and light and intriguing heavy tools and, as far as I've ever been concerned, magic.

"Aunt Gina? Are you okay? I heard . . ." I stop, mouth open.

Shards of glass in every color and various sizes cover the floor. Swirled red and black and glints of milky white, as if she had a massive creation in progress and it all blew to pieces. Sometimes that happens. Things get too big, don't stick together. Pieces accidentally drop, break, or shatter.

That's not what happened here.

I know, because standing in the middle of the jagged sea of rainbow glass is my tiny aunt, wearing only a tank top and overalls in the lingering heat of the furnaces and blowtorch, dark hair in a messy bun on top of her head, clenching a hammer in her fist.

It's too late to go before she sees me because the door creaks when I move it. Her eyes flick up and her face is red and blotchy.

"Auntie," I mumble. "I'm sorry." I've intruded her sacred space and seen something I'm not supposed to. I want to run, hide, duck under the covers in my bed so this monster, the shadow, the horror of seeing my adult aunt in this grief, can't get me.

She looks equally as horrified that I'm here. But I can't leave now.

"What happened?" I take one step down into the room and she aims the hammer at me.

"Hunter, stop, you don't have any . . . shoes." Her arm drops. She stares at me, realizing what she said. "Oh God." She sinks to the floor, throws the hammer aside, and buries her face in her hands. "I'm sorry, Gage."

Heart pounding, I cast around and spot a broom a few feet away, and creep on tiptoe through the mess to grab it and sweep myself a path to her. I kneel to offer a hug and she breaks into a hard sob, leaning against me. Her tears threaten to crack the case around my own.

"I'm sorry," she mumbles. "Oh, baby, I'm sorry. I shouldn't do this to you."

"It's okay." It's all I can manage, and I know my dad is right. My aunt is here trying to work, to try to make something, and I should be doing the same.

She pats my arm and leans away, staring at the gruesome mess. I settle carefully next to her, cross-legged on the floor. The room is stuffy and the scent of fire and dust is the smell of my aunt, of home, of better times.

"Remember when he asked if I would make him a pipe?" Aunt Gina laughs, swiping her wrist over her eyes.

A rough laugh chokes in my mouth. "Yeah." I can barely think of him without falling apart, much less scrounge up and articulate a memory.

Her smile crumples. "I should have. Of all the silly things. He was such a good kid. You both . . . you too." She rests a warm hand on my bare foot and I have to close my eyes. "Thank you for checking on me, Gage. You don't have to."

"Yes I do," I murmur.

She sighs in defeat. Her strong hand, scarred from molten glass with nails short and dirty, squeezes my foot. "Is your mom still up?"

"Yeah. Yeah, she's reading."

She nods, but neither of us gets up. She looks how I feel. Spent. Done. I wrap an arm around her shoulders and she leans against me.

"I think I'll have to bow out of this show," she says, and my heart aches. Before Hunter died, she'd gotten a huge grant to participate in a show in Seattle featuring artists from all over the Rockies. "I had this . . . this." She gestures at the shattered glass. "But it wasn't working. And I can't fix it by next weekend." She sweeps both hands over her messy hair, unwinds her bun briskly, then re-twists it. "Just as well, really. It was crap."

I forgot the show was next week. She and my parents were going to drive to Seattle and make a weekend of it. Before Hunter died, it was going to be an epic family road trip.

I don't have an answer for her. I look around and try to figure out what abstract thing she had going.

The soft light of the studio catches the edges of the glass, glimmers of fire and swirls of snow. A breathtaking emerald fragment peeks from under the white. The texture of broken shapes mesmerizes me for a minute. There's something soothing about sitting in the middle of the mess, finding interesting shapes and small pieces of beauty in the light and the brokenness.

"It's kind of pretty just like this." I reach out to touch a cool piece of black glass that looks like volcanic onyx. "Even broken."

It probably sounds like I'm reaching. She had a sculpture here, something new and amazing, but had to destroy it. I know the reason because it hits me sometimes. The rage. The realization you have to keep doing things like going to work and eating food and washing your clothes when the person you love most is missing.

Aunt Gina lifts her head, her gaze traveling over the gleaming shards. "You know, you're all right." She wraps her wiry arm around me to squeeze before she stands. I push myself up with her. "Always look for the good stuff," she murmurs. Then she blinks at me, and her eyebrows snap together. "You're out here in bare feet and a T-shirt? Go home, Gage!" But she's amused, raw but still laughing.

"I was walking Justine back. Mom said she took her own little ski tour today."

Aunt Gina sighs. "Still wandering off?"

I shrug. Plenty of kids wander the ski hill and the town on their own; we're just super sensitive about it now. "I think she was bored or frustrated. I told her I'd get her a milkshake and walk her home from dance tomorrow."

Aunt Gina rubs her cheek. "You don't have to do that."

"I want to," I insist.

She peers at me, then bows her head, looking around at the mess she's realizing she has to do something about. I stoop to grab the broom.

"I can help—"

"Go home, Gage." She swipes dark strands from her forehead and smiles at me grimly. "We clean up our own messes in this house." She holds out her hand and I reluctantly return the broom.

"Yes, ma'am."

It's weird to leave her there, but Aunt Gina is not one to lie about how she's feeling or what she wants. When she says go, she means it.

Back at my house, I find Jack in his man cave, a tidy office that is eighty percent dedicated to Warhammer models and game guides, and the other twenty percent is his PlayStation, TV, favorite books, and painting table. He's working on a Space Marine when I knock on the doorjamb, and he swivels his chair to greet me.

"Hey, Gage." He assesses me, folding his hands over his stomach. "You want to talk about any of it?"

I appreciate his bluntness and the offer. In the eight years he and Mom have been married, he never forced a father-son thing. He didn't have to. We liked each other without trying. He's also never let my dad and our stumbling relationship be an elephant in the room and the older I get, the more I appreciate it. "Not really. Thanks, though."

I consider telling him about my encounter with Olivia,

as if noticing girls again will prove I'm okay, but I don't. That's only for me right now.

His eyebrows crook in sympathy. "That's okay. You know I'm here, though."

I fidget against the ridges of the door frame. "You said you wanted to show me something?"

His face lights up. "Yep, come on in." He stands as I enter the room and grabs a couple sheets of paper off his printer to bring to me. He's a hand shorter than me, which is weird when you've spent almost half your life looking up to someone.

"Okay." He grips my shoulder, but in an entirely different way than my dad grabs me. Jack is grounding. "Don't take this as me pushing you out of the nest. You know how your mom and I feel, and you're working, and you can be here as long as you want. All that said . . ." He meets my gaze through his glasses, intense and excited. "This came through my news feed today, and I feel I'd be negligent not to share it with you."

Jack is even keel. I rarely see him worked up in one direction or the other, so the palpable eagerness vibrating off him stirs my curiosity. Heart rate climbing, I look at the papers. It's a job application. I've seen a lot of those recently—schools, internships, a facade of papers pretending I'm moving forward with my life. The letterhead on this one silences me.

An opening for prep cooks this summer at Redwood House, chef Michael Andrus's flagship restaurant.

The first time I ever pointed my skis down a black diamond trail and felt the hurtling exhilaration and terror is nothing compared to the fear and thrill blossoming in my chest at the thought of putting my name on this piece of paper. Granted, Andrus himself probably wouldn't ever see it. His executive chef might, though. I could stand at the line where he once called orders, chop an onion that ends up on a table in a restaurant he founded with his own two hands, get real experiences, training, connections. . . .

This is it.

This is my way out. My way forward. Out of Clark, out of Hunter's shadow, out of my grief. A way to stop spinning my wheels, coasting, moping.

If I can do this . . .

If.

Gratitude cinches my throat, anxiety snugly behind it. "Wow. Jack—thanks. Uh, thanks for showing me." If I talk more, I'm going to crumple and bawl on his shoulder and I'm not even sure why.

"That's your guy, right?" He pokes the name on the paper. "Andrus?"

My mouth tightens, warm heat behind my eyelids. "Yeah, it is. That's—yeah."

"San Francisco!" Jack squeezes my arm, lighting up when he sees I'm interested. "You loved San Francisco." I did. When we visited Jack's parents the first time, I did love it, but the thought of what it would take to get there now is daunting, to say the least.

"It's just . . ." I look at the paper, the address. "Uh, far away."

"It's not that far, promise." He pats my arm. I meet his eyes, and the emotion and pride in his face makes me think uncomfortably of my dad telling me to man up. Jack's never said anything like that to me, but he must be thinking it. This is a hint. He thinks it's time for me to move on too. And he's right. I swallow as he keeps going. "This is meant for you."

I read over the paper and look hesitantly at him again. "What if I don't get it?"

He squeezes my arm. "You have to try. I know it feels huge and scary and far away. Especially this year. I know. But you're a big fish, Gage. You need some bigger water to grow, you need to see what else is out there, at least. If you hate it, you can always come home. Always. But I think you should try, don't you?"

I know he's saying the big fish stuff to praise me, but all the steps involved—the application, the wait, the move, if I get the job? It swamps me like a tidal wave.

But . . . if I *get* the job . . .

This is my chance. My heart pounds and I can't even read the words on the application.

Jack's still talking, he's got it all figured out. "You could stay with my folks or we can help you with a place, to start—"

I can't handle actual planning right now, so I scoop him into a hug instead. This didn't just "come across" his news feed. He found it. He's been looking for stuff for me and he found this specific, perfect thing. I've been coasting and he's been looking for things for me, for solutions.

"Thanks, Jack," I whisper. Now is not the time to unload all my doubts and fears. I can't think when would be a good time. Maybe never. "I'll do my best."

He pats my back before pulling away to make sure I take the application. "You bet. I know you will. If you need a proofreader, ask your mom." I laugh and he grins confidently. "You can do this. Obviously, the others didn't pan out because you're meant to do this."

Guilt stabs me. Right. All the other jobs I applied for that didn't pan out.

I force a laugh, rub my eyes, and manage to swallow it before good feelings morph into other feelings. They're all woven so closely now, one strand tugs another, and anything—happiness, sadness, anger—might unravel me. "Thanks."

"Anytime, Gage. Love you." He pats my back and I give him a squeeze in gratitude.

"Love you too."

As I'm leaving he asks, "Are you still making snacks for our game tomorrow?" He motions at his Warhammer stuff. Wednesday nights are Warhammer sessions at our house.

"Oh. Yeah. Definitely." That might be a perfect chance for Bryson to try cooking something too. "I might have a friend over."

"You bet." He retrieves his wallet from the table and I shake my head. He frowns. "For groceries." He peers at me sternly over his glasses. I've been doing the food for his sessions for a while as a way to test random recipes, but he still doesn't want me to pay for it since it's his deal.

"You can Venmo it."

"Ah, right." He tosses his wallet back onto the table and grabs a pen, making a note on his hand, then holds it up with a grin. "Got it on the PalmPilot. I'll send it tomorrow."

I hang my head with a grin. "Thanks, Jack."

He waves me away and I head upstairs, leaving him to his painting.

A shower washes off the diner, the walk, the bowling

alley, the stress of my dad's visit. I have my way forward. Time to get on it.

I crack the window in my room for some frosty air because I always wake up hot no matter the season. My window looks over the breezeway between our houses, straight across to Hunter's window. Sometimes we'd flick our lamps or a flashlight at each other, before we had phones, just to say, "Hey, thinking of you too."

Of course, his window's been dark for a year.

I drop to my chair at the desk, guilt over Jack's support and enthusiasm worming through me, and lay out the job application. It looks like it's printed from an online form, so I'll have to apply online, but I can use this as a rough draft. I open my laptop and the email folder where I saved the responses to my other applications, which I told Mom and Jack were nos, and scroll through them, stuffing my guilt and trying to use them to boost my confidence.

Dear Mr. Bryant, we were impressed with your enthusiasm and would like to offer . . .

Attn: Gage Bryant: Welcome aboard! We enjoyed the creativity displayed in your . . .

I click through them all. In a way, Jack's right. They didn't pan out. Every acceptance sent panic and fear shooting down my stomach. Leave the diner? Leave Clark? Get in a car, a plane, and go live somewhere, alone? Leave Justine, my mom, Aunt Gina, and LWDA? Although Imogen would be appalled to find out I never accepted any of these offers, some of them not that far away, both in Washington and right here in Idaho.

Even one of the swanky restaurants up on the ski hill that has a Michelin star said they would give me a chance.

Maybe I should've taken that one. Still have to get in a car, though. And if I failed at that, everyone in town would know. The manager knows my family. What if they offered it out of pity?

Your mom and your aunt and that little girl need you. They need to know you're okay.

The warm hive feeling prickles my neck and I huff a short breath. "Man up," I mutter, slap my laptop closed, and set the papers for Redwood House in front of me neatly.

"*Do or do not,*" Hunter croaks in a poor imitation of Yoda in my memory. Nerd. I rub my eyes.

There's some shouting outside, up the street, then the crackle and flare of fireworks. Looks like someone saved a few from New Year's. It's tempting to wander out and see who it is, but then I'd have to talk to people.

This is the hard time. Dark time, with Hunter's dark, empty window staring at me twenty feet away. I stare at the application until the words look like they're in another language. I need help.

I need Hunter.

I shove away from the desk to make sure my door is locked, then crouch by the bed and pull out a box my old ski boots came in that's now full of sentimental stuff. Printed photos, recipes I devised from *The Hobbit* and *Game of Thrones*, a battered copy of *Assassin's Apprentice* signed by Robin Hobb, and a woven bracelet my first girlfriend, Rowan, gave me.

At the bottom, in a leather case embossed with the White Tree of Gondor, is Hunter's phone. Aunt Gina let me keep it after I helped them copy all the photos and stuff from it.

What they don't know is I also reactivated it with

a plan I pay for myself, so I can text it and feel like he's texting back. I'm pretty sure that is not a healthy coping mechanism, but I really don't care. It helps, and I'm trying to handle this myself. I've erased all the contacts but me in case anyone still has him in their phone so I don't accidentally send someone a message from Hunter and give them a heart attack.

I settle on the floor and lean back against the bed, pulling out my own phone.

Me: Hey. Found this awesome job opportunity today. And met a really cute girl.

I rest my phone on my stomach and use his to answer.

Huntsman: Using the Force like a boss. Go for it!!

The soft jolt of happiness at seeing a text from him relaxes my heart.

Me: Which one?

Huntsman: Both, coward :P

Part of me wants to look up, to see the light in his room even though I know it's me. I know it's me. I know he's gone. There's no denial or anything. The phone is just cheaper than therapy at less than fifty bucks a month and it's so good to feel like he's there.

Me: I'm just scared.

Huntsman: "Fear is the mind-killer. I will face my fear."

Me: I know. Sorry to bug you. I just

My fingers stop and I close my eyes for a second before finishing.

Me: I just feel alone a lot. I think everyone's ready for me to be over it and I'm not. I miss you

I stop. I didn't mean to type the last part. I close my eyes briefly, then pick his phone up again and rest my thumbs on the screen, staring at our fake conversation. I know what he would say. *Lone wolves die alone.* Or maybe not. I don't know. My eyes sting. I don't type anything. Maybe he wouldn't say any of that. Maybe he would tell me I should get some sleep, get a life, move on too. He would. He would want me to be happy and productive, to live.

And he would be right.

My throat clamps, breath shuddering as frustration heats my face.

I hold the power button until the screen goes black, stow it in the box again, and shove myself back to the desk, to the application, to work on the first step of actually getting on with my life.

AT FIVE IN THE MORNING, the dark air of the breezeway is thin and frozen. Stars blaze over the neighborhood and my breath puffs in silver clouds.

As I climb the porch and ease inside, Cassidy's claws *click, click, click* to greet me and she sticks her nose in my face as I sit on the floor to pull traction cleats over my shoes. The frozen morning also prompts me to put on Cassidy's booties so our walk isn't cut short by frozen paws.

"Good girl," I murmur, tipping my face away from her attempts to wash it, and wrestle her paws into the booties. "Yes, who's a good old boof? Who's my Cassie bear? Look at these big bear feet." Her tail waves. Hunter tried to give her an epic name from a book, but she only answered to her shelter name, so Cassidy she remained.

She was Hunter's dog. Now she's Justine's, and mine, and everyone's. When Aunt Gina first told my mom how sad it was that Cassidy would sit by the door all day waiting for Hunter, I knew I had to do something. If you say his name, she still perks up and looks at the door.

We walk every morning about the same time, so now she sits and waits for me. We have to go early because it got harder and harder to walk the neighborhood and have people look at me warily, mournfully, walking my dead cousin's dog. Now we go in the small, dark hours of the morning when we are completely alone.

After I get the last hind paw strapped into a bootie, she lands a lick square on my mouth. I push her away, then clip the leash and head out.

The neighborhood is suspended, still and silent like a paused movie, the air so dry and cold it would squeak if you could run your finger down it. The snow that fell yesterday sits lightly as a blanket of feathers across yards and alleys, a dry, sparkling powder.

I'm bundled against all of it. I love it. Me, the stars, the snow, the dog. Feeling good. I researched Redwood House last night and reread some of Andrus's blogs and looked over the application until I finally fell asleep, and it feels right.

We pick up to a slow jog along a forested patch at the edge of the neighborhood that leads into some walking and bike trails. Snow and hoarfrost cake the pine trees and skeletal white aspens. My own secret Lothlórien, wreathed in silver and the gold of streetlamps.

Even though Cassidy's almost fourteen, she's all for an easy run. No matter how badly I sleep, how tired I am, no matter the weather, I know Cassidy is sitting at the door, staring out, waiting for me. I can't let her down.

I can't let any of them down.

I started the walks as a service to Hunter and Aunt Gina, but now it's also for me. The icy, dry air aches in my lungs, but I know if I push through this part, if I get my blood up, and Cassidy's, it'll keep us going for the rest of the day.

Cassidy stumbles and her front paws slide, and that's the only warning I get to alter my gait for ice—but it's too late, too hard and slick even for my cleats. My heel hits and slides and my elbow smacks the pavement, cracking red pain and anger through my brain.

I shriek an f-bomb right in the middle of the frozen morning and Cassidy skitters away from me, jerking the leash, tangling her feet.

"Stop!" I bark at her, and she cowers while I sit there swearing and shaking. Pain throbs through my elbow and against all my desperate will, tears thaw my face. I swallow back a frustrated sob, and another, half choking and crying alone where no one can see. Almost no one.

Cassidy ventures in and licks my face vigorously, whining. Guilt washes over everything else. I hug her neck. "I'm sorry," I whisper. "I'm sorry, good girl. You're a good girl."

It's tempting to sit there and let the tears come while the dog comforts me, but I manage to pull it together. I have to. I can't be this easy to crack.

The persistent, nagging terror that I'm actually just weak gnaws at my heart.

I clench my teeth against another sob. I don't want to ask. I don't know who to ask. I can't burden Aunt Gina, or Mom. Jack will tell me it's okay to feel this way, but I don't know if he means it anymore, and it doesn't feel okay at all.

Cassidy sits and leans against me heavily and lifts her silver muzzle to the air, sniffing calmly. Protecting me. I stare at the ice we slipped on, revealed now from under the snow.

It's clear, black ice, distinctly rippled like moving water, but frozen hard. I'm mesmerized by it like I was Aunt Gina's glass. The air warmed enough yesterday for some snow to melt and flow, then it froze solid again.

That's how it feels in my chest. Like the grief was flowing, and now it's solid and icy. Stuck. That's for the best, I guess, if letting it flow makes people uncomfortable and holds me back.

I know the moment it froze too.

A couple weeks after I got out of the hospital and Dad came to pick me up to go see a movie. The first time I got in a car not loopy on pain medication. Half a block down the road from the house I couldn't breathe, I started crying, my pulse was racing, and I thought I was having a heart attack.

And Dad. Jerking the truck to a stop so I could escape, but then . . .

Cassidy sticks her cold nose in my ear and I startle back to the moment, realizing we're both shivering in the middle of the sidewalk. Definitely not productive. I don't need to sit here thinking about every bad thing. Cassidy snuffles my face, tail wagging, until I take a deep, full breath.

"Sorry, bear," I mutter, and with a throb of pain in my elbow, I drag myself up to keep walking.

"NO ONIONS ON THAT ONE, GAGE," ANDY SAYS OVER THE NOISE of the diner.

It's just past two o'clock in the afternoon and Nan's has been packed since we opened. People down from early-morning skiing and people on their way up, all converging here. The clatter of spoons and clinking milkshake glasses drowns out the oldies music in my own personal symphony. High school kids on winter break cover all the stations—milkshakes, tables, scooping ice cream, cashing people out. It feels weird to be the second-oldest person here sometimes.

"What?" I pause with my spatula full of grilled onions, hovering over a patty with cheese. Andy has owned Nan's since the nineties—a short, wiry, scruffy old white Boomer who always smells like cigarettes and cooking meat and has a fierce dedication to specialty licorice and good, simple food.

He flicks a hand against the ticket. "No onions."

I hate waste, so I stand there a second, trying to decide what to do with the onion. I could finish the burger and give it to Colby, who's hanging out at the end of the ice cream bar. Then I remember he picked the onions off the other one I gave him. And I'm stuck, staring at the grill and unable to decide what to do.

Andy flips burgers, bacon, checks the fries, then aims his spatula at my burger patty. "I think it's done."

The scent of charring meat snaps me out of it and I grumble, scooping the burned patty. Usually we're like surgeons at the grill, a well-oiled machine. Not sure what makes me think I could hack it in a Michael Andrus kitchen, where they probably measure the chopped onions by the millimeter, when I can't even keep five orders straight here.

Andy watches me sidelong. "You stoned or something? You've been on Mars all morning."

"Yeah, just didn't sleep much. I mean, no, I'm not stoned." I slap the burger together, then pause. I can't serve that. I want to be proud of what I'm doing. And no part of me is proud of this blackened piece of crap.

I glance down the way at Colby again—but I can't serve a bad dish to anyone. It goes in the compost bin the waitresses convinced Andy to get a year ago, and I start another one as Mikaela approaches. She is Imogen's younger sister and pretty much her mini-me, pale white and freckled, except her hair is blazing red, currently swept into a neat ponytail.

She points at my discarded burger. "Was that table eight?"

"Yeah. A couple extra minutes, sorry."

"Whatever." She leans on the fridge near the grill and grabs her Italian soda for a sip. She started here on Christmas break, the youngest of the crew. "They can wait, they're jerks."

I look over my shoulder at the table. Three guys in their thirties, I'm guessing, all white touristy dudes with a lot of tan for January, a lot of money, a lot of attitude. Irritation sparks in my chest. "Jerks how?"

She shrugs with a glance at Andy, then at me, then down to her soda. "Just weird."

"Ignore them, kiddo," Andy advises, and Mikaela purses her lips, plunging her straw idly in and out of the soda. Andy steps back and wipes his hands on his apron. "You got this for a second, Gage? I've got to see a man about a dog."

"Yeah." I look away from table eight to tend to my food. "Mikaela, can you do the fries?"

"Sure." She leaves her straw in her soda and slips up next to me.

"What'd they do?" I ask, and she sighs.

"Just gross—flirting and saying stuff. Asking what time I get off."

Anger and protectiveness warm my neck. The bruise on my elbow flares when I make the specific movements required to rapidly assemble a trio of burgers. Pickles, lettuce, tomato. "Did you tell them to stop?"

"Not really." Her face is flushed from the fryer, or embarrassment, and she shrugs. She jerks the fry basket from the sizzling oil and I grab tongs to distribute fries alongside the burgers, then sprinkle a pinch of salt on top. She glances the way Andy left and tucks a wisp of hair behind her ear. "I just laughed."

"Okay." A group floods in from the sidewalk, another busload down from the hill, and the noise in the room doubles. If someone was hassling Imogen, they would have a drink in their face and be out the door already. But Mikaela isn't Imogen, and Imogen's not here. I am.

I finish the redo of the last burger and tug the ticket to read it. "These are all for them?"

"Yeah." She piles everything onto a tray, but I take it before she can.

"I got it."

Her eyes widen. "Gage, don't, it's okay."

I lift a reassuring hand, settling the tray on my other arm. "I'm just taking the food. You're done with that table."

"Don't do anything," she says sternly. "It's like a fifty-dollar table. Andy will kill me."

Wow, a whole fifty dollars. That does it. I lean over. "If Andy has a problem, he can talk to me."

"It's not that big a deal."

The more she argues, the bigger a deal it becomes to me, stoking my anger that she has to deal with them at all. "It's all good. I'm not going to do anything." I smile even as nerves rattle my core. Honestly, I mean that. I'm the least confrontational person I know, including my whole family. There are always rude customers, and we usually shake it off and take their money. But I can't today. I can't let the jerks get away with it. If I die tomorrow, Mikaela has to know I had her back.

"Watch that pork chop and make another basket of fries, okay? I'll be right back."

She looks at me in a mix of horror and gratitude, then turns to the grill in determination. I head over to eight with their tray of burgers.

"Three classics, no onion?"

"That's us," says one of them. "Three classics."

They snort and laugh and part of me wonders if they've already been drinking this afternoon.

"Where's our girl?" One of them with douchey swept-up blond hair leans his chair back to peer toward the grill.

I move to block his view. "On break. Let me know if I can get you anything else."

"You can get our waitress back."

"She doesn't want to serve you." I keep my tone level so it blends into the cheery noise of the rest of the diner. My stomach feels like ice and my face is hot. "And honestly, I'd like you to leave, but I hate to waste food."

They stare at me, then erupt into laughter and macho *ooh* noises. A guy with slick black hair rolls his eyes. "Dude. Relax. We were just talking to her."

I grip the back of an empty chair and lean forward, glaring at him even as my fight-or-flight response amps but veers toward flight. "Dude. She's fifteen."

He narrows his eyes, red flushing his face. Then Blondie laughs and nudges him with an elbow. "Oh man, jailbait!"

The others laugh, and angry resolve jitters through me as if I'm about to storm Normandy, not deal with a table of entitled jackasses. "Wow."

Their laughs fade. One drops his gaze to his fries.

Then the blond guy comes up with "What?"

"I said wow, I can't believe you said that." I hate confrontation. I hate it. I might puke on them. I should've dropped the food and left.

One guy leans toward me and speaks slowly. "We were just. Joking."

"Well, now you can just. Eat." I motion to the food.

"Okay, we got it." Blondie shoos his hand at me. "See you on Yelp."

That little gesture pops anger in my head, but I've said what I needed to. The second I turn away, they start talking over their food.

"What an asshole."

"Someone should tell him she's not going to blow him for standing up for her."

"It was a *compliment*," the blond insists.

I pause. I roll my shoulders and crack two knuckles with my thumb as a sliding, warm compulsion clamps over my brain to prove . . . something. To prove something, anything, to anyone. Possibilities dart through my brain. Throw the food in his face. Upend the table. Smash a fist into his smirking mouth.

But the younger kids are watching, and I need a thinking man's solution. An Aragorn solution, not a brute reaction. I know what Hunter would do—call them out. But I only have until Andy gets back from the bathroom.

I turn back around, appalled at myself and the blend of discomfort and thrill that's coming from picking a fight.

They look up at me as I approach the table, and Blondie spreads his hands. "Yes?"

"Listen—" My voice hitches. I clear my throat. "Take that back now and apologize to her, or get out."

He stares at me, lips parting, while his friends sit back, amazed. "Excuse me?"

"You heard me fine." I grip the back of the chair where they've stacked their coats, loom in, and point toward Mikaela, over behind the counter. She presses both hands to her mouth, gaze darting between us. "Apologize for making her uncomfortable and stop acting like a sleazebag, or leave."

Blondie makes a short, choked sound of disbelief. He glances around for support, but his friends are suddenly fascinated by their fries. Conversation in the room dwindles as people watch us sideways.

"Now," I say quietly, meeting his eyes, clenching the chair until my knuckles whiten so he won't see my hands shaking. Adrenaline shoots down every limb. I should probably stop now. But I don't. I am not about to tolerate these scumbags. "Or I can post your picture on all the local sites so everyone knows we've got a pedophile in town."

He looks as if I slapped him with the word. "Hey, can you keep your voice down?"

"I don't know, can you keep it in your pants?"

"What is *wrong* with you?"

"Dude," one of his friends mutters. Blondie looks at him, betrayed when he realizes they're no longer on his side. "Just . . . come on."

"I'm sorry," Blondie snaps, then looks toward Mikaela, watching in flushed horror, and raises his voice, spreading his arms. "Sorry, okay? No disrespect, I didn't know. I'm sorry." He glares at me, crimson creeping up his neck. "Happy?"

"Yeah." My heart throttles and I release a slow breath, palms slick against the chrome of the chair. "Don't let it happen again."

Red washes his face and he braces as if he might stand, but then he just waves sharply at me. "Get out of my face, man. I got it."

"Good." I push the chair against the table to punctuate my point, but I'm rattling with nerves and shove harder than I meant, sending his drink into his lap. Blueberry Italian soda soaks the front of his pristine, name-brand, white ski shirt and he jumps up with a shout, his chair clattering to the floor.

I lift both hands, palms out. "That was an accident!"

Three things happen at once—the diner falls silent but for Elvis crooning "Suspicious Minds," Andy emerges from the back, and Blondie chucks his soda glass at my head. I block it with one arm and it smashes on the floor.

Rage sears the reason from my body, I lunge around the table, grab Blondie's collar, and haul him toward the door.

The younger guys working the counter shoot their fists into the air and hoot their approval, while the girls gasp and laugh and customers scramble out of my path.

"Whoa, whoa!" Andy shouts, weaving around tables. "Gage!"

Blondie wrestles and squirms and lands a kick on my knee, but I've got a couple inches on him in every direction so I plow straight through the aisle between the tables and the ice cream bar. Sheer momentum bashes us right out the door and into the snowy street.

I think my best bet is to keep ahold of him; I've never been in a real fight and I didn't do sports in high school. I can't let him go and I don't want to punch, so it's mostly a chaotic grapple of elbows, arms locked and heads bowed, bodies twisting like battling elks while he shrieks profanities at me.

He finally wrenches hard enough that the bruise on my elbow flares with pain. I release, and he staggers free of my grip. People on the sidewalk scurry around us, then stop to stare and whip out their phones. His fist comes at my face. As if someone else has taken over my body, I jerk back, grab his arm and swing around, using all his momentum to throw him to the ground.

Our onlookers make a collective sound of astonishment, the kids inside start clapping, and he hits the packed snow on the pavement at precisely the same moment a local police cruiser turns up the street.

6

"THOUGHT I WAS COMING UP the street to a Harting boy." Deputy Dwight Larsen shakes his head at me, yet his demeanor suggests he finds the whole thing hilarious. Imogen got her height from him, her build, her hair, her freckles. I wonder if he still sees me as a kid, as Imogen's little hiking buddy. "Not you, Gage."

"I'm sorry," I mutter from my spot, sitting on the curb. No one called him; he just happened to be driving by on his route. I can't believe it. People edge by, the click of ski boots on the sidewalk infiltrating my head. *Tck tck* . . . I pack some dirty sidewalk snow in my palms and press it to the back of my neck.

No one in the diner is eating, or working. They're watching through the big windows. Andy hovers over me like a mother hen, silent, shocked, and probably wondering if this is going to be good or bad for business.

Blondie talks heatedly to another officer while I sit in shame on the curb. I hunch forward, trying to be invisible. I wish they would turn off the flashing blue and red lights even though they're washed out in the daylight, but I think Imogen's dad enjoys the spectacle.

"Are we about done?" Andy asks him. "I still have customers."

I stare at the police cruiser, a big white SUV with a gold star and banner emblazoned along the sides. What if I have to get in it? I curl my arms over my stomach, counting backward from one hundred.

"Well, that's up to him." Deputy Larsen nods to Blondie. "And if he wants to press charges."

My head jerks up. "What? Press *charges*?"

"For assault, Gage," he says almost gently, brow furrowing.

Blondie stomps over to us. "You bet I do."

"Come on, Dwight," Andy mutters uncomfortably to Deputy Larsen. "He's a good kid. You heard what happened."

Before Larsen can answer, Blondie points at me. "Yeah, he attacked me. He was harassing us." I gulp air, then close my eyes against the flashing red and blue. "And I heard that little bitch in there say she was going to spit in our food. Just because we're not from here."

"Hey now," Andy growls.

"That's a lie!" I shove to my feet. Larsen lifts a hand, and Andy pushes between us, arms wide like he could stop me. "He threw his glass at me first, is that assault too? Do I get to press charges?"

Andy pats my arms, trying to contain me. "Okay, okay, Gage, it's okay."

"Easy now, everybody." Deputy Larsen's eyebrows draw together and he looks up at the window where the waitresses are peering out at us, including his wide-eyed, mortified youngest daughter. "Which little 'bitch' was that again, sir?"

"Mikaela," I answer for him, loud and clear. Larsen raises his chin, red creeping up his neck and face.

Blondie hesitates, glancing between us. I watch it dawn on him that the restaurant owner and the sheriff's deputy are on a first-name basis, that this town could fit in the palm of his hand. "Maybe. I . . . I don't remember. You know what, forget it." He lifts his hands and drops them. "Forget it. I don't need to press charges. He's obviously going nowhere anyway." He glares me up and down as if to remind me he's doing me a favor, and I look away before I give him something real to press charges about. "Am I free to go?"

Larsen glances at Andy, then at me. I shrug, folding my arms over my stomach.

Andy nods sharply. "Don't come back here. Any of you. Or I'll have you for trespassing." He looks at Deputy Larsen, pointing a finger. "Got that, Dwight?"

Larsen nods, eyebrows up. "Oh, I've got it all."

Blondie scoffs. "Believe me, we won't be back." He rejoins his friends, who've taken their stuff from the diner. I bet they didn't even pay. I guess they never got to eat, though.

Deputy Larsen pats my shoulder once, awkwardly. "All good here? I'm not going to write you up, unless you need a lecture?"

"No, sir. Yes, I'm all good. Thanks." I can't look at

him. He was there. He was there, the night of the crash. Paramedics were helping me out of the car when he arrived and we were all painted in flashing blue and red lights. He saw me sobbing and screaming and trying to get back into the car with Hunter.

I close my eyes.

He hesitates before leaning close, gripping my shoulder. "Say hi to your folks. You know you guys can call me or Rachel if you need anything."

I nod once, glancing at him with what I hope is gratitude, but is probably just numbness. I wonder if he approves of me attacking the guy.

I wonder if he has nightmares, like mine.

Probably not.

He heads inside to talk to Mikaela. I turn to follow, wishing I had a cold pool of water to dive into. Maybe I can submerge my head in the sink for a couple seconds. This town really needs a pool that isn't attached to one of the luxury vacation lodges.

Andy catches my arm, but when I look at him, he averts his gaze. "Hey, Gage. Why don't you . . . why don't you take the rest of the day off? Or a couple days?"

"What?" The words bring me fully to the moment.

He pats my arm and motions up the sidewalk. "You know, take the rest of the week. Take a break. You've been full-time since—uh—graduation, so why don't you relax?"

Amazement clears my head. "Are . . . are you firing me?"

"No!" He looks up quickly, then his eyes dart away. "Just take a few days. You're always welcome here, kiddo. I know this is, uh, a rough week for you. I'm sorry I didn't realize you were stressed."

"I'm not, I'm okay. I'm sorry." Heat and embarrassment and frustration gather hot behind my eyes. I clench my jaw. "I'm really sorry, Andy, it'll never happen again. I really want this job, I love it here."

"I know." He pats my shoulder firmly. "I'm not firing you, Gage, we're all good. Take a few days. Start fresh next week. Monday, Tuesday, whenever."

He takes the last word and heads back inside, while I stand there and stare at the people who are still looking out the window. One of the younger guys, Noah, gives me a thumbs-up and holds up his phone to assure me he got the whole thing on video. Great.

Andy tried to make it sound like a favor, but it doesn't feel that way. I can't keep my act together, so he's sending me to the corner.

I force my feet to move and cut through the alley between the diner and the art gallery next door to slip in the back and grab my coat. There's no way I'm walking through the diner now. I can't talk to anyone after that, not even Mikaela. Especially not Mikaela. She asked me not to do anything and I did anyway, but the worst part is I know I only half did it for her.

Something snapped in my brain somewhere in the interaction, when I stopped doing it for her and for principle, and started doing it for myself—but that didn't even work. I don't feel proud of it. I don't feel righteous. I don't know if I feel anything. I want to curl up in bed for three days.

Maybe Andy's right.

He walks into the break room from the kitchen, and I'm just standing there with the door open to the cold alley.

I pull on my coat as if I have a plan for where to go. "I started the candy order. It's on your desk."

"Okay," Andy says. "I'll find it."

"The hard candy's doing okay, mostly gummies and chocolate, probably—and Noah said there's this sour candy challenge on TikTok, so I'd stock up on that."

He crosses his arms, smiling. "Okay, I'll ask him about it."

"And the lettuce is looking iffy." I wiggle my hand so-so. "So you might want to call the co-op."

"Got it."

I zip my coat, grab my hat from the hook, and turn, then pause. "Oh, Pat from the restaurant supply called last night—"

"Gage." Andy levels a stare at me. "I'll see you next week."

For a second I hang in the doorway, but he promised this isn't forever, so I lift a hand and duck out, shutting the door firmly behind me.

The afternoon stares back at me in bright, snowy emptiness.

I'm reluctant to go home since I promised Justine I would walk her back from dance practice, and she'll be out at four, and that's more walking than I want to do in a day.

As the upcoming days of *nothing* spread themselves before me, my breath hitches and I squeeze my eyes shut. My phone buzzes and I yank it out with relief. Maybe it's Andy, realizing he can't do without me.

DadB: Probably won't make it to the diner for that burger this week, safety trainings.

I close my eyes, grateful he wasn't there to see the fight,

and text him back not to worry about it. As it's sending, another comes through.

Imogenesis: Mik told me you just went full Hulk on a customer LOL you okay???

Air huffs out my nose. Clouds drift off the sun and it blazes across the fresh snow in the alley, the parking lot nearby, the cars with their mounded snow hats, and I duck into the shadow of the building to avoid getting blinded.

Me: Did she tell you what he said?

Imogenesis: She told me everything. Sounds like he needed a high five in the face.

She sends a fist emoji.

Me: It wasn't worth it.

Cold seeps through my coat and I get moving, walking up the alley, even though I don't know where I'm going.

Me: I just got so angry. You should've seen this guy's hair.

Imogenesis: Lolol what? Was it a faux-hawk? Did that send you over the edge? GAGE SMASH >:O

I halt with a snort and rub my eyes.

Me: Andy gave me the rest of the day off. Want to hang out?

Imogenesis: Aww booo! Mia and I are halfway to the hot springs. Wow, I should've raged at customers more often, Andy never gives anyone time off.

Me: I think he was embarrassed.

Mindlessly, I text and meander my way through the alleys and side streets, avoiding tourists and locals alike.

Imogenesis: Mia said she'd turn around and get you if you want to come. Half hour maybe.

Me: Can't.

Imogenesis: The roads are great, dry.

Me: I'm making snacks for Jack's Warhammer thing tonight.

Imogenesis: :|

Me: Thanks though. Hey will you ask Mia if she has any allergies and if she eats pork?

She sends a GIF of a suspicious chicken. Then her ellipsis pulses, stops, and I imagine they're trying to figure out why I'm asking. I chuckle, letting them enjoy the mystery. I emerge from the back alley at the end of the main avenue of shops and restaurants and turn up the corner toward the library. Outside, I claim a seat on one of the cold metal benches the Visitors Bureau paid a bunch of money to sprinkle around town a few years ago. Dad gripes that there's better things to do with tax money, but at that moment, I'm grateful for a bench outside in the sunny, frosty air.

Imogenesis: She says yes pork, no allergies.

Me: Cool thx.

Imogenesis: Whyyyyy? :O

I send a dude-shrugging emoji, then:

Me: Have fun at the hot springs.

Imogenesis: We will. And maybe you and I can hang out soon, before I go back to school. Miss you :)

I gaze at the text. I miss her too. But it's harder with her because Hunter is all woven between us.

Me: We will, promise.

She doesn't answer and I wonder if they're talking about me. Or the pork thing. Or maybe she lost service.

My brain doesn't let me sit there for long in silence because I'll go down a dark road, even in the sunlight. I send Bryson one of the recipe ideas I found last night, grasping for the feeling of being useful and competent. It takes him so long to answer, I'm shivering by the time my phone buzzes and I wonder if he's decided he doesn't want to anymore.

Brywolf: That does look fancy, and yet not easy

I grin because the image of banh mi lettuce wraps probably does look intimidating to a person who doesn't cook.

Me: It's easy. Promise. You cook meat, make two sauces, chop some things, and put it all in the lettuce. Like tacos.

Brywolf: . . .

Me: I thought we could do a practice run tonight.

Brywolf: Oh cool. We're on the hill, I should be down around 5.

Me: Just come to my house. Jack's got his friends over for gaming and I always make stuff for them.

Brywolf: We're cooking FOR people?!

Me: It's chill. Easiest customers you'll ever have. Easier than running a football fifty yards. I have faith in you. 8)

He doesn't answer for a minute. I probably shouldn't have said that. Football is too tied up with his dad maybe, abuse, his injury in the last season.

Or he's thinking how much he wants to impress Mia.

Or he literally just said he's skiing and maybe can't answer right away. Maybe everyone else is able to move on after they're hurt, and it's only me, stuck in my rut of grief and fear forever.

Bryson answers, proving this final guess correct.

Brywolf: Okay see you there. Thanks!

A warm, happy relief that he's coming blooms in my chest, along with a spasm of guilt over missing Hunter. I know that's normal. Some guilt. But Hunter would definitely want me to have friends; it's not like I'm trying to replace him. No one could and I wish I could tell him that.

I should have told him. Maybe he knew.

A lump solidifies in my throat and I need to move again.

As I stand up, another text buzzes in.

Brywolf: Oh hey, promise you won't throw me out into the street if I screw up.

Followed by several laughing-hysterically faces and a link to Noah's Instagram, where he's already posted a Story of me freaking out. And he tagged me. I stare at myself bursting out of the door with Blondie and throwing him to the ground, trying to pry apart the mortification while also kind of being impressed with myself.

Then it occurs to me it's not a great look when I'm applying for a job I really want. But surely Redwood House isn't going to dig far enough to see some kid's Instagram in Podunk Idaho. Still. Worry spears my chest and I untag myself, then send a quick message asking Noah to take it down before it spreads too much.

Bryson sends a GIF of the Hulk pitching Loki through the air, and I sink to the bench again with a hard laugh.

Me: I can make this recipe harder you know.

Brywolf: Please no. GTG heading down Zeke's Run. See you in a few.

I sit there overthinking my threat, and I hope he knows it was a joke. I wouldn't sabotage anyone. But I leave it at that because Zeke's Run is a black diamond trail, dizzyingly steep and riddled with moguls, named after one of the founders of the hill, and I don't want to distract Bryson.

For a second I gaze at the cold bluebird sky, watching my own breath crystallize in the air. When another shiver racks me, I finally give up and head into the library to flip through some books and maybe feel like my problems aren't all insurmountable.

After a couple hours, it's time to pick up Justine from dance as promised. The walk back through downtown is peaceful and soothes the last of my nerves. I'm looking forward to spoiling Justine a little with a milkshake, hanging with Bryson, and cooking for Jack's friends tonight. Feeling normal again.

Except when I get to the theater, Justine is already gone.

JUSTINE'S DANCE TEACHER REGARDS ME apologetically, his arms crossed. "I'm sorry. She said you told her you were going to get her a milkshake and she was meeting you at Nan's, so I let her leave."

Did I say that? Or that I was getting her here? I don't remember. It's only like five minutes after four. She shouldn't have left. And I have no way to contact her because Aunt Gina's not a huge fan of giving kids phones and screens, and probably won't let Justine have her own for years. A distinct, hard pulse taps up my neck. "Thanks."

He frowns at me in concern. "So she's probably there."

I try to snap out of the panic of discovering Justine is not where she is supposed to be. She's probably fine, just being a little rebel. Or maybe I told her to meet me. My mind spins and I clamp down on my thoughts. This should not be a big deal.

I smile at her teacher. "Right, probably. Thanks."

"Mm-hmm. Sorry, next time I'll make sure she stays."

"No worries." I turn back up the street, thinking of how she ditched Mom skiing, and now she's wandering downtown by herself. *It's not a big deal*, I try to remind myself. Not this time of year. Plenty of kids run around through town and it's pretty safe, but still. She's running off. I should tell Aunt Gina.

It's only a few blocks from the theater where the classes are and back to the main street, but I speed up to a jog as all sorts of unreasonable, terrible scenarios crowd my head.

It's weird to enter Nan's through the front door and I can't remember the last time I did. In the lull time between lunch and the early dinner rush, only a couple people occupy the tables, and the crew is busy cleaning and restocking. Noah punches the air when he sees me and grins. I shake my head.

Justine is not there.

Mikaela is wiping down the counter and I stomp snow from my boots before striding over to her, breathless. She looks startled and I lift my hands to say, "I come in peace." "Hey, sorry, have you seen Justine? Did she come in here?"

"Um—yeah, she did, looking for you. But then she left."

"You let her . . . She left?" I glance over my shoulder at the door, anxiety wriggling through my chest.

Her eyes are wide. "Sorry? When I said you weren't here, she said, 'Oh okay,' and left, like she knew where to go."

I stare at her as unease and failure turn my stomach, and close a fist to hide my trembling hand. I promised Justine a milkshake and a walk home and couldn't even manage that. "Did she say if she was going home or what?"

Mikaela looks out the window, then sheepishly to me. "I didn't hear. I don't know."

"She went to Mugs."

Both of us turn to look at Colby, who's sitting at the end of the bar and reading another car magazine as if he lives here. I can't believe he's still here. I shouldn't have fed him once.

"What?" I ask, trying to focus.

He leans against the counter. "She said, 'Oh okay, I'm going to get coffee.' And she went to Mountain Mugs."

Mikaela snickers, then covers her mouth when I look at her in clear distress. "Sorry, Gage. Just, saying she's going to get coffee. It's cute."

I rub my forehead as an ache pulses through the thin scar there. "You're fine. Thanks, Colby."

"Sure. Um . . . I was wondering if . . ." He fidgets, hands disappearing into his too-long sleeves.

I lift both hands and drop them in defeat. "Yeah. Mikaela, can you have Andy make him a burger? No onions. Tell him to take it out of my check or whatever." Then I point at Colby. "And you can take out the trash and wipe down the candy bins. They get dusty."

Colby looks around the diner, then to Mikaela, who tosses him a rag. To my surprise, he hops down from the stool and gets to work without complaining.

"Nice," Mikaela says, amused.

"I think he'll be okay."

She smiles. "We'll watch him."

"Thanks." Maybe I don't look like a horrible monster to her after all. Or maybe Imogen told her not to make a big deal out of it since I'm so stressed, apparently.

"Hey. I'm sorry, if—"

"We're cool," Mikaela says, cocking her head at me. "Thanks for saying something." She smiles ruefully, and my anxiousness eases.

With that settled and Colby making himself useful, I pat the counter once, then head out to jog up the street after my wayward cousin before she wanders to another destination.

THE BELL JINGLES AS I SHOVE INTO MOUNTAIN MUGS—NOW hot and sweaty. It's not far from Nan's, but simultaneously jogging and trying to convince myself Justine is fine has worked me into a state. The place is bustling as people stop in after their ski day, although it looks like most are taking their coffees to go. The sudden heat and loud alt-eighties they have playing split across my head.

Meanwhile, Justine is perched happy and calm as you please at one of the high bistro tables near the window, sipping from a big white mug. Exasperation and relief bloom across my brain.

"Hi!" a sweet voice calls from the counter, and I turn to see Olivia—who I am once again unprepared to encounter. She beams at me, brown eyes sparkling. "Gage with a *g*."

My mouth opens, but no sound comes out. She looks adorable again, no hat this time, brown curls framing her face, a knitted lavender sweater. I want to make sure I say something especially intelligent and charming.

So of course I fail to say anything.

"Gage!" Justine waves at me and I scowl at her.

"Oh, she's yours?" Olivia's still smiling, seemingly entertained by my baffled and hopefully rugged-looking silence. She points to Justine, who is eating whipped cream with rainbow sprinkles off her beverage with a spoon. "I wondered."

"Yeah, she's mine—I mean, she's not *mine*." My brain scrambles at that math. "She's my cousin. I was supposed to walk her home, but she wandered off." I say that last part louder for Justine's benefit, and out of the corner of my eye, I see her tip her head back with a world-weary sigh.

Olivia considers me, and the room's so warm, I have to shed my coat. "That's sweet of you. She said you would pay for her drink." She grins and rings it up, motioning me to the counter.

I venture close, folding my coat over my arm, but leave my hat on because I'm sure my hair is a sweaty mess. "Thanks." I conjure up a smile. "I hope she wasn't bugging you or anything."

"She's an angel," she says mischievously, lifting her eyes to mine. "Are you getting anything? Quad shot?" She holds up a twenty-ounce cup. "Did you get a lot done last night?"

I think of the evening—my dad, my aunt and her shattered sculpture, Jack finding that job opening—and rub my forehead. "Yeah. It was busy."

Her smile fades and her brow crooks, as if she's worried about me. Great. "And tonight?"

"Tonight?" My brain blanks.

She leans forward with a tiny smile. "Big plans? You need a big coffee again?"

"Yes." She remembers me and my order. Maybe that's

a good thing. I hope. "Yes, please. The same."

She shakes her head playfully. "No rest for the weary."

If only she knew. But I really don't want her to. It's only small talk and somehow I'm all spun up, but in a good way, my pulse slick. I just want to say things that make her keep smiling like that. I manage a normal breath and remember who I am and what's happening, even though mostly what's happening are her big brown eyes.

"Actually, yeah. It's kind of a fun night. My stepdad games with his friends and I cook for them."

"You cook?" She scribbles my order on the coffee cup, along with another doodle, while we talk. There's no one behind me this time. Justine is enjoying her luxurious hot cocoa. I relax slightly.

"Yeah, that's kind of my thing." I remember Mia's high opinion of guys who cook, so I make a point of it. "So I make them cool snacks and experiment with recipes."

She looks me over with another smile. "Huh. That's really neat. What game are they playing?"

"Warhammer. It's kind of like D&D."

"I know Warhammer." She's still drawing. "Fantasy or 40k or what?"

I feel like at this point even Jack would throw his own advice to the wind and tell me to go for it. "40k. The ninth edition, I think. I . . . What about you? Did you just move here?"

"Oh right, I'm new in a small town." She smiles at the cup. The flow of the Sharpie around the surface, making cool leaves and flowers and now a bird, hypnotizes me. Her nails are painted a soft lavender. "I'm here for the season, through Wild Range."

Wild Range is the umbrella company that runs the ski resort, Silver Mountain, along with the summer attractions there, and a couple of hotels on the lake. The Landry family owns that and half the town, including Mountain Mugs.

They hire people from all over the world for their seasons, so I've met young people from everywhere. They drift in and out for their adventure and I've thought about trying something like that, somewhere else.

It seems cool and brave that Olivia just packed up and came here.

Instead of saying that, though, the words that come out are "So you're here alone?"

She blinks at me, reassessing. "Well. There's the rest of the work crew." Her gaze drops back to the cup. "And my roommate."

Too late, I think of Mikaela and the douchebags hassling her, and I wish I could rewind ten seconds because I realize how my question sounded. I hate that she had to assess me, the risk of me, before answering.

"I just meant that's really cool," I mumble. My heart pounds. *Why did I ask if she was alone?* "Like, adventurous. I really didn't mean to be nosy. Maybe I'll see you around."

Her eyes lift, and her mouth quirks in what I interpret as a relieved, reassuring smile at my awkward apology. She relaxes again. "Possibly."

"Um, how much?"

She finishes her drawing before passing the cup down to the barista. "It's seven fifty, with the hot chocolate."

"Thanks." I feel stared at and look around to see Justine watching us over her mug as she takes a long drink from the hot cocoa.

"So." Olivia brushes curls off her cheek and I suppress a physical compulsion to reach up and tuck them behind her ear. Delicate gold roses pierce her ears, which are also unfairly pretty. "Where's around?"

"Around?" I jerk my gaze from her ears. "What?"

"You said you'd see me around, so where's around?" She motions a circle. "Where do the cool kids hang out?"

"The cool kids?" A grin surprises me on my own face. "I have no idea. I can tell you where the awkward nerdy ones hang out, though."

She laughs and it feels like I won the lottery.

"Ga-age," Justine calls, drawing my name into two syllables and swinging her feet. "Come sit with me."

"Just a second." I look from her to Olivia, reassured I didn't creep her out too badly. But I still tread carefully. "You know. It's a small town. I'll just . . . probably see you around."

"Hm, true. You did today, after all." She offers a more hesitant smile that sends a hundred signals to my body, but I remind myself she's in customer-service mode.

"Gage!" Justine calls again.

"Better go," Olivia murmurs. "Duty calls."

"Yeah. Yep. Have a good one." I turn around too quickly, run into a chair behind me, and nearly overturn a woman's coffee on that table.

"Sorry!" I grab for her mug to keep it steady and she stares at me in horror as if I crawled out from under her shoe. Her bougie twist of blond hair and gold-and-pearl jewelry indicates I should back away immediately and not touch her table any more than I already have. A glance over my shoulder shows Olivia with her hand over her mouth and her eyes wide with mirth.

Oh God. Oh... My brain dissolves into profanity because she's so nice and I'm acting like a clueless jerk.

"Justine. Come on." I don't trust myself to navigate the café after that. "We have to go."

Justine scowls. "Why?"

"I have to go to the store. Do you want to shop with me? I'm making snacks for the game thing tonight. You can help me pick stuff out." I'm not above a bribe at this point.

"Yeah!" The anger clears from her face and she nods eagerly. She hops from her stool and takes two steps, leaving her mug.

"Hey." I point. I've bused too many tables to let her get away with that. "It goes in the tray."

"Gage!" The barista plops my drink on the counter and I duck over to add sugar and thank him. Then I pause, remembering I didn't tip, again. Olivia is studiously cleaning the area around the register and straightening the expensive candies and packets of biscotti.

I slink back to the register to tuck a couple of bills in the jar, which usually has a different funny sign on it every day: "Aiden's Dog Food Fund" or "Monte's Mountain Bike," and today's is "Snacks for Starving Artist Olivia." She's drawn a wreath of birds around the words.

"That's really pretty," I murmur.

She looks up with that tiny smile again. "Oh, thanks."

So are you, my brain adds silently, but I think of Mikaela, angry and blushing and laughing along even though the guys made her uncomfortable, and I can't believe I asked Olivia if she was here alone. "Have, um . . .

have a good night. Afternoon."

"All of the above." She rests her elbows on the counter and props her chin in her hands. "See you tomorrow?"

Justine tugs my hand, then twines around my arm, hanging. "Let's go!"

"Yeah," I say to both of them. "See you . . ."

"Olivia," she says, pointing to the jar.

Warmth flushes my cheeks and the back of my neck, but it's good warmth, pleasant and thrilling instead of harsh and terrifying. "No, I remember. Olivia."

"Gaww!" Justine hooks her arm in mine, leaning away to try and drag me, but I'm planted, and offer Olivia a final wry smile.

She grins. "Looks like you'd better get moving."

Justine humphs and I tug my elbow gently to straighten her up.

"Yeah, looks like. Thanks again." I balance my coat and coffee and turn attention to Justine. "What's with you running off? Didn't we just say you had to tell people where you're going?"

"I did!" she insists as we head out, the bell jingling our exit. "I told Mr. Darren and then I told them at the diner."

"Okay, but . . ." I try to explain to her that doesn't mean telling random people like Colby where she's going, and she argues semantics, and when I glance back over my shoulder, Olivia is laughing at us through the window, and lifts her hand to wave goodbye.

BRYSON STANDS CLEAR OF ME with his arms crossed, watching me assemble miniature cheese sandwiches I plan to grill.

"That looks like something from *Downton Abbey*."

I grin at him over my shoulder. "Justine, butter."

She comes forward eagerly with her spatula and bowl of soft butter and Bryson gets out of the way. *Nurse, scalpel*, Hunter would mimic me, tipping his chair back and waving his hand like a conductor. I close my eyes, breathe deep, grappling the shadow back to its corner.

"How do you keep it all straight?" Bryson's voice brings me back. Here, now. Surrounded by good things. The robust voices of Jack's friends fill the living room with life and vigor. Mom and Aunt Gina have retreated from game night to watch their latest K-drama at Aunt Gina's house, make fiddly cocktails, and "solve the problems of the world" as Mom says.

"How do I what?" I ask Bryson.

Bryson motions around the kitchen and the four dishes we've got going, in various stages of completion. "How do you know exactly when to do everything?"

I set a pan on the stove for the pork he's about to make. "I don't know, practice? Like anything else. Figure out how long something takes and stack it together in my head."

"Huh." Bryson looks impressed, which gives me a supercharge of confidence. But then, that's what being in a kitchen usually does.

"Okay, let's do this." Edging around Justine, I motion Bryson to the counter with his ingredients. "Do you learn better watching or doing?"

He grabs a notebook he brought and flips to a fresh page. "Watching." He looks nervously at the ingredients— a pound of pork, a bright green head of butter lettuce, gorgeous red radishes, a cucumber, two carrots, and all the bottles to make the sauces.

"Okay, first you want to slice the vegetables because they're going to sit in the rice vinegar." I pause while he writes stuff down. "Really thin, like this." I demonstrate on a radish, swiftly rendering it into neat julienne slices. "Or if your mom has a mandoline, you can—"

Bryson laughs. "A what?"

"It's like a . . ." I flick the knife. "You know what, maybe stick with a knife."

"Yeah, I pictured, like, a mandolin." He mimes playing a small guitar and we both bust up laughing at the idea of trying to chop vegetables with it.

"Sandwiches are buttered," Justine announces.

"So you chop these all up—or you can shred the carrot. It's faster and has a softer texture."

"Gage," Justine says, tapping my hip.

I give her a one-armed hug, holding the knife clear. "I heard you, thank you, just a second—"

"And the sugar, right?" Bryson is writing. I'm impressed he read the recipe beforehand.

"What else can I do?" Justine peers at the vegetables and it's like I'm back at Nan's, directing the ballet of kids between orders.

"Um." I look around for something. "Oh. See this?" I point her to the lettuce. "I need you to pick off all the best leaves and wash them." She watches me earnestly, a very serious little sous chef. "We're not making a salad; we're using them like tortillas, so try not to break them."

"Okay!" She grabs the lettuce and carries it, like a sacred object in both hands, to the sink.

"Okay, Bry, now we start the pork."

We work through the recipe and the sauces—one goes on the meat, the other is a spicy mayo to drizzle on top once the sandwiches are done. I multitask with the grilled cheese while Bryson handles the pork.

A chorus of shouts erupts from the living room at some exciting event in the game as I start piling grilled cheeses onto a platter. Justine crowds in next to me. On the counter, she has laid ten beautiful lettuce leaves along a couple of paper towels. "Those are perfect, nice job. Now plate these."

"What's that?"

"Make them look pretty on the plate."

"Oh." She takes the sandwiches gingerly and starts stacking them up like a pyramid.

"Looks good," I say. "Take them out when you're done." She's beaming, proud of herself. The good stuff. I glance around the kitchen, taking stock, and turn to check on Bryson. "Ready to make the wraps?"

"Let's do it." He grins proudly at the pan of seasoned pork. "I feel like I'm on *Chopped* or something."

"Smells amazing!" one of Jack's buddies shouts from the living room. Then there's happy noises when Justine arrives with the grilled cheeses.

I hold the pan while Bryson painstakingly spoons meat into the lettuce, then we sprinkle the chopped vegetables on top, drizzle mayo—"And they're done," I tell him.

He writes something in his notebook. "It looks just like the picture."

"That's the idea." I nudge him with an elbow and he grabs me around the shoulders in a quick hug of thanks before we carry the food to the living room.

I don't play Warhammer, but I get the gist of it, and tonight they're doing a one-off to introduce a new guy to the game. Around the table are Jack; their GM, Meaghan, who looks like a Crossfit model with her dazzling flamingo-pink hair in a thick braid over one shoulder; the new guy, Chase; and Jack's oldest friend, who I've only ever known as Tank. He's Meaghan's husband, a big guy with a solid tattoo sleeve up his left arm, a tidy military fade of graying black hair, and a perpetual grin. The living room furniture is pushed around to make room for his wheelchair and the gaming table.

Bryson and I present the banh mi wraps. "This one's new," I tell them. "So tell us what you think. Any critique, or whatever."

"Smells delicious," Meaghan says.

"My man," Tank says, not shy about starting.

Hands dive into the wraps and they're gone in two seconds with grumbles of approval. Tank wipes his fingers daintily on a napkin, then says around a mouthful, "They're really good. A little bitter."

Meaghan elbows him. "Ingrate."

He lifts his hands. "What? He wants feedback."

"No, it's helpful," I say. "Thanks." I turn to Bryson, pointing at his notepad. "Probably too many radishes."

Bryson writes it down. "Fewer radishes. Got it."

I hand the empty plate to him. "Better go put some more wraps together."

He grins and retreats to the kitchen.

"You raise good kids, Johnny," Tank says to Jack, who offers me a thumbs-up.

"I agree."

Justine flops onto the couch. "Why do you call Uncle Jack 'Johnny'?"

"That's his name," Tank says over his shoulder. "Jack is short for John."

"How is Jack *short* for John?" she demands, eyes narrow.

"A question for the ages," Meaghan says, then tries to draw everyone back to the game. "Chase," she addresses the new guy, "you can roll to fire on those lashworms."

"Oh, it's my turn?" This guy is younger than the rest of them, all fit muscle with fresh pink scars that look like burns lacing one side of his face. He seems at ease and like he's enjoying the night. I think he might stick around; sometimes they stay and become part of the regular crew, sometimes not, but it's one of the ways Jack reaches out and interacts with his peer group. His work with Wounded Warrior Project is really what gave Hunter and me the idea for LWDA. Making sure no one falls through the cracks.

Chase's roll is inadequate to deal with the creatures, and the others groan.

"Well." Tank leans forward to scoop up the dice while Meaghan moves the ruler. "That's what you get for sending a squid to do a grunt's job."

Justine giggles even though she probably doesn't know what any of that means.

"So while he's doing that," Jack instructs Chase, "you can think about your next move. Just communicate with the rest of the squad so you guys are all working together. You know all about that."

Chase smiles faintly, his gaze ticking to one side. "Yeah."

"Or provide support"—Tank rolls the dice—"for those of us who know what they're doing."

"Like Meaghan?" Chase says easily, and she and Jack chuckle. Tank points at him as if to say touché.

"Ignore Tank," Jack says. "He's still mad about the last campaign—"

"Do not," Tank advises, and the others snicker, except for Chase, who looks between them, intrigued. "We do not speak of it."

"Why do you call him Tank?" Justine asks, hopping from the couch to stand near Jack.

"That was his call sign," Jack says. I glance over my shoulder, hoping Bryson didn't get lost on his way to the kitchen. I'll let him figure it out. It feels good to be in this room, surrounded by life and jokes and normalcy.

"What's a call sign?" Justine leans forward to peer at the table and Meaghan shoos her back before she accidentally moves pieces on the game board.

There's a crackling outside, fireworks up the street. Chase glances toward the window and shifts restlessly.

"It's what you call someone over the radio," Jack says, "to protect their identity."

Her face lights up and she looks around the table. "I want a call sign!"

"Okay." Tank rests his hand on the top of her head. "I vote Hobbit."

"No!" She bats his hand away.

"Peanut? Mouse?" He grins and Justine crosses her arms, looking at Meaghan, then Jack, for support. They are chuckling, but focused on Jack's move. My gaze is drawn to Chase, who hasn't said a word in a minute, isn't laughing, and hunches forward slowly in his chair, rubbing his forehead.

"Chase?" Meaghan asks quietly. He nods, lifting a hand but not his head.

"How about Tinkerbell?" Justine says, and they laugh.

"Hey," I say, and they look up at me. "Tinkerbell's cool. She fixes stuff and she can make people fly." Justine looks at me like I personally placed the stars in the sky, then sticks her tongue out at Tank.

"Yeah, Tank." Jack grins, leaning forward. "Can you make people fly?"

Tank lifts his bushy eyebrows. "I can if—Justine, earmuffs"—Justine obediently covers her ears—"if I push them off a high enough building." He dives his hand downward. "Whoosh."

"Whoosh?" Meaghan echoes incredulously, and Tank bares his teeth in a proud grin.

"That's the noise, yep."

"I can hear you," Justine informs him. He throws up his hands in defeat.

Something crashes and shatters in the kitchen, Bryson swears, and at the same time, a battering cacophony of firecrackers erupts practically outside our door.

Chase lunges to his feet, sending his chair backward and almost upending the table. Justine squeals and leaps to the couch and I fall back a couple steps, bracing as if I could do something. Tank's and Meaghan's hands shoot out to grab his wrists.

"Hey, brother," Tank rumbles, "you're okay. Johnny—"

"Yep." Jack heads to the front door to tell whoever's out there to knock it off.

"Chase," Meaghan says, firm and warm. "It's okay. You're here. You're safe."

For half a second I stare at Chase—short of breath, his eyes unfocused, face flushed.

I know that look, that feeling, like when I was in the car. My meltdown.

But this is not how my dad handled it. Chase stares at Meaghan while she says his name again, squeezing his arm, and tells him where he is. Tank pushes over slowly to pick up the chair, then pats him firmly on the back a couple of times.

Chase hangs his head.

Meaghan rubs his back, then stands and joins Justine on the couch while Tank leans close to Chase, speaking too low for me to hear.

This is not my business. I don't want to stare. I slink away from the table and out of the room, pulse pounding.

In the kitchen, Bryson is picking up pieces of a platter from the floor. He looks at me, wide-eyed. "Man, I'm sorry. I was trying to heat up the pork, then I moved too fast and knocked—"

"It's okay." I grab a broom from the pantry and help him, rattled and wanting to keep him out of the living room until Chase has chilled out. The sight of his panicked face is burned into my brain. Is that how I looked when I panicked? No wonder Dad told me to keep it together.

"I can replace this," Bryson is still apologizing. I must look distressed, and he thinks it's about the broken plate.

Keep it together. "It's really okay. I think Mom got it at the dollar store." I force a reassuring grin. It's quiet in the living room, and Bryson and I assemble some more wraps with what's left of the lettuce.

When we take them out, Meaghan is explaining things to a terrified Justine on the couch, and Tank's at the table, writing something. Jack is still gone, and now so is Chase. I glance inquiringly to Tank, who lifts his chin toward the side door.

"You want to grab us a six-pack, Gage? They're in the outdoor fridge." He grins. The outdoor fridge is the snowbank off the side of the porch. As Bryson sets down the food he says, "Hey, thanks. Johnny says you were a running back?"

Bryson runs a hand through his hair with a small smile. "Oh, yeah."

"Defense, myself," Tank says, inhaling another wrap. "Going to play in college?"

"Hopefully," Bryson says, sitting again. "Just letting my shoulder heal up, and dealing with some family stuff."

"Good man. Who do you like for the Super Bowl?"

Bryson lifts his hands. "Seahawks."

Tank laughs. "But really."

They start talking teams and I watch Justine for another minute, her upset, worried face, decide to let Meaghan handle it, and head to the porch.

Jack and Chase are out there, both with their arms resting on the railing.

". . . afraid she's going to leave me if I can't get it together." Chase's voice is choked and soft, and I freeze. I should leave them alone.

I don't.

Jack shakes his head. "You're doing everything right. That's why you're here. Allison knows that. New mission, right?"

"Yes, sir," he murmurs. "I know."

I rest a hand on the door frame, knowing I shouldn't eavesdrop but unable to turn away.

"Your priorities right now are"—Jack ticks things off on his fingers—"healing, loving Allison, then camping trips when that baby girl is big enough."

Chase smiles, rubbing his knuckles, and nods.

Jack grins. "Right? That's the goal. But you can't skip step one."

"Yes, sir," Chase murmurs again.

My throat feels like ice as I watch Jack.

"We've all been there," Jack says quietly.

"I know." Chase stares out at the snow, the streetlamps, the air. A warm and tense silence unfolds until he draws an immense sigh and rubs his scarred face, smiling wryly to Jack. "When does it get better?"

I hold my breath, leaning forward.

Jack rests a hand on his shoulder, squeezes, and doesn't answer.

A text buzzes on my phone and I jump, and Chase looks over sharply. Heat flushes my face and I lift a hand in apology, then check my phone.

DadB: Heard you kicked some prick's ass at the diner. Nice work, proud of you.

My eyes close for a second. Instead of pride, frustration crackles in my chest. I decide not to answer right then because he wouldn't like whatever I have to say.

Instead I step out onto the porch and shove the phone back into my pocket. "Sorry. I told Tank I'd grab some more drinks."

"Come on out, Gage," Jack says easily. "We're just talking."

Chase and I lock gazes briefly; there's a flicker of challenge and I realize he is really not much older than me. Rather than look away as if I'm embarrassed by his pain and mine and whatever else we're feeling, I follow Jack's example and nod in acknowledgment. Chase smiles faintly, but I have nothing to say, and no help to give, so I edge by them to grab the beers from the snow.

WHEN I RETURN WITH THE SIX-PACK, EVERYONE LOOKS UP AT me with wide, knowing smiles.

"Uh." I set the beers on the coffee table near Tank.

"What's going on?"

"Sooo," Meaghan says, "Justine tells us you have a new lady friend."

I whip around to glare at Justine, who's settled on the couch with her drawings. "Justine!"

"What? It's true."

"It's—it's not like that. I don't . . . *Justine.*" I press both hands to my face. Mom and Jack I could handle. But a whole room full of people? Meaghan reaches over to pat my wrist.

"Who's the lucky lady?" Tank inquires before he stuffs another banh mi wrap into his mouth. Bryson has taken up half the couch and he's grinning expectantly.

The last thing I want to do is share more information. "Uh . . ."

At that moment of course, Jack and Chase return.

"Her name is Olivia," Justine tells everyone on the planet, "She works at a coffee shop and she's really nice."

"Who's nice?" Jack comes up short by the table, patting Chase's shoulder as he resumes his seat. Tank offers him the last of the wraps and he hesitates before taking it, then a beer, eyes darting around warily until he seems satisfied that no one is staring at him.

They are not, because they're staring at me now.

"So?" Meaghan demands. "Did you ask her out?"

"No. She was . . ." I look desperately to Jack to save me, but he tilts his head with an inquiring smile as he sits again. "You know, she was working. I didn't want to bother her."

"But you're going to?" Bryson urges. Maybe he feels better about asking Mia out if I'm dating too.

"Not at work, right?" I look at Jack. "You said not to hit on women when they're working."

Tank cracks a beer. "Good rule of thumb."

"But not always accurate," Meaghan continues for him, holding out her hand. Tank purses his mouth, hands her the beer, and gets another for himself. "It's okay, you just have to figure out if the flirting is welcome or not."

"She *obviously* likes him," Justine says, impatient.

"Obviously," Bryson says, motioning to me with a grin as if to say, "What's not to like?" I would appreciate his loyalty more if it didn't feel like everyone was laughing.

"It was so embarrassing." Justine crosses her arms and rolls her eyes. I wonder when Aunt Gina is going to enroll her in theater classes to use up some of this dramatic energy.

"Okay, how do you know?" I scowl at Justine. But also, since the whole thing is out now and everyone is grinning at me like I'm a specimen in a zoo, I might as well get advice.

Meaghan starts to speak, but Tank, oblivious, leans forward, sliding one hand in a line through the air. "First you establish a baseline for her, right? You know what I mean by that?"

"Yeah, like, situational awareness." I cross my arms. "What's normal." I glance to Jack, who nods to confirm.

Tank grins his approval. "Yep. Nice. Nice work," he says to Jack, approving of his parenting. "So, you figure out how she's treating everyone else and if she's treating you the same."

"Well, yeah, she's nice to everyone."

Meaghan sits back and crosses her arms with an amused smile. "But is she extra nice to you?"

"I . . . I don't know."

Justine sighs loudly and trots to the kitchen.

"Oh wait." Bryson sits forward on the couch. "Is this that girl at Mugs? Yeah, she's cute. You should go for it. I could ask Aiden if she——"

"No!" I rub my forehead. "Please don't help."

Justine returns with my now empty coffee cup covered in Olivia's pretty doodles. "Look! She drew this on his cup!"

There's a collective "Ooo!" and I consider wading out into the snow, never to return.

"Let's see," Meaghan says, holding her hand out for the cup.

"Damn," Tank says, leaning in close to her to peer at the doodles. "I should commission her to do some designs for my right arm." He lifts said arm, naked compared to the intense ink on his left. They pass the cup around while I wonder how long I could survive in a tent in the woods.

"What do you know about her?" Jack asks mildly, as if he's not completely interested in me doing something positive and brave like asking someone out.

I fold my arms over my chest. "She's working the season for Wild Range."

"So you've talked?" Jack is calmer than the rest, but I can tell he's happy about it. Relieved, maybe, that I'm showing signs of life.

"Yeah," I mumble. "A little, while they're making my coffee."

"What's this?" Meaghan points at the second *g* in my name, where Olivia once again drew a smiley face. I hadn't noticed before.

"Oh, that's . . . It's a joke." Everyone continues passing

the cup around. "She got my name wrong on the first—"

"You already have inside jokes?" Bryson sits forward, raising both fists. "Bro, you're in!"

"I found a heart!" Chase points triumphantly at the cup, and fire engulfs my face and neck so thoroughly that sweat springs on my scalp. Justine squeaks and crowds in close.

Tank leans over to look, then shakes his head. "That's a butterfly wing."

"Let me see!" Justine shrieks.

"It's obviously a heart," Chase says, eyes narrowing.

"Let's see," Jack says, peering over his glasses, but Justine has the cup now.

"Okay." I pluck the cup from her hands and hide it against my chest. "Thanks, everyone. I'll . . . Thanks. I'll think about it."

"It sounds like you should go for it," Meaghan advises patiently, and as she is the only grown woman in the room, I want to trust her opinion above the enthusiasm of the men, as well-meaning as they are. I meet her eyes and she smiles encouragingly. "Just, if she says no, respect it."

"Right," I agree.

"Let me know if you need any advice," Tank offers.

"What qualifies you?" Chase wants to know.

"Me?" Tank leans back, stretching an arm around Meaghan. "Twenty years married to the woman of my dreams, that's what." He grins and Meaghan laughs, but she rests a hand on his thigh and leans over to kiss his cheek. Tank points at me. "Door's open, brother."

"I'm good," I mumble. "Thanks." My heart pounds and it takes all my willpower not to peek at the cup and see if there is indeed a butterfly wing or a heart.

Jack pats his hands firmly against the table and finally saves me. "Can we play now? Before the swarm kills us all?"

They agree and leave me in peace, and instructing Chase in the game takes enough focus and friendly ragging that it seems like they've stopped thinking about me at all. Bryson and I hang in the living room for a while. He worries Mia hasn't answered her phone and I let him know she and Imogen are at the hot springs and might not have service until tomorrow, unless they come back late.

Eventually Justine gets bored and I escort her home, and later it's a cluster of goodbyes and putting on coats and people shuffling out the door, leaving the house buzzing in the sudden quiet after a good evening.

Jack and I roll up our sleeves and start on the dishes.

For a minute there's contented quiet; he washes, I dry.

"So," he ventures. "Anything on your mind?"

This ritual started when I was a kid. Mom's the original cook of the family, so we would clean up, and Jack made it our time to bring up anything I didn't want to talk about over dinner.

"The usual," I say, hoping he doesn't ask about Olivia again. Or Hunter.

"Mm." He scours the buttery pan where the grilled cheese rested. "Do you want to talk about why you turned all Gordon Ramsay at work today?"

Oh. I wonder who told him. There's one degree of separation between any two people in this town, so it could've been anyone. Andy. Deputy Larsen. Maybe Imogen called my mom. People circling me, talking about me, worried. Shame and uncertainty sweep my chest when I realize he might've been wondering about it all night, and not said a word.

I stack the plate back in the cupboard. "Do I have to?"

"Nope." He sprays down the pan. "It's just really unusual for you and I was worried."

My harsh sigh surprises even Jack, and he looks at me over his shoulder, sprayer in one hand, pan in the other.

"Gage."

I've hunched up near the counter, wishing I had a shell to disappear into. *Don't ask if I'm okay, don't, please don't.*

His gaze drops to the sink full of soapy water, and he clears his throat. "I'm not sure when you and I stopped talking, but I miss it. And I don't know if it's something I did, but I want you to know you still can. Okay?"

"Okay." I stare at the toast crumbs on the counter, then wipe them off with my hand.

He waits a second, then focuses back on his work. "Okay."

With his back to me, it's easier to start. "I'm just . . . I'm not proud of it."

Maybe sensing if he looks at me I'll close up again, Jack just hands me the pan. "How do you feel about it?"

"Embarrassed," I mumble, rubbing my towel listlessly against the pan. "Everyone thinks it's great and funny and maybe he deserved it, but I don't know. Then Andy told me to take a week off, so I'm pretty sure I shouldn't have done anything."

Jack nods, listening, and I remember why I used to talk to him more, when I was younger. Before we lost Hunter, when talking helped and answers made sense.

He's stacked up more dishes, the sauce bowls, a spatula, while I take forever drying the pan. Now he watches me in the reflection of the window over the sink. "Do you want to know what I think?"

"Sure." I work on all the smaller dishes and for a minute it feels like I'm fourteen again and he's offering advice about my discovery that my friend Rowan is pretty and smells good.

"So this is my opinion," he says, calm and clear, which is how he has prefaced his advice since the day I met him. "I think, at least as far as speaking up, you did the right thing."

Relief floods me in a cool rush. I didn't realize how afraid I was that Jack was mad at me or disappointed until now. "Really?"

"Really." He glances at me, the warm kitchen light glinting off his glasses. "Sometimes it's hard to do and it doesn't feel like a big deal, but it was. As far as fighting . . ." A brief shrug before he smiles. "You were there, I wasn't. That's a situation you have to judge every time. I think it's best to avoid a fight when you can, but sometimes you can't. You have to be careful, though, because it can seriously escalate, accidentally. If he'd cracked his head on the sidewalk or one of you hits too hard"—he snaps his fingers—"done."

I shake my head. "I don't think I should've. Not that time. Like, in Andy's restaurant and when I was mad about other stuff that had nothing to do with those guys."

Jack nods with a slight smile; he approves of me coming to a conclusion on my own. "Well, remember that next time."

"You've been in fights, right?"

He barks a laugh and points at me, flinging a clump of bubbles. "Oh no, sir, we're not getting into my history."

"Come on." I grin, my heart uncurling. Right. This is Jack. "Let's hear it."

He examines a whisk for specks of soap. "I'm afraid that information is sealed in the tomes of parental confidentiality."

"Okay, I'll ask Tank."

He laughs and shakes his head, tossing me the whisk. "On pain of death, boy."

We continue in quiet. When the dishes are put away, I wipe down the counters, the desire to let it all out climbing up my chest.

"So," he says, squeezing out the sponge. "What other stuff were you mad about?"

"What do you mean?"

He leans back against the counter. "You said you picked a fight because you were mad about other stuff."

"I . . ." My throat locks. "I don't know. Just everything. Hunter. You know."

"I know," he says. Not pushing, listening.

"It's . . . it . . ." Before I can melt down in front of him, alarms flash in my head and I pivot topics swiftly. Maybe I can get help without being obvious. "What's going on with Chase?"

"Chase?" He turns in surprise and plucks off his glasses, wiping steam from the lenses, head tipped down. "Hypervigilant. Sometimes he has panic attacks, flashbacks."

Panic attacks. I don't want to ask too much more

because then Jack would know. "Is he going to be okay? Like, you can get over that, right?"

"He's doing okay. It's hard work, what he's going through." He's watching me too closely. "Some people never overcome those things."

"Oh." I know which people he means. People who aren't strong enough.

I fidget with the dish towel, then move past him to hang it on the oven handle. He steps aside, turning to continue facing me. There's so much on everyone's plates. Jack works with the veterans and I don't want to give him one more person to worry about when those people have been through so much worse. I'm afraid he's going to suggest therapy again, and I just . . . can't. I also don't want to lie to him anymore, and those two compulsions emerge as a word without a plan.

"Jack—"

"Listen, Gage—"

He smiles crookedly and reaches out to grip my arm, but I'm afraid if I talk more, I'll start crying and I can't let him see that.

Before either of us can continue, Aunt Gina and Mom parade into the kitchen from the side door, both of them pink in the cheeks from their cocktails, grinning like they really have solved the problems of the world. Jack draws a breath through his nose, holds my gaze a second, then smiles at them.

Mom gasps in happiness. "Look at my men in here cleaning the kitchen." She saunters over, gives me a squeeze, then slides her arms around Jack and kisses his shoulder.

"Hey now, lady," Jack says warmly, kissing her hair,

"my wife will be home any second." He looks at me over her dark hair, eyebrows crooked up. I nod, wave my hand for *later*, and look away.

"We have an announcement," Mom says.

Aunt Gina has a wide smile, and she spreads her arms as if she might hug the whole world. "I'm going to do the show."

"Wow!" Jack grins, looking between them. "That's great. But I thought you wouldn't have time to make something?"

"I do. I have a new idea." Aunt Gina beams at Jack, then at me, eyes bright and excited, and clasps her hands behind her head. "Because my nephew is a genius."

"Me?"

"You," Aunt Gina confirms.

"This calls for a celebration," Jack says.

We finish up cleaning, they crack a bottle of wine, and we all head into the living room to hear the idea. Aunt Gina sits cross-legged on the floor near the fire, her hands painting the vision in the air.

"It's about grief," she says, which makes sense. I don't think any of us could work from anything else right now. "I'm still working on the title, but I'm thinking 'In This Brokenness,' or something." She flicks a hand, and goes on to describe the installment.

It will be a walk-through display of glass fragments, all shining black but progressing to gray and white as the viewer moves through. The path is circular, from dark to light to dark again, and again, as many times as you want to walk through it.

Shards of glass jutting from the floor, suspended from

the ceiling, a maze of treacherous, beautiful pieces, with a trail of crushed glass leading the viewer. I close my eyes as she speaks, picturing it. Tumbled glass crunching underfoot, walking among shards, leaning away from sharp-edged objects.

"Like moving through grief," Aunt Gina murmurs, and sips her wine.

I see it. Precious, dangerous thoughts—good memories, sadness, the fear of knowing the sorrow could slice you open any second. It's brilliant. It's definitely not my idea, but if saying her broken sculpture was pretty got her there, I'll take it. I glance to Mom and she is bright-eyed, watching her sister proudly.

"All right," Jack says, leaning forward and resting his hands on his knees, hands folded. "Let's talk logistics. The Tahoe can haul a trailer. . . ."

As he's talking, the entire day hits me like my dad's Mack truck. I stand, making them pause. "I'm tapping out." I kneel by Aunt Gina to hug her and she clamps her arms around me. "It's a really cool idea," I murmur. *I wish Hunter could see it.* "It's going to be amazing."

"Thank you," she whispers, and pats my back before releasing me.

Jack stands to offer a hug, then Mom. I retreat and their voices float up the stairs after me.

I enter the sanctuary of my room, close the door, and lean against it, glad Mom and Aunt Gina came home before I spilled my guts to Jack. They know I still struggle with cars; he doesn't need to worry that I'm going to break down if I hear a turn signal, if a guy makes me mad, if a smell reminds me too sharply of Hunter. Aunt Gina needs to focus on her art, Mom on her work and her sister, Jack on his veterans.

I can do this. I *have* to do this.

I distract myself with the job application. One question asks the applicant what they would do with a list of ingredients. Potato, leeks, fish. It's not a trick question per se, but I'm a hundred percent sure I'm supposed to squeeze as much out of those ingredients as possible, not just a single impressive dish. I study the menu for Redwood House to get their vibe, then sketch ideas for some different appetizers and a main course until I doze, head on my desk.

The bleak familiar nightmare darts forward from the dark. The car horn, careening across the road, Hunter's face—

I jerk awake.

A raw breath brings me back to the room, the moment. I sit up slowly and press the heels of my hands to my eyes.

"You're okay," I mumble, then drop my hands to my lap and stare at the Redwood House application for a second to pull away from the memories.

A cramp twists down my neck and I roll my shoulders before tapping my phone to check the time. Just after three in the morning. I switch off my lamp, sitting in the dark as a frosty wind trickles in through my window.

Out of habit, I glance idly to Hunter's window, and flick my lamp on and off twice.

For a moment it's dark, freezing, empty.

Then across the breezeway, Hunter's lamp flicks on, and off again.

AUNT GINA KEEPS A CROWBAR by her side door for just this occasion, and I grab it as I creep into her kitchen.

Cassidy is nowhere to be seen and I remain on intruder alert, heart pounding. I know it's not Hunter. It can't be. But it is someone. I didn't imagine it.

The smart thing to do would've been to text Aunt Gina. Or wake up Jack. Or probably anything other than stalk over to her house to see who's in Hunter's room. But I take control of the situation and slip through their house in the dark as easily as if it's my own house, up the stairs. Their floor plan is a mirror of ours. The cool air of the hall smells familiar, Aunt Gina's laundry and all her sandalwood diffusers. I step wide over a creaky board in the hall and pause outside Hunter's room. It's dark.

With the crowbar clenched in one hand, I ease the door open, holding my breath.

There's a small gasp and it feels like my heart ascends out of my chest.

"Justine?" I rest the crowbar outside against the wall so she doesn't see it, but I don't step into the room. Belatedly, Cassidy gives the softest *woof* from inside the room, tail thumping. "What are you doing?"

"I couldn't sleep," Justine whispers, and turns on the lamp. She's wearing her She-Ra pajamas, perched on Hunter's bed. Cassidy is curled at the end of the bed and huffs a sigh at the light. "What are you doing?"

"Same." I rest a hand on the door frame, pressing my thumb hard against the ridges of wood. We haven't really touched Hunter's stuff yet. Aunt Gina's not ready. I'm not ready. Nobody's ready, so the room remains as it was the night we were driving back from the movie theater, except she's cleared the trash and his laundry. "Then you turned the lamp on, and I wanted to see who was in here."

She squints at me. "Who did you think it was?"

I smile wearily. "I don't know. Batman. Come on, let me tuck you back in."

She hugs her knees to her chest and stares at me. "I want to stay here. Sometimes I sleep in here. Mom says it's okay."

I rub my thumbnail against the wood. His room smells exactly as it always has, like a library: books and an almond diffuser. It feels like he's there. "Yeah, of course it's okay."

A single step into the room doesn't send alarm bells through my head, and I take a steadier breath. This is a safe place. Sad, empty, but safe. Not like the car. Hunter's room, covered in movie and fantasy posters and crammed with books on homemade cinder-block shelves and a closet full of handmade Lord of the Rings costumes, is a good place.

I feel happy here, not devastated, and with vast relief I step in and sit with Justine on the bed. She leans against me, and I wrap an arm around her.

"Did you have fun tonight? You really helped in the kitchen."

"Yeah." Her soft voice is muffled against my shirt. "But I miss Hunter."

My eyes close and I give her a squeeze. "Me too, Tinkerbell." I give her new call sign a try.

She giggles against my chest. "How come you never talk about him anymore?"

"Oh." My mouth works, quivers. It feels like he's chilling with us there in the room. But he's not. "It just . . ." Words that aren't mine come to mind. *It doesn't do any good. Why drag up sad things?* That's Dad, not me. *Crying doesn't do any good.* I clear my throat roughly. "You know, it hurts."

She's quiet for a second, and I scramble to keep myself together. It's not panic, it's only tears. But I can't. I can't, not in front of her. I think of her bewilderment, watching Chase's panic attack.

"It hurts not to talk about him too," she finally says.

I try to think of something that won't send me flying to pieces.

She picks at my shirt. "If I die, will you stop talking about me?"

My heart crumbles and I suck a sharp breath against a horrified sob, and close both arms around her. "Oh no, Justine. I will. I would talk about you all the time. Promise. How funny you are and what a great skier you are and—"

"Hunter was a better skier," she says, and my mouth clamps tight.

I do want to talk about him. I do. I want to shout from the rooftops what an amazing person and friend he was. What a good brother, a good cousin, a good son, one of the only guys I knew who truly believed in magic.

But when I do, the words dissolve into sorrow.

It isn't just that he died a year ago. It's that he dies again every day, every time I think of him. I don't know when it transforms into loving memories, into moving forward. Maybe never. Maybe I'm fighting a losing battle. Aunt Gina's glass installment will be circular, so unless they walk out, the viewer keeps circling through the sharpness, the dark and the light, the good and the bad.

Maybe she knows it will never end.

"Justine . . ." I swallow hard against my tight throat. "How about if you talk about him for a while? Maybe about when Hunter took you skiing in the trees? Tell me a story?"

"And then you," Justine says, and I gather my sadness into iron bands and clamp them tight, wrenching down until my chest aches, so I can be here for her.

"Okay. I will. You tell a story and then I'll tell a story."

She pulls away and kneels, facing me. "When I was eight, he said I was big enough to go through the trees and he showed me the trails. He would ski behind me, and he told me about the tree wells." She tells me this to assure me she's capable, even though Mom was worried. "So I know how to be safe. And one time, he pretended to run into a tree and all these people stopped to help. It was so funny."

I nod, my mind drifting as she speaks, to whipping down the hill with Hunter and Imogen. I like straightforward blue runs, cruising downhill, but he was the better skier, tackling trees and moguls and knee-deep powder. Plowing into life.

"Now you," Justine says, and I snap back to her, scrambling for something that won't make me cry. Not skiing.

I scoot farther on the bed to lean against the wall, looking around the room. Almost all my memories involve Hunter, so it's a challenge to parse one from the rest.

My gaze falls on the sword I got him for his sixteenth birthday, which is the centerpiece of his whole room. All the old happiness and wonder swamps me, our love of books and movies and the belief that old powers might be real, and that good and nobility will overcome. Hunter made it real, loved it, was never embarrassed that he believed in magic. My brother, my captain, my king.

I point. "Do you see that sword?"

Justine peers over and nods, resting her cheek on her knees to look at me.

"It's from Middle-earth, and it's called Andúril, the Flame of the West. The sword of the king of Gondor."

"Nuh-uh." She peers at me suspiciously and I lift my chin and point again to the sword, which is a truly beautiful replica of the movie sword.

"Yeah-huh. Hunter told me it was the best present he

would ever receive for the rest of his life."

Justine looks again at the sword, eyes wider. I saved for months. It's a fully functional weapon—maybe not really crafted from the shards of Narsil, but well made by a reputable forge, not a cheap Amazon knockoff. Hand-forged, dual hardened and sharpened, with the sun, moon, seven stars, and runes inscribing the inner fuller. I hope I always remember his face, the ear-to-ear grin, the shameless bellow of glee when he unwrapped it. The bone-crushing hug.

I clear my throat, cross my arms, and remember to tell the story out loud. "You remember that camping trip? When we had our birthdays out in the state park?"

Justine grins. "Yeah! We jumped off the rocks into the river. I didn't want to, but Hunter said it would be okay because he'd done it a million times."

"Yeah," I say. "Hunter was fearless."

The tightness in my chest eases; I breathe more freely, and any feelings of panic have slipped away in that happy memory. Something new whispers in my chest, but I don't recognize it yet. It's like hope, but not. Maybe this is the path out. Please let there be a path out.

We're both quiet for a minute.

Then out of nowhere, Justine erupts into tears and curls up against me, sniffling and burying her face in my chest. "I miss him," she whispers.

My throat aches and a noise comes out. I hug her again and rest my cheek in her hair, squeezing my eyes shut. "Me too. It's okay, Justine."

But she keeps crying and a wave rolls forward in my head. She so rarely cries anymore, I strive to keep it together. *Later, later, not in front of her.* She's usually bright and strong—and now she feels so frail and small. I know she's not, my little skier daredevil cousin, running off on her own, rolling her eyes, speaking truths in rooms full of adults. But I guess I'm safe enough to melt down on because she shudders and cries and all I can do is sit there numbly and pet her back and her hair.

That little girl needs you.

"Hey." I try to clear the ache from my voice. "It's okay."

But it's not okay. It will never be okay again. Hunter's never coming back. The golden warmth and peace that came from remembering good times is swallowed in the dark. I shove my pain to the wall and rack my brain for a comfort for her. And it comes to me.

"Hey." I pat her shoulders, make her sit up so I can see her red tearstained face. "I have something for you, okay? Stay here. I'll be right back. It's okay."

"No, stay," she pleads.

I edge away, off the bed. "I'll be right back, I promise. Stay right here."

She stares at me, drawing Hunter's pillow close to hug instead. Cassidy looks up at me as if she's irritated by all the moving around, then drops her head to her paws with another sigh.

On my way back down the hall I snatch the crowbar to put it away, move stealthily back through my own house, to my room, pull the box from under the bed, and retrieve Hunter's phone. She needs it more than I do. I need to let go of it.

I delete all the apps and lock everything else down with a password, turn off the data and Wi-Fi just to be safe, and grab the charger. I know Aunt Gina doesn't want Justine to have a phone, but this is different.

I pause over the fake text conversation, steel myself, and swipe to delete the whole thing.

When I return to Hunter's room, Justine is curled around the pillow under the blankets, eyes closed. My step into the room opens her eyes.

"Hey." I sit near her on the bed to offer the phone. She takes it and runs her fingers over the silver embossed tree with a smile. She knows what it is. "This has all the pictures Hunter and I ever took for the last few years. If you're sad, you can look through them. And there's music on here he used to listen to."

She wipes her nose on a corner of the sheet and props herself up on an elbow. I show her how to look through the albums by year, and we scroll through a few until a smile lights her face again and my chest relaxes with triumph.

After she's smiling, I squeeze her shoulder and start to go.

"No, stay!" She grabs my arm while her other hand clutches the phone.

"I need to go to bed." I pat her hand. "It's okay. Why don't you come over in the morning and help me make breakfast?"

"You said you couldn't sleep," she argues. But I can't sit there and talk about Hunter with her. She's fine now, and I will end up a mess. I know it in my bones.

Instead I close my eyes, there in my best friend's room, and sort out what he might do. But I don't know. He wouldn't do anything; he wouldn't have to, because if he were here, this wouldn't be happening. We'd all be asleep in our beds because everything would be okay.

My eyes open and come to rest on the sword. Beneath that is a bookshelf, his shrine to our favorite authors, whose words and worlds shaped us and made us better able to deal with our gray and mundane existence.

I start to stand and Justine grabs my shirt.

"Hang on. I'll stay." I pat her hand again and she releases me warily so I can cross the room. I pull Hunter's dog-eared, dirt-stained, battered copy of *The Hobbit* from the shelf, and rub my thumb over the embossed letters on the cover. On the title page there's a thumbprint stain from when we took the book camping and read it after we'd eaten s'mores. I press my thumb over the print, which is Hunter's, then return to Justine and sit on the bed. "Hunter and I read these books a million times. What if you and I read it together?"

She appears skeptical. "It looks long."

I nudge her with my knee as I draw it up comfortably onto the bed. "You'll like it."

"Did Hunter like it?"

"Yes." I rub my thumb over the cover again and again, tracing the letters. "But his favorite book was *The Two Towers*."

"I want to read that one, then."

I grin. "Nope. You have to read them in order." She sighs, but settles back in and watches me expectantly. I touch Hunter's phone. "Can I see this for a second?" She hands it back and I open his music to his Shire playlist, ignoring my pounding heart. Once the soft flute surrounds us, Justine cuddles the phone back to her chest and pulls her blankets up with an eager smile, and I press the paperback open carefully with my thumb.

"'In a hole in the ground there lived a hobbit . . .'"

Justine gazes at me while I read, and eventually her eyes close.

While we're still in the midst of the unexpected party, the bedroom door cracks and Aunt Gina peers in, brow furrowed. She sees us and covers her mouth, then turns her hand to indicate I should carry on, and slips back out.

I keep reading until my voice is threadbare, Justine and Cassidy are snoring, and the playlist has gone quiet.

JUSTINE STARES IN AWE AS I CRACK AND OPEN EGGS ONE-handed into a bowl, something I've been practicing since I was her age.

"Pay attention to your knife," I warn. She looks back to her cutting board and resumes carefully slicing cherry tomatoes in half. "Those look great."

She beams and her feet do a quick tap-step of victory, carrying on while I pour the eggs into the big cast-iron skillet that Mom got me for my fifteenth birthday.

Snow falls, piling up on the kitchen windowsill, the porch, the streets. Mom wanders into the kitchen in her winter robe, fluffy white with silver snowflakes, rubbing her eyes, dark hair in a cloud around her shoulders. "What's this?"

"We're making a frilala!" Justine says. Mom grins, sliding in to wrap an arm around both of us without disrupting the work.

"Also known as a frittata," I say wryly, "in some parts of the world."

"Well, that sounds delicious." Mom smooths Justine's hair.

"Hakuna frittata," Justine sings as she chops tomatoes. "What a wonderful egg . . ."

Mom and I both laugh. "That's pretty good." I nudge Justine.

Mom rests her hands on Justine's shoulders. "Can I invite your mom over?"

"Yes," Justine says.

"That was the plan," I inform her. "Since I'm on vacation now, I thought we'd make breakfast." I smile at Mom over my shoulder and she rises on her tiptoes to kiss my cheek, then the top of Justine's head. Then she moves back to pull her phone from her robe pocket, text Aunt Gina, and start a pot of coffee.

Justine continues singing "Hakuna Frittata" and Mom helps improvise new words, and before we're finished Jack has come downstairs and Aunt Gina arrives, still in her pajamas and slippers, with Cassidy at her heels.

Admittedly, it is good to hang out in my own kitchen with the family instead of trudging off to prep for Andy. I thought being out of my routine would throw me off track, but it's calming and cozy with the snow, with everyone in the same room. I hold on to that feeling—here, safe, instead of thinking about the rest of the day. The scent of coffee and toast hangs snug in the air and the walls.

They talk about the trip to Seattle again, gradually deciding to make a whole vacation of it, if Mom can get the time off. As a private lactation consultant, she has more flexibility than a regular nurse, and some of her stuff she can do over the phone or Zoom.

"It will be good to do some of the work there," Aunt Gina says while Justine and I chop spinach. "Some spontaneity. My friend David has a studio, so I can get fresh pieces from him and use his kiln."

Mom chuckles. "And if something breaks in transit, you can still use it."

"Well." Aunt Gina smirks. "Most of the shapes are intentional. Not random broken glass."

"Mm-hmm." Mom reaches over to pat her knee in a reassuring big-sister way.

"So I called the gallery, and I can start installing as early as Sunday."

"Which is what you'd like to do?" Jack seeks clarity and a plan.

Justine and I scoop tomatoes into the skillet, and I give her a spoon. "Spread them around so they're . . . yeah, even. That's great."

"Ideally," Aunt Gina says. "And do some work throughout the week while you guys go be tourists."

"Sounds good," Jack says.

"What do you think?" Mom asks.

Justine opens the oven for me and I slide the skillet in. We high-five, and when we both straighten up, the adults are looking at us expectantly.

Mom smiles. "Gage?"

I realize the earlier question was to me, but I draw a blank. "What do I think about what?"

"I should know better than to address you while you're cooking." Mom leans forward with a gentle smile, fingers closing around her coffee mug. "We would like to go to Seattle with your aunt and see the show opening, and support her. We're leaving Saturday and coming back next Sunday, and we thought it might be a nice family trip. Do you want to go? Do you have the time off?"

They're not trying to stress me out. I know it. Really trying not to pressure me, especially after Dad marched in and invited me to ride in his rig. Still, I can't believe they're even asking. Almost seven hours in a car on winter roads? Snoqualmie Pass? A crowded city packed with other cars? My throat dries up even as cold guilt washes over me.

"Might be good, Gage," Jack says gently. "You can post up in the back of the Tahoe for a few hours with a book and music, we can cover the windows—"

"I can't." They hold their expressions carefully neutral while I try to keep my voice steady. "I . . . I'm sorry, Aunt Gina. I can't."

Her brow furrows in worry. Disappointment in myself and my cowardice wells up through my chest.

Mom smiles and I know she's being gentle, but she looks sad. "We just wanted to ask, to include you."

"Gage," Jack says, "it's all right."

Is it? My dad's voice pings around my brain. *Is it?*

They're going to ask more. If I'm okay. What I need. They're going to know I'm barely holding it together.

"Do you want one of us to stay?" Mom asks, and I straighten, forcing my head up since I obviously look pathetic.

No. I can't let them plan their life around my failure to move on. I have to be okay, or they won't go, and I won't go to San Francisco even if I get the job; I'll just walk in my sharp circle of grief forever and they'll be stuck there with me.

"It's not the car thing." I lie so fast, I surprise even myself. Jack raises his eyebrows and Aunt Gina and Mom lean forward. "I . . . it's, you know. Next week is . . ." I remember the LWDA meeting. Mia, suggesting we do something for Hunter. "I thought I'd do, like, a memorial thing for Hunter, with my friends. A movie night on Monday. We already planned it. We're going to watch all the Lord of the Rings and make some food." The words of this nonexistent plan come so easily, it must sound real. "Is that okay? If I have them over?"

Mom smiles, surprised. "Of course."

"No drugs, no booze," Jack chimes automatically, with a small grin, because I am the least likely person in my whole town he'd have to say that to.

Aunt Gina looks so pleased for me. "It sounds wonderful, Gage. I'm sorry we'll miss it."

"I'm sorry I'll miss your show," I say honestly. "I . . . I didn't think you were going or I would've planned a different night." The ease of the lie spreads like a balm over my fear, and they're buying it. Perfect. It's perfect. It sounds like exactly something I would do, and the adults' faces are all lit up and Mom smiles. Excellent.

Relief relaxes my chest as I picture what will actually happen: a few days to myself. A respite where I don't have to look anyone in the face and pretend I'm okay. Maybe I can try a couple recipes, play some *Mass Effect*. Read a new book. Or lie on my bed and stare at the wall without anyone knocking on my door. I'll see if Andy can give me some of next week off too. He seemed pretty eager to get me out of his hair.

Maybe that's what I really need. Some rest. Some time before I launch into my new life.

I'm proud of myself for handling that so easily, and looking forward to my time alone.

"So." Aunt Gina reaches her hand out to Justine, and she leans against her. "Just Uncle Jack and Aunt Lizzie and you and me, huh?"

"No!" Justine says, and Aunt Gina's dark brows lift. "I want to stay with Gage and do the movie night!"

My gaze hops from her to Aunt Gina, and she must see the desperate *no* in my eyes. "Oh, honey, I don't think Gage wants to babysit for a whole week—"

"I'm not a baby." Justine twists out of her arm and sets her hands on her hips. She does look like a stubborn little Tinkerbell in that moment. Under the table, Cassidy thumps her tail as if she, too, is excited for a memorial movie night. "Please?"

"Gage," Aunt Gina says, "you do not have to do this."

My pulse thumps like a drum in my neck. "Um . . ."

"You would have a great time in Seattle," Mom says to Justine. "And it would mean so much to your mom if you were there, to see—"

"I try not to use guilt as a motivator," Aunt Gina says evenly to Mom, who purses her lips and has a drink of coffee. Aunt Gina motions to Justine, but her feet are planted. "But you really should come with us, honey. It'll be fun."

Jack leans forward. "Have you been to Pike Place Market? It's—"

"I don't want to." Justine pivots and looks up at me with her big hazel eyes that might as well be Hunter's eyes, and a shining smile. "Please? I've never seen the movies and I can help you make the food, and I'll be really, really, *really* good. Please?"

All I see is my house full of people, talking about Hunter, watching the movies Hunter loved most in the world, while I'm dying inside.

"Um."

Justine gazes at me as if I'm holding the whole world together.

"Justine," Aunt Gina says firmly, standing up. "We don't negotiate. I said—"

"It's okay," my mouth says, while my brain cowers in the corner. Hunter's there at the front of everything. Hunter, who will never get to spend time with Justine again, who would do anything to take care of his family and his friends.

That little girl needs you.

Dad's right. I know he is. Everyone else is holding it together. I don't know why I can't. I can. I have to. Aunt Gina is doing her show. Mom and Jack are working. Even Justine is holding it together, and she's a kid. She deserves a movie night.

I cinch down on my rushing pulse and the ticking in my head, and focus on Justine, who stares at me like her life depends on spending the week with me. The promise of quiet alone time evaporates.

I'm talking, watching myself from some distance.

"It sounds fine. You can stay if your mom says it's okay." I look at the adults with an easy smile, some other part of me operating my face and my limbs. "I'm not working and Andy can probably give me more time off, if I ask."

"Gage," Jack murmurs, eyebrows crooking in. "Are you sure?"

"I'm happy to." I look at him, lifting my chin, man-to-man. This is my chance to prove I'm okay. That I can handle it. Somehow my voice is light. "It'll be fun."

"I'll pay you," Aunt Gina insists. I wave a hand and shrug.

Justine squeals and throws her arms around my middle and squeezes with all her strength. I pat her shoulder, breathing slow and even.

"That's very generous of you," Aunt Gina says pointedly, more to Justine than me. "Justine, tell Gage thank—"

"Thank you, thank you!"

Jack leans back with a warm nod of approval.

"Well," Mom says with a hesitant smile. "That's settled. That's great."

"Yeah," I echo, resting a hand on Justine's shoulder. "Great."

I KNOW PEOPLE AREN'T REALLY STARING at me as I walk down the main street, but it sure feels that way. Like everyone knows about my outburst and throwing a customer out of Nan's. The locals probably do. Stuff like that doesn't stay quiet long. I hope Noah took down that video because gossip is bad enough.

After agreeing to watch Justine for the week and with the excuse that I need to run errands and coordinate my now-happening memorial movie night, I escape for a walk.

The day continues damp and gray with flurrying snow, and downtown is sleepy because everyone's probably skiing. It feels bizarre to be walking around in the middle of the day, not working. I pass Nan's and don't stop, a particular destination in mind.

I have plenty to do, now that my brain is reorganizing

the week. If I can't have alone time, I will work on getting my head together and enjoying myself in other ways. Like asking Olivia out. I will ask her out, apply for my dream job, host a memorial night for my best friend, take care of my cousin. That's what I should be doing.

Snowflakes melt on the back of my neck, and the thought of Olivia's smiling face gives me a twining rush of hope and fear. *See you tomorrow.*

This time, I'll be prepared. I might even succeed in being charming.

Mom gave me a couple errands while I'm out, including refilling the kitchen soaps, so I get that out of the way first.

Silver Mountain Soap Co. has been in business as long as I've been alive, a staple of downtown where they have locally made bath stuff and essential oils and skin care. Never a place someone like my dad would step into, but it's the best place to buy presents for my mom and aunt.

The rush of clean, soapy, herby fragrance as I open the door kicks me back to high school and I stomp off snow before proceeding inside. A couple of old ladies are peering at the soap on one shelf and trying to determine if it's locally made.

"Hi, Gage," calls a familiar voice.

My head flies up and I look to the counter, where I did not expect to see Rowan, but should have. I should've checked if she was working before I came. Her mom's best friend owns the store and I'm certain it's Rowan's ambition to take it over one day because she is genuinely into all of it. She is also a big fish, as Jack would say, ambitious and smart, but I know she enjoys our little pond.

Her whole family is that way—driven. Her mom has a successful lifestyle blog and her twin brother was captain of the soccer team and I'm not sure what her little sister's up to, but it's probably gold star, straight-A type stuff too.

Rowan is what my mom calls "striking": clear olive skin, long, tumbling waves of black hair, and surprising blue eyes currently outlined in dramatic black liner. I was completely in love with her sophomore and junior year, along with half my class. I wonder if she still has the Evenstar pendant I gave her, in my hopeless devotion.

Probably not.

She checks me out top to bottom and she smiles. "You look nice. New coat?"

"Thanks, yeah." It is. Not my old puffy winter jacket, but a black wool button-down. My next stop is Mountain Mugs. "Mom got it for me for Christmas. She needs some refills." I shrug with a lopsided smile and head to the counter with the reusable bag of soap bottles.

"You got it. Anything for you? Aftershave?" She grins as she pulls the empty bottles out of the bag and grabs her gallon of soap to refill.

"No, I'm still good." That's a fib. I'm out of aftershave; I just didn't want to come here, so I started using a store brand.

She looks me over again, smiling as if she knows something. "You sure?"

"Uh, yeah?" I stuff my hands into my coat pockets, cracking one knuckle. The old ladies are looking at me now and smiling, like it's cute that I practice personal hygiene.

"You don't want something new?" Rowan tosses her hair and crosses her arms. I should've told Mom I couldn't do her refills. "Don't you have the same smell you've been wearing since high school?"

"Yeah? It's fine, I like it."

She tsks and wanders to their vials of fragrance and essential oil testers and starts sniffing. They have a product line they can mix custom scents into and it's all we use—hand soap, shower gel, lotion, my aftershave. Hunter never got into it, but dating Rowan did teach me all the exceptional advantages of smelling good.

"No," she says, tapping her lips thoughtfully. "I don't think so. Let's do something new. New year, new you. Scent is the strongest memory trigger, you know. You don't want to smell the same your whole life."

I wander closer in spite of myself. New me sounds good. "Really?"

"Yes. Look." She pops a glass amber vial under my nose and it's whatever vanilla tobacco scent they use in my aftershave. It hurtles me instantly back to getting showered and ready for school, sitting in class—and Hunter. And Rowan.

"Wow." I tip my head away. "Okay, maybe something new. I, uh . . . have a date." It's a fib too, but maybe if I say it, it'll be true by the end of the day.

"I knew it!" She pokes my chest. "You never dress up." She beams triumphantly while warmth swarms my face. "What do you want to smell like?"

"I don't know. Good?"

She rolls her eyes, waves me away, and tosses her hair again, wafting me with rose and myrrh. "I'll make something for you."

"Thanks."

I wander the store and wonder randomly what Olivia smells like while Rowan does her thing. She has to pause to help the old ladies, gets them checked out, then they dawdle and ask for a lunch recommendation. She sends them to Nan's while winking at me. When they finally leave, it's just her and me and soft jazz floating through the store while she takes her time concocting a fragrance, then refilling Mom's soaps.

"Who's your date?"

I pick up a bottle of face product and put it back, fidgety. "Her name's Olivia. She's—"

"From Mountain Mugs? Aw, she's nice. She's really funny."

I turn to stare at her. She sniffs the scented oils she's been dripping into a bottle, seems satisfied, and grabs the gallon of aftershave. I cross my arms. "How do you know her?"

"Do you think you're the only person who gets coffee, ever? They have the best roast." Rowan grins, shaking my bottle of aftershave like a bartender with a cocktail. "Also, I dunno, maybe she asked Aiden about you."

"She—wait, why were you talking to Aiden?" I head to the counter.

She flicks one black eyebrow up. "Why do you think?"

Sometimes I love my small town. Sometimes not. "You're dating Aiden? He's like twenty-five."

She tops off my bottle of aftershave and sticks a label on it. "One, none of your business; two, he's twenty-one. And Olivia's really nice. You would be adorable together and have beautiful brown-eyed babies and you have my blessing."

Heat flashes up my face. "Uh, thanks. I think I'll shoot for a first date and maybe learn her last name before we talk about babies, is that okay?"

"Smart." She winks again. "Smell this." She tips the bottle toward me. It's really good, like spruce and wood and citrus.

"That's . . . Wow, thank you. Yes."

"Suits you." She smiles, pleased. "Better than smelling like burgers." She shakes her head. "I'll never eat a hamburger again without thinking of you."

I lean on the counter. "I guess I could have a worse legacy. So, what, uh . . . what did Olivia ask about me?"

Rowan smiles slowly as she rings me up. "Just getting the scoop. Making sure you're cool."

"Oh, great."

She rolls her eyes. "Don't worry, he talked you up. Okay, it's twenty for this."

"All of it?" I want to know what else Aiden said and how he talked me up, but asking might make me look desperate.

She smiles, softer. "Friends and family discount."

"Thanks." I pat the counter and try to make a quick exit after I pay, but she trots around the counter with her phone.

"Wait, wait, can I borrow you for one second?"

I almost escaped. Irritation flutters up my chest and I rub my face. "Rowan—"

"Please? It'll only take a second. I need something for the store's Instagram today."

Rowan is the social media queen, and she's great at it, an up-and-coming young businesswoman just like her mom. An actual influencer, with legions of followers and her own YouTube channel on skin care and makeup. I know it's not all Likes, sunshine, and fun, though. I've seen some of the comments people post on her stuff and I don't know how she keeps it together. I'd lose it. But she'll probably be basking in the tropical sun on her own yacht somewhere while I'm still chopping tomatoes on the line. I think it's great.

I just don't want to be a part of it.

She did give me a discount, though, so maybe I owe her. "One picture, but don't tag me, okay?"

"Obviously. You have like nine followers and you never post anything." She floats over and I start to take my coat off, but she touches my sleeve. "No, leave it on. Hm. Have you ever thought about growing a beard?"

"No."

"You should, if you can."

"I *can*." I brace myself as she picks a couple of dog hairs off my shoulder, turns my collar just so, aims her phone, then clucks her tongue in dissatisfaction and herds me under a different light.

"I really appreciate it. We're trying to promote the men's stuff." She plucks my wool hat off and fusses with my hair, finger-combing it into an acceptable arrangement while I withhold a sigh. "I like it shorter like this. It's a good length for you. Mm-kay, tip your head down, no . . ." She steers my head to a specific angle where I'm jutting my face out unnaturally. "Now press your tongue to the roof of your mouth so your chin is less . . . Yes—ooh, keep clenching your jaw like that, that's good." She tips her mouth up near my jaw and it's all very clinical to capture some perfect imaginary moment, some version of me that doesn't exist.

"Rowan—"

"Shh, hold still."

"Do you remember why we broke up?"

"Yes. We broke up because you're moody and emotionally unavailable." She rests her lips stiffly near my jaw and takes a picture.

My brow furrows. "I'm what?"

"Oh, that looks good—leave your mouth open. Not that much—okay."

I release a soft breath, neck cramping from holding the bizarre angle of my head. She takes several pictures and then hops away, patting my shoulder. "Perfect. Thank you so much. Look how hot you are."

She holds up the phone to show me the best picture of the batch. Not my full face, but three-quarters of us—an anonymous male jaw and a girl's mouth. Honestly, it could be any guy's face with her lips hovering close. I guess that's the point. It does look pretty good, like a Calvin Klein ad. It's just not *me*, and it reminds me why I've been avoiding this place, and her.

"My chin is hot?"

She rolls her eyes. "You don't get it."

"I really don't." I never did. We had two relationships: the real one and the one on social media, and it was exhausting. I already wear different masks for people, and that was just one more. A big reason I avoid Instagram and Snapchat and whatever else she's on, and all my friends have to deal with plain old texting.

But that was two years ago and I really don't want to be thinking about it, and now Rowan's frowning and I don't want to upset her. She's just being Rowan. I step back, lightening my tone.

"So that's a good look? When I ask Olivia out, I should . . ." I tip my head down and forward in the awkward angle, hang my mouth open, and she laughs, shoving me lightly. "What, that's not hot?"

"Just trying to give you a boost of self-esteem. Leave your hat off. You're having a good hair day. I really wish you'd let me do an account for you." She sighs, long suffering, twining a raven lock of hair around one finger. "I don't think you understand how much your social media can help you. Or hurt you. If you even send me pictures of the food you're making, I can—"

"I'm good, thanks." I head to the door, then pause. "Hey, tell Ash he should come back to LWDA sometime. We miss him."

Her expression softens at her brother's name, and the invitation. Ethan was on the soccer team, and his suicide hit them hardest, next to his own family. "You tell him? He'd love to hear from you."

"You should come too," I add, watching her. "I know you've got it all together, but we can always use the inspiration."

"Right." She laughs, gaze darting to the side. Then she flips her hair and smiles warmly. "Thanks, Gage."

"And tell Aiden hi." I grin and she rolls her eyes.

"I will." She hops back onto her stool, all into her phone now, editing the picture. "Oh, and, Gage?"

I pause at the door, stuffing my hat into my pocket as advised, and look back, but she's still tapping at her phone. "Yeah?"

"If you go out with Olivia, don't talk about Hunter too much."

Surprise flicks across my brain. "Uh, yeah. Why would I talk about Hunter at all, on a first date?"

"I don't know. You seem stressed out." She brushes hair off her shoulder and doesn't look up even though she's talking to me. Another reason we broke up. "It's sad, just don't talk about it too much, you know, if she asks."

I turn fully back to her. "Why would she ask?"

"Hm?" Her head tilts, eyes on her phone.

"Rowan." At last she looks up, blinking soft black lashes, and I grip the door frame. "Why would she ask?" Her lips press tight and I take two steps forward, frustration sparking. "Did Aiden *tell* her—"

A cluster of women decked out in expensive winter clothes and jewelry streams in behind me, barraging the air with laughter and talking. I move out of the way while Rowan slides from her stool again with an apologetic shrug and smile, then turns her dazzling attention to the customers.

"Hi, ladies! Let me know if I can help you with anything."

Breath tight, I wade through the women and back into the cold air of the street.

Small-town gossip. Two days and half a conversation with Olivia and she already knows the worst thing in my life. Amazing. I roll my shoulders and turn up the street, grasping for the determination I had before going in there. My phone buzzes.

It's from Rowan. An extra picture she took. It's black and white and of my whole face, my brow furrowed and stern, eyes lifted to some indeterminate place beyond the frame. In context, I know I look like that because I was irritated. Out of context, it's dramatic and cool and makes me stop in the middle of the sidewalk.

Rowanstar: Thought you should have this one ;) Didn't mean to be a downer, I just want you to be happy <3 Go get her.

My irritation settles at her good intentions. I would like to be happy too.

The photo doesn't look like me at all. Whatever filter she used, and the light. But it does look like a guy who has his life together, dark hair and eyes stern and strong. Maybe I can pretend to be that guy today.

I dig the new aftershave from my coat pocket and rub some onto my neck—not that Olivia will be that close, but it does smell great, invigorating. It helps me cling to my plan. I'm going to ask out a pretty girl, apply for Redwood House, host a memorial for my friend, man up, and get on with my life.

And it's going to be great.

MY ADRENALINE IS UP BY THE TIME I WALK INTO MOUNTAIN Mugs, which is packed for lunch. A line snakes around near the door. Voices, laughter, and the hiss of the coffee machine and whirr of the Frappuccino blender all jangle together.

Wait in line or head to the counter? I don't want to look rude. I step to the end of the line to give myself time to chill out and run the hopefully witty line I thought of through my head a couple of times.

I'm so distracted, nervous, realizing it doesn't matter what I smell like now because I'm just one more person in the packed place, that I don't see it's not Olivia taking orders until I'm face-to-face with Aiden and his shining white teeth.

"Hey, Gage!" Aiden looks like he stepped out of a ski magazine. Lean and tall in a fitted Henley with stylish leather bracelets, a slouchy black hipster beanie, and a short, immaculate beard. He probably looks amazing on Rowan's Instagram.

I should have gotten eyes on Olivia the minute I stepped in, and a glance to the side shows she's not making coffee, either. What if she's not even working today?

See you tomorrow. She should definitely be here.

"Off today? How's your family?"

I turn my grudging attention back to Aiden. "They're great. How's yours?"

He blinks at my gruff tone and I lift my chin, irritated he's been spilling my business, all my anxiousness about seeing Olivia contorting smoothly into anger at the nearest target. I've never really had a beef with Aiden, except he's here and talking and Hunter is not, and apparently he's telling people my personal stuff.

He smiles, gaze flicking over me. "They're great, thanks for asking. What can I get you?"

I hadn't planned to order coffee, just stroll in, flirt, snag a date or not, and go. My plan fractures. "A shot of espresso, I guess."

"For here?"

"Sure."

I look at the tip jar, which has "Aiden's Dog Food Fund"

on it, then around again for Olivia. I stuff my hands into my pockets and lower my voice. "Hey. Is Olivia working?"

Aiden smiles knowingly, drawing more irritation out of my chest. "She's on lunch. Should be back soon. Want me to tell her you asked?"

"No." I tug my wallet out to pay, disappointment twining around my frustration with Aiden, even though it's not that big a deal. I know it's not. I can wait. "But, since you asked, could you not tell everyone my business?"

He tips his head at me, genuinely confused. "What do you mean?"

"I mean if people ask about me, maybe don't pick Hunter as one of your top five facts to share?"

His groomed eyebrows lift, and he frowns. "I'm sorry, I didn't know it was a secret—"

"It's not, just . . . don't. Thanks." I fold a dollar and drop it in the tip jar, then hover by the bar until a girl slides my espresso over. I empty a sugar packet into the froth and down it in one gulp because I can't see myself sitting there with the miniature mug, sipping for half an hour while I wait for Olivia.

I try to chill out.

Maybe I am moody.

I'll come back later.

I weave around the tables and people, wishing I'd shed my coat as the room starts to feel sweltering. Motion catches my eye in the archway that leads to their kitchen, a bright laugh, and Olivia steps out from behind the counter, tying on her apron.

She hops right in next to Aiden, and even though I explicitly told him not to mention me, he nudges her and tips his head my way. Irritation and uncertainty wash over me and I feel like a stalker—then she looks over, and her whole face lights up and she cocks her head with a curious smile.

The smile pulls me right back in, skirting the line to meet her around at the other side of the coffee bar, away from people.

"You're early today. I just never know when you're going to pop up."

I chuckle and run a hand through my hair before remembering how carefully Rowan had it styled. Oh well. "I like to keep people guessing."

"I see." Her gaze follows my hand through my hair, then she motions at me. "You look nice. Going somewhere?"

"Just here." Reassured that I didn't imagine all her smiles and the spark of energy between us, I manage to capture some of the feeling of the cool dude in Rowan's picture who's me but not. "Actually, I got a tip about where the cool kids hang out."

Pink suffuses her cheeks and she leans in. "You did, huh?"

"Yeah. So . . ." I clear my throat and restrain myself from fidgeting with the edge of the counter just as the espresso hits my bloodstream. "So I thought we could avoid them, maybe, and I . . . maybe I could take you out for dinner."

The relief and terror of getting the question out almost takes my feet out from under me, until her smile deepens and she tips her head up, cheeks pink and eyes shining. "That sounds fun."

I'm not sure what I expected her answer to be after our nice interactions, so instead of a cool response, all I have is

"Really?"

She laughs and touches my arm. "Yes. I would love that."

"Wow." I grin, feeling ridiculous, but she's still smiling, so it's all good. Everything is going according to plan. "When's a good time for you?"

She leans her hip on the counter and I realize she's supposed to be working and Aiden is letting us chat and flirt. My anger at him smooths down. "My schedule's weird, so you tell me, and I'll tell you if it works." She grins and I laugh softly. I know about weird schedules.

I don't want to wait too long. I don't even really want to leave the coffee shop now, I want to just stand there with her smiling at me and looking like she wants to touch my coat again. I'll have to thank Mom for it one more time. "Tonight?" God, that probably looks too eager, like I don't have a life.

She beams. "Tonight is perfect."

Oh. My heart is pounding. "What time do you get hungry?"

She laughs and touches my arm again, picking off a dog hair in an entirely different way than Rowan did. "Seven? I need time to get pretty."

"No you don't," I blurt, and she tips her head up again with a smile. "I mean, seven it is. Where are you staying? I'll pick you up."

"You know the employee housing behind the Lodge?"

I nod. Not too far from downtown. "Cool. Do you like Italian?"

"I like every kind of food." She grins.

I laugh and duck my head. This is the good stuff. "Me too."

She pulls out her phone and unlocks it. "Here, add yourself. I can't wait to see what the resident chef thinks is a good place to eat."

"Resident chef?" Maybe Aiden talked me up after all. I don't think I've grinned like this since . . . well. I make myself a contact in her phone; *Gage with a g,* to keep our joke going. "I'll try not to disappoint you."

She takes her phone back, and types something for a second. "I'm sure you won't."

My phone buzzes with a text from her and I meet her eyes, but finally Aiden calls her over as the line creeps toward the door. "I'll see you later."

She grins and bounces away back to work.

I'm two blocks down, with snowflakes melting on my face and the world lighter than it has been in a year, when I realize what I said to her.

I'll pick you up.

Shit.

MOM'S AT WORK AND JACK is in the living room on the phone with Veterans Affairs when I get back.

"I understand. Can you connect me to someone whose hands *aren't* tied? I've got a woman who's—Yes, I'll hold." He has his sharp, hard first sergeant voice on, the tone he uses when he's pushing the rope, as he calls it. I've only heard it when he's talking to military people or when I've done something really ill-advised.

I poke my head in to let him know I'm home, and he lifts a hand but doesn't look up from his paperwork.

It's warming up outside to a balmy forty-something, so I stow my coat back in the hall closet, slip the keys to the Tahoe from their hook, and head out behind the house. The big tan SUV crouches like a dormant beast in the gravel spot by the alley.

"It's just sitting there," I tell myself firmly. I can do

this. It's not even the same car we wrecked in. The Honda was totaled. Adrenaline whisks through me when I touch the handle, so I rest my hand there for a second. Like wading into a freezing mountain lake, a little at a time.

I can do this. I have to do this.

I leave my hand there until my body seems reassured the danger has subsided, then take a deep breath.

"'Fear is the mind-killer,'" I whisper and open the door.

Unlike Bryson's truck, Jack's Tahoe doesn't smell like vanilla. It smells like clean car because the man goes over it with a Q-tip every couple of months. Maybe Rowan is onto something with the scent memory-trigger stuff. I stand there, breathing, looking at the soft beige seats, the instrument panel, the dried mud and salt on the floor mats, as my heart beats into a jogging rhythm. I wait to calm down, but that doesn't happen. I think this is as good as it's going to get.

"You're fine," I growl at myself. Dad's voice: *Don't be so dramatic.* I remember Meaghan calming Chase. "You're here, you're safe."

My body is convinced I'm neither here nor safe, wary of mortal danger as I climb into the driver's seat and lean back slowly. Different car. Not even moving—I'm safe— my heart rate climbs and it feels like all of a sudden my shirt is sticking to me with sweat. No buildup, just like a bucket of sweat has been dumped on me.

My soft mantra of "You're safe, you're safe" dissolves into panting breaths. I stay right there. Maybe this is as bad as it will get. I close the door firmly.

I can get through—I can—I glance to the passenger side.

The panic is not gradual.

It smashes me in a burst of heat and sweat, strips my breath, flares incomprehensible warnings in my brain. The tires shrieking. The seat belt digging against my chest as we spun. Headlights, the thunk of my own head on glass—*Hunter*—

A strangled noise comes out of my throat and I fumble at the door with numb, locked fingers.

What's wrong with you? My dad's voice, rough and bewildered as he swerved the truck to the nearest parking lot.

My chest squeezes like a heart attack. *No, no* . . . layered over the accident, the panic, seeing Hunter's face—oh God—now there's the memory of Dad barking at me.

Calm down! What's wrong with you?

I wrestle out of the Tahoe and stumble out, slam the door, lurch away to sink to my knees into the snow near the apple tree in the alley.

Sun sneaks through the clouds, glittering hot silver on the snow. I squeeze my eyes shut, gulping air.

Get it together, bud. Don't be so dramatic. Dad, hauling me to my feet after my first meltdown. My panic attack. I know that's what it is. He forced me back into the car to a doctor to make sure there was "nothing" wrong with me. Big, solid eighteen-year-old guy dissolving into tears and heart palpitations even though nothing happened.

Dad brushed it off, sure I'd get over it.

You'd better not let your mother see this happen. She doesn't need that. You're okay.

I press two handfuls of snow to my face, clawing my way to the present.

You can't do that meltdown shit you did to me.

You're okay.

I remember hugging Hunter as his dad drove away. *Big boys don't cry.* I choke a hard laugh. Apparently I was stronger when I was nine.

Anger and failure burn out the panic and I curl over myself, breathing hard. A scream snags in my throat and I manage to swallow it, forcing my breathing to slow down. I've balled myself up in the snow under the tree in the fresh air, with a slant of cold sunlight on my sweat-soaked shoulders.

I have to get up. I have to get up, before someone sees me.

A rhythmic buzz nearby draws me up from the pit of self-loathing and frustration.

My phone.

Must've launched from my pocket when I fell out of the car, and it takes a minute to find it in the snow.

Forcing my body to uncurl as the anxiety and anger drains, I remain sitting on the ground, wipe snow from the phone, and swipe.

"Hey," I croak, "what's up?"

"Dude!" Bryson's voice pitches high—he's shouting. I hold the phone away from my ear. "She said yes! I'm making Mia dinner tonight. Thank you so much for the help, man."

"That's . . ." I rub a hand down my face, so happy for him that I want to cry. Or maybe I want to cry in general. "That's awesome, Bry. You've got this. I hope you have a great time."

"Thanks, I—are you sick? I went to Nan's and you weren't there."

"No." I clear my throat. "No, I'm fine. Andy gave me a few days off. Good luck tonight."

"Thanks. You rock. I'll catch you later."

"Bry," I say quickly. "I was thinking about doing, like, a movie night next week. For Hunter. If you—"

"I'm in." His voice changes, lower, sincere. Like he's soothing an animal. "That sounds awesome, whatever you want to do."

"Great." I stare at the dazzling snow. "I'll text you."

"Sounds good!" Back to elation. And he hangs up.

The snow has melted and my clothes are soaked against my hot skin, but I finally start to shiver and drag myself up and into the house. I throw the keys back onto their hook. Jack's still on the phone, so it's easy to escape to my room. I change into dry clothes, listen to a couple loud songs, pace. I wish I had Hunter's phone, but I left it with Justine.

That's fine. That's good. That's a step.

I'll try the car again later, again and again until I figure it out, even if it's not today. Time to handle my business. Walk it off.

I blast all my contacts in LWDA with a text inviting them to marathon all three of the original Lord of the Rings movies at my house this coming Monday.

Imogenesis: YES!!! Sounds amazing I'm in!! What can I do?

I stretch out on my bed, trying to shove some sense of determination through the spectacle I made of myself in the Tahoe. At least no one saw it. That's all that matters.

Me: Just show up. I'm going to make a bunch of food and we'll just chill.

Imogenesis: Okay I'll help pay for food and get $$ from everyone.

Me: Okay :P

Imogenesis: I'm so happy you're doing this. It'll be really fun. Everyone will be psyched. I'm so coming in costume.

I stare at her text, then rub my itchy eyes. She's right. My fear and emotional instability are no excuse not to honor Hunter and everything he meant to everyone. This is what Dad means. Sometimes you have to gut it out for others' sakes. It might be good for me, too. It will. It will be great. I'll be the leader they need and it will mean everything to Justine.

A few more texts fly my way with people offering to help and I finally delegate drinks out to Bryson, money collecting to Imogen, and follow-up to Mia, because she's good with directions and nudging people. I get ten RSVPs within twenty minutes and part of me is thrilled.

The rest . . .

I stare at the ceiling, then sit up and stare toward Hunter's window, trying not to think too much about a house full of people.

Finally I text Olivia.

Me: Hi! Bad news, I have car trouble. Hate to ask but how does a walk to the restaurant sound? It would only add ten minutes ():)

I know she's at work for a few more hours, so I don't expect an answer right away, but it comes anyway.

Olivia: No worries!! We can take my car if you want. I'll pick you up ;D

My exhausted heart jolts. I stare at the text, picture her sweet face, and imagine trying to get into her car. I don't even need to be looking at a vehicle to know what will happen.

My throat clenches as my brain scrambles. It's easier to fake it in a text, at least.

Me: Actually there's something really cool on the walk, if you're up for it.

This time there is about ten minutes before she answers and I'm pretty sure I've blown it. I'm about to text her again that it's really a ploy to spend extra time with her when she finally texts back.

Olivia: I'll wear my snow boots :))

Relief gives me a full breath. She doesn't deserve all the baggage I come with. I will make sure everything else is perfect.

I'm on the phone leaving a message with the restaurant for a reservation when Jack knocks. I walk over to open the door and motion *just a second*. He grins when he deduces I'm making dinner plans. I hang up.

"Hey," Jack says, and I can tell he's trying not to be nosy. "Can you help us load the trailer on Friday?"

"Yeah, sure." I run a hand through my hair while his gaze darts over me, critical, and I straighten up. "Of course."

"No plans?" he inquires slyly.

A smile finds my face. "Not Friday. But . . ." I hesitate, and he leans against the door frame and folds his arms in his magically interested but unobtrusive way. No wonder all the vets pour their hearts out to him. "But I did ask Olivia out tonight. I'm taking her to Belle Vite."

His grin is warm and wide. "Solid choice. Let me know if you want—if you need anything." His brow furrows slightly and we both know what he didn't say. *Let me know if you want to borrow the car.*

"Thanks. I think I've got it."

He rubs his chin, then looks at my carpet. "Gage,

listen. I know it's a rough week, and I'm really proud of how you're handling everything, and how you're taking care of people. But——"

"Thanks," I murmur, his praise as warm and heavy as gold.

"But," he continues, eyes lifting, "you tell me if *you* need anything. Okay?"

My jaw twitches and I rest my arms over my stomach. I know my family is there for me. That's the problem. I don't want them to be. I want them to be able to live their lives without worrying about me. "Sure thing. Thanks, Jack."

He watches me a second, leans in the room to grip my arm briefly, then sees himself out, shutting the door behind him. I have some hours to kill, so rather than work myself into a state over Olivia and what she must think of walking to our date, I hop online to start crafting a Lord of the Rings–themed menu for the movie night.

If I keep moving forward, eventually the bad stuff will have to fall behind me.

THE WEATHER GODS ALIGN TO KEEP THE EVENING MILD, AND snow falls like feathers through the streetlamps as I approach the employee apartments behind the Lodge.

The Lodge is really Silver Mountain Lodge & River House Restaurant, but that's a mouthful and no one calls it that. It's a hotel and restaurant, condos for snowbirds and part-timers, a spa and conference center. It perches along the river that runs on the north side of town toward the lake, dominating a quarter mile of riverfront and spilling light onto the water, which is sluggish with snow but not frozen.

I check the apartment number Olivia sent earlier and head up the exterior stairs, down a walkway, and knock. I showered, tried the new aftershave, wore the good coat, and I'm almost feeling like the guy in Rowan's moody picture again, confident, together. Even though I'm making my date walk. Maybe she'll think it's romantic.

She opens the door and a blast of Taylor Swift and the scent of a lavender room freshener and cheery light spill over me. A girl I assume is Olivia's roommate peers past her to get a look at me before I step back so Olivia can come outside. She's in soft pinks again, a fuzzy touchable sweater and skirt and wool leggings with penguins on them and, as promised, snow boots. "Hi!" Her curls are pinned up elegantly, drawing all attention to her rosy face, soft lashes, lips shiny with gloss.

"Hi. Wow."

She grins. "Right back at you." She grabs her coat and I move automatically to help her put it on, and she glances over her shoulder and up at me with a smile.

I push the version of myself who was curled up like an infant under the apple tree to the back of my mind when she smiles like that. That's not me. This is me. A man with a plan and a beautiful date and a perfect snowy evening and a good meal to look forward to.

We're both quiet until we're a couple blocks from the Lodge, and I lead her away from the main road to a walking path that loops down along the river and ends up downtown.

"I'm really glad you asked me out," she ventures, with that dimpled smile.

"Yeah?" I look down at her and she's gazing at the river, then up at me, with snowflakes landing in her hair. "I am too. I thought I was bothering you."

She laughs and nudges me before skipping ahead in the snow. "Nope." She turns, walking backward with her hands in her pockets, framed by snow and golden streetlamps. "What's this neat thing you wanted to show me?"

"Up ahead. It's kind of silly." I'm mesmerized by her light, warm energy.

"I like silly." She waits for me to catch up and turns to walk in step again. For a minute I'm tongue-tied, but she seems content staring around at the snow in the air as it falls to melt on the water.

"So where are you from?" I finally ask. "Why Clark, in the winter?"

"Hm." She folds her hands behind her back. "Do you want the long version or the short?"

I chuckle. "Short now, long over dinner?"

"Florida," she says, looking up at me. "Sort of. And I picked Clark because I wanted to see a real winter for once in my life."

"Wow, that's a change." It's taking everything I have not to brush snow from her hair. She looks so touchable. "What do you think so far?"

"Of Clark?"

I motion around. "Clark. Winter. Everything."

"I love it." She beams and I'm happy we're walking so I have more time to see her just being her. "So far it's everything I hoped it would be."

We come to a Y in the path: one option crosses a foot-bridge over the river toward an older housing development, and the other branch leads downtown. I touch her elbow to turn us onto the bridge. No one has walked on it since it started snowing, and the soft press of our feet in the snow and the whisper of water below are the only sounds.

"Okay, here's the thing I wanted you to see."

"It's so beautiful," she breathes, staring upriver and breathing deeply. Wood smoke from neighborhood houses drifts in the air along with the frosty, fresh snow and the scent of pine. She grips the rail to peer down at the water.

I step in close and lean in. "So, legend says if you make a wish on this bridge while it's snowing, it'll come true."

She peers at me. "Legend, huh."

"Yep." I stick my hands in my pockets and fail to look serious.

"You literally just made that up."

A laugh huffs out of my chest. "Maybe. But you should make a wish anyway. You never know."

Her eyes sparkle in the faint glow and she cocks her head. "Okay. You have to too."

"Already did."

"Ooh." She glances me up and down. "Hope it was a good one."

"It was." I grin and, since we're already being cheesy, offer her my arm—then my phone buzzes. I ignore it because there is a beautiful girl looping her arm through mine.

"Why, thank you, sir."

My phone buzzes again. Her gaze drops to my coat pocket, then up to my eyes. "Do you need to get that?"

"Maybe I should. Sorry, let me check." I touch her arm and pull away, irritation flaring.

Brywolf: Dude I think I screwed this up?!

The second text is a picture of pork browning in a pan. I brighten my screen.

Me: Looks okay? What's wrong?

He's calling.

I look at Olivia. "Do you mind—It's sort of . . . I'm sorry, it's, like, a culinary emergency."

"A what?" She looks intrigued and delighted, then waves both hands at me to answer.

I step away farther along the bridge. "Bryson? What—"

"Oh my God, thank you for answering." He sounds frantic. "I think—bro, I put the wrong sauce on the meat."

"You what?" I rub my forehead.

"I put . . . Does the mayo thing go on the meat or not?"

"The mayo?" I glance over my shoulder at Olivia, who is trying to catch snowflakes on her tongue, and my brain spins to a happy and useless stop. I turn away.

"Yeah," Bryson says. "I put the mayonnaise on the pork?"

Mayo. Right. "No, you're supposed to dollop it on top once everything is in the wrap."

He swears and I hold the phone away from my ear until he quiets down. "Oh man. I put it in the meat and cooked it. What do I do? She's coming any second and I don't have enough pork to make it again."

I rub my mouth. "Don't freak out. It's probably fine."

"It's *probably* fine?"

I grit my teeth to keep from laughing because he sounds really upset and I know the feeling. Pressure's on. I should have told him not to cook on a first date. Too high stakes. "I mean, taste it? See if it tastes okay."

"Taste it? Okay." There's a shuffle, utensils clinking as he mutters swear words. Then a pause. "It tastes good. It's really good. Wow."

"There you go, put the wraps together like that and call it good."

"It's not, like, going to poison us or anything? Sautéed mayonnaise?"

Then I do laugh. Olivia's watching me curiously and I mouth "sorry," but she shrugs with a smile and starts building a miniature snowman on the railing of the bridge. "No, it's fine. Mix the other sauce in so it's got the spice and it'll just be really rich. It'll probably be delicious."

There's a sizzle as he pours in the other sauce. "I can't believe I did that."

I can't really either, since we practiced making it, but watching Olivia being adorable and knowing how Bryson feels about Mia, I could see being nervous and getting things out of order. "It's fine, Bry. She'll love it. You might've even improved the recipe."

"Should I make more mayo to put on top?"

"I wouldn't. Too rich."

He's recovered. "Dude, thanks so much. I owe you one."

"Sure thing. Good luck—"

"Wait, one more question," he says quickly.

"Yep?" I press my lips together and watch Olivia sticking twig arms into her snowman.

"I made some rice to go with the wraps, but I don't know how long to cook it before I drain it."

I stare at the river. "Before you what?"

"Before I drain the water?"

"Um." He's cooking rice like spaghetti. I don't know whether to laugh or cry, and remind myself most of his life and talents don't involve cooking food. "Just, uh . . ." I rub my forehead. "Test it. Taste it. When it's soft and chewy, it's done."

"Got it. Thanks, man!"

"Yep."

We hang up and I return to Olivia, unsure if the moment has passed when I can offer my arm again, but she tucks her mitten into the crook of my elbow right where we left off.

"What was *that*?" She grins.

"I'll tell you on the way. Who's this?" I point at her snowman.

She smiles mischievously. "That's Gabe."

"Thanks, I hate him."

She laughs, loud and bright, and we stroll on to the restaurant.

BELLE VITE IS COZY AND I like it because they don't have any tacky faux Italian décor. It's simple and elegant, all dark woods and cozy candlelight, with great food. They honored my request for a table by one of the massive picture windows overlooking the main street, so we have snow and a pretty view. Every table is candlelit and they don't play music, so it's only the warm murmur of people talking, glasses and flatware clinking.

The host seats us and tells us the special, paccheri al forno with their own hothouse cherry tomatoes and house-made mozzarella.

"Okay, what's good?" Olivia flips over her menu—a single page front and back, which I love. *Do a few things really well* is one of Michael Andrus's mottos, and I agree.

She's so bright-eyed and excited, I feel like I've flown

her to Italy for the night. Maybe I look excited too, I don't know, but her enthusiasm warms me right to the core. A brief, sharp ache of wishing Hunter could meet her flows up—and ebbs, to my relief.

"If you like calamari, their fried appetizer is really good. Actually, everything is good. I like it because they've got it by region, see? There are different northern and southern dishes and styles. And they make seasonal changes." I lean over to point out the descriptions to her. "I like the gnocchi, but it's really rich."

"What's a gnocchi?" She tips her head closer to me and I discover she smells like oranges and some kind of flower, and for a second I can't for the life of me remember what a gnocchi is.

"It's . . . it's like a mini dumpling. Made with potatoes."

"Sounds yummy. What are you getting?"

"Probably the special. Their tomatoes are, like . . . You know when you eat a cherry tomato right off the vine? That tangy, earthy taste? They always taste like that, and they make their own mozzarella here, and all the pasta. Usually if there's a special, it means the chef was inspired by something, so it's probably amazing. Like they were feeling creative."

She's smiling at me, chin propped in her hand.

Heat creeps up my neck. "What?"

A slow grin illuminates her face. "You're just super passionate about food. I think that's really cool."

I clear my throat and drink some ice water. Maybe I should tone it down. "Sorry."

She blinks and sits up. "For what? I just said it was really cool. I meant it."

"Oh. Thanks." I glance to the menu as weird anxiousness at showing my love for food taps my chest, a dark twin to not letting anyone see me cry. That's new. I will *not* be embarrassed by my one true calling. I sit up. "It's . . . I don't know. It runs in the family. My mom cooks, my grandparents on her side were into it. The Italian thing, I don't know. And there's this chef I like who's really inspiring, Michael Andrus. He says food is like a service."

She looks intrigued. "Service?"

"Yeah." All the books and blogs by Andrus fling to mind and I try to sum it up. "Feeding people is basic, and important, right? And so is honoring the things that went into the meal. The ingredients, the plants and animals, the people who farmed and grew and transported them." I clear my throat, smoothing my hands over the cloth napkin as an undefined emotion wriggles up out of nowhere. "So I think about that when I cook and when I eat, and all the different ways you can get the most out of a food, and it makes it kind of . . . um, sacred." I guess going off the rails about food is better than rambling about Hunter, but I press my lips tight, feeling like I said too much.

Olivia gazes at me, nodding slowly. Then she reaches over, hesitates, and touches my hand. Before she can respond to all that, the waitress comes by, an older lady who seems amused by us.

"Have we decided?"

Olivia sits up, moving her hand from mine. "Well, he's convinced me to get the special. Please." She grins at me and maybe my monologue didn't scare her off after all.

"Same," I murmur to the waitress, completely distracted. "The special."

"Good choice," she says and collects our menus. "Anything to drink besides water?" She peers at me, poised to ask for ID.

"Water's fine for me."

"Strawberry lemonade?" Olivia grins. And off the waitress goes again.

Enough about me. "So you're from Florida? What's the long version?"

She laughs and sits back, folding her hands in her lap. "The long version is my dad travels for work, so I was born in France, but we've been all over."

"Wow. What does he do?"

"He's a business consultant." She says it in a warm but practiced way. "Like, for startups or old businesses trying to rebrand. Sometimes we're in a place a few months, sometimes a couple years. And I guess when they were dating, Mom said there was no way he was leaving her at home while he traveled the world." She grins.

"That's so cool." I try to comprehend that lifestyle, compared to my whole life in Clark. "So if I wanted to start my own restaurant, he could get me off the ground?"

She grins. "Exactly. I'll schedule you a call with him."

I laugh, looking around Belle Vite, and try to imagine owning or running a place. "I think I'll stick with the line, for a while. And . . . you were born in France?"

"Don't get too excited," she says wryly. "I don't remember any of it. And we moved a lot, but Florida's the most recent stop and the longest. I think he and Mom like it there." Her expression scrunches up.

"But you don't."

"It's okay. But somehow with all the moving, we always

managed to skip winter. And . . ." She pauses, eyes lifting to mine, and they are so deep and brown. I feel like she's going to share something hard, so I lean in, just listening, the way I've seen Jack listen. "My grandma died last fall and it's been really hard for my dad. Then he felt bad, like he was dragging everyone down, so he pretty much kicked me out of the house to have an adventure. And I chose winter, and here I am. Ta-da."

She shrugs and I feel like someone kicked my stomach. I want to relate—but that would bring up Hunter. That would change the topic to me. And now I know she's here to get *away* from sad things.

A drink of cold water clears my throat. "I'm sorry. That's really rough. Did you . . . Were you close to her?"

"Not really." She looks rueful. "We moved too much. I saw her once a year or so."

I nod, focusing hard on her face.

Don't talk about Hunter. It's sad.

"It was mostly hard seeing my dad so sad, you know? I couldn't do anything."

"Yeah." I definitely won't talk about Hunter.

Her eyes widen, looking me over. I try to relax the grimace from my face as she says, "I'm so sorry. I didn't mean to bring things down."

"You didn't," I say quickly. "It's just life. You can talk about anything you want to."

The waiter drops off the lemonade and Olivia considers me, reaching over to touch my sleeve playfully. "Your turn. You're from here?"

"Born and raised, yep. I'm boring." I grin, heart pounding as I touch her hand in return. It just feels natural, easy, and she smiles. This must be what people mean when they say "chemistry."

"I don't think that's boring. Your mom's Italian? You said the 'Italian thing.' "

"Kind of." I chuckle. "I mean, in a vague ancestral way. We don't speak Italian or anything. But yeah. And my dad—my bio dad, Mom remarried—he's born-and-bred Idaho too. Third generation or something like that. I'm, like, half Italian, half Idaho . . . potato or something."

"Half Italian, half potato." She nods slowly, playing with the straw in her lemonade, her other hand near mine on the table. Her pinkie brushes my wrist. "So you're a gnocchi."

The laugh catches my whole body by surprise and I hang my head in defeat. "Yes, exactly. I'm a gnocchi."

She laughs, then there's a faint buzz from the pocket of her coat, draped on the back of her chair. She looks startled, then amused, as if she's just remembered something. "I have to answer this."

I have a brief flashback to Rowan on her phone, but I took a call from Bryson in the first ten minutes of our date, so I nod while she pulls her phone out.

Her eyes lift to me. "Sorry, it's just a rescue text."

"A what?" I pause, water glass halfway to my mouth.

"My roommate said she'd text in case I needed a reason to escape the date. What should I tell her?" She grins.

"Tell her you're being held hostage listening to me drone on about pasta and she should come immediately."

She sits back with a laugh. "Gage, I would listen to you talk about food all night."

"Good, because I probably will."

She laughs again and answers her roommate, then puts the phone away.

"As long as you have time to eat before you escape," I say.

She leans forward and touches my arm. "Sorry, you're stuck with me for the duration."

"Darn," I murmur, and for a minute we both gaze at each other, and while I know I've only had one girlfriend, I feel like this date is going as well as a date can go, as long as I can keep it together. *Talk about her*, Jack's advice bubbles to the top. *Listen more than you talk.* Not only is that sage advice, it will help us avoid Hunter.

My phone buzzes and she motions me to check it. Maybe she thinks it's my rescue text too.

Brywolf: Mia loves the food!

Me: Great!! Is she there? Get off the phone and tell me later!

Brywolf: Lol bye

I put it away and grin at Olivia. "Tell me more about where your family's traveled? And also, very important, what are your favorite books? And your art—are you, like, going to school for that?"

She laughs and stirs her lemonade with her straw. "I don't know about the art thing? Right now I think I'm happier making lattes and drawing whatever I want. I see so many artists online burned out, or not able to break in, or not making the stuff they really want."

"Oh," I say. "Sorry."

She smiles reassuringly, the light from the candle in her eyes. "Oh, no, it's not a bad thing. I think it's . . . you know, everyone's trying to make money on everything, and I just like *doing* it. As a hobby. Seeing what my dad does,

I have a really good idea what it would take to make art a business, and I don't think I want to."

I think that over. And remember Hunter, laughing, wishing he could read books for a living. "Yeah. That makes sense. Working in a kitchen can be really high pressure. I can see how it might make someone jaded—same for art, I mean." She smiles softly at me, seeming relieved. I wonder how many people ask her if she makes money on her art. I sit forward, wanting her to know I understand. "My aunt's a glass artist, but most of the time she's doing production stuff—vases and ornaments and things, not the big sculptures she really wants to make."

Her eyes light up at the mention of Aunt Gina's work. "Exactly."

"Maybe . . . you can show me some of your other stuff sometime?"

She blushes, which is intriguing. "If you want."

An answering warmth hits my cheeks, too. "Yeah, I'd love to see."

She grins, pleased, and has a sip of her lemonade. "Then I will. But cooking is definitely your thing, huh? Career-wise?"

Butterflies stir up my chest. "Yeah. I don't think I'd burn out like an artist. I mean, I like the challenge of doing something I might not try on my own. Like if I had to figure out emu tartare or—"

"*Emu tartare?*" She bursts out laughing and I feel like I'm washed in gold light.

"Uh." I laugh. "Yeah, it's a thing. One of the local restaurants . . . So wait, you were born in *France* and we've got one over on you here in Clark, Idaho?"

"Apparently!"

She laughs again, pelting me with more questions. So I tell her about the fine dining up on the ski hill, and Clark, in general. She swaps stories of her family's travels, and the falling snow outside turns the whole restaurant into a snow globe.

When the food arrives, it's to die for, as I hoped. Rustic and rich and artful, and we can't shut up about it even on the walk back, until we get close to the bridge. I can't tell if she's genuinely interested in me talking about how they air-dried the pasta or if she's being nice, but either way, it feels like I'm winning. Easy and safe. I keep my attention there instead of at the edge of things, where it's dark and sharp, where Hunter is.

The snow has stopped, but the air is humid and cold, and Olivia keeps her arm looped through mine the entire time.

"Next time we have to save room for dessert," she says, and all I hear is *next time*, and my heart skips to a harder beat. Before I can smoothly transition to asking for a second date, she gasps in surprise and peels away from me to trot out onto the bridge. "Look!"

I stride to catch up, and see that her small snowman has endured, and someone else has added a dozen snow people of various sizes all along the rail.

"Gabe has friends! Aw." She's delighted. I am too, really, but even though her joy is infectious, I doubt she wants to see me squealing over some miniature snowmen. *Keep it together, bud.* "Do you think it was one person or a bunch of different people making them once they thought it was a thing?" She's so cute, I can't stand it, and I manage not to make some incomprehensible sounds, stepping in close behind her.

"Probably a bunch. It's definitely something people would do here."

She's still staring at the snowmen, mittens clasped together. "I love this place so much."

Heart pounding, I take a chance and wrap an arm around her. "Hey, should I be jealous of Gabe?"

She turns in my arm and rests both mittens up on my chest, face somber. "Probably. He seems pretty popular."

I scoff, trying not to stare at her lips, warmth in my cheeks. "Bet he can't cook."

"How do you know?" Her eyes sparkle and her face is tipped up expectantly, and I rest my other arm snugly around her, just like that, pulse in my throat.

"He'd melt."

She giggles and burrows her face against my chest and I know this will go down as one of my favorite moments in my whole life. "No he wouldn't, he's magic."

"Yeah? Hope he can fly. Get lost, bud." I touch the tiny snowman's head, threatening to push him off the rail into the river.

Olivia gasps. "Not Gabe, noooo!" She grabs my coat and drags me to the middle of the bridge to spare her snowman. I gather her close again and she looks up at me, her arms around me, her face close, smelling like oranges and flowers and a whisper of pasta, and everything else in the world spins to a stop.

"Olivia," I murmur, voice stuck in my chest.

"Yes please," she whispers.

That's all I need to tuck in close and kiss her softly on the mouth. I haven't kissed a girl since Rowan. Somehow being a homebody who likes to read and cook does not afford me the dating opportunities one might think.

Then there was the accident. Hunter.

I press in close, here, now.

Olivia's lips are soft and full and she's smiling against my mouth as my body remembers how good all this is, softly waking back up. Clouds of triumph and happiness float across my head and warmth flushes my whole body.

I lean back, heart pounding. Her eyes are closed. "Huh," I murmur.

"What?" she breathes.

"My wish came true."

She laughs and pushes my chest, then comes close again, looking at me from under her lashes, which sends electric alerts flashing across my brain. "You should make another one."

"Okay." I close my eyes again. "Done."

She kisses me while my eyes are closed, this time parting her lips, offering. I try to be cool and keep it light and romantic even though my body kicks into a second, excited gear.

After a heart-pounding second, I pull back just enough to speak. "Hey, it happened again."

She snickers and touches her mitten to my chin. "Wow. You should wish for a million dollars."

"I'd rather have another kiss."

"Oh my gosh." She laughs and leans back, arms still around my waist. "What's the catch?"

"The catch?"

"Yeah." She tips her head up, studying me. "You're a nice, fun guy who likes to cook—what's the catch?"

The compliments should make me feel ten feet taller, but out of nowhere I feel suddenly, coldly, like a fraud. A breath leaves my chest and I hope it sounds like a laugh. Fear and nerves claw up my head. I clamp down on a burst of hysterical laughter.

I can't ride in cars.

If you say my dead cousin's name, I'll start crying. Or screaming. Or punch someone.

The catch?

I'm broken.

"Well, you haven't tasted my food yet," I joke weakly.

"Word on the street is it's good," she says, smiling, brows knitting as she reads me. I remember she knows about Hunter.

"No catch then," I mumble, touching one of her curls, as I've wanted to since day one, wrestling the despair down to the pit of my stomach. "Unless you count being able to quote every Star Wars and Lord of the Rings movie by heart—"

"That's not a catch." She grins. "I would make popcorn."

"So. What's the catch with you? Nice, adventurous girl who's fascinated by my opinions on tomatoes?"

"No catch," she says, dimples appearing. "I'm as amazing as I appear."

The fear eases back, though I'm washed in sweat now and so grateful for deodorant and aftershave, which she seems to be enjoying, staying close. "I thought so."

"Unless you count me being a tourist," she says.

"You're not a tourist." I grin, beating back my fear and grief, punching it back to its corner, hopefully to stay for the rest of the night. "You're a seasonal hire."

She smirks, petting a button on my coat. "Seasonal,"

she reminds me.

I can't explain to her that it doesn't matter if we date for a day or a month or forever, that we have to take our happiness now. That we have to take what we can, now, because we don't know what's coming, how long it lasts, or when we might not have tomorrow.

Instead I tug off a glove and touch her cheek. "We'd better make the most of the season, then."

"Wise." Her gaze flicks to my mouth again. I lean in for another kiss, and another one, until we both start to shiver and head off the bridge toward the Lodge.

We're quiet on the walk in the afterglow of the date, and the handful of what I would judge as perfect kisses. Olivia stays tucked close to me the whole time as if she feels happy and safe with me, and I try to feel worthy of that, but somehow everything is warping into worry and frustration.

What's the catch?

You're moody and emotionally unavailable.

Where did Rowan come up with that? It sounds like something from BuzzFeed. I can't believe I went to her shop on the same day I asked out someone new. Choice move.

We ascend the stairs outside the employee apartments and I walk Olivia to her door, where she turns in close again, tipping her face up. "I had a really fun time. Thank you. Um . . ." She bites her lip and I hope it's because she wants to see me again.

"Me too. What are you doing this weekend?" I take charge, and she smiles. "Friday I've got family stuff, but do you work Saturday? I've got some time off, so I can do whenever." That probably looks too eager again, but she's the one with the schedule, so I might as well be honest.

"I work Friday and Saturday, but I get off at four. If . . ."

"Yes. Let's do something."

"I've heard there's a really good burger place in town." She smiles slyly and brushes a mitten over her curls as one comes loose from its pin.

I chuckle. "Would you be sad if I said I didn't want to go there on my day off? Especially not on a date when all the kids I work with would be watching us?" She laughs and shakes her head, then the brilliant idea comes to me. If it's good enough for Bryson, it's good enough for me. "I could . . . make you dinner on Saturday, instead."

She pauses, then smiles, considering. "Here?"

"Here. Or my house. Wherever you're comfortable."

Behind her door, we can hear her roommate, belting along to what sounds like a Russian pop song. Olivia's dimples deepen and she leans close, wrapping her hand around mine. "Maybe your house. What time?"

"As soon as possible," I say, which makes her grin. "I'll text you the address."

"Sounds good." She squeezes my hand and I lean close to kiss her soft cheek.

Then I remember Justine. "Oh. There's one little complication—"

"I knew it," she breathes, but laughs. "What?"

"I'm sort of babysitting my cousin for the week. I'll see if I can get a friend to watch her for a while, but if not . . ."

"Is this the cousin who came into Mugs and ordered herself a hot chocolate like she owned the place? She's funny."

"Yes, that's her. Justine."

Olivia reaches up to brush at my hair with her mitten and ten pleasant lightning bolts zing down my body even though she looks disappointed. "Whatever you need to do."

"I don't mean cancel. Just, do you mind if she's there? I'll put on a movie for her or something."

"Oh." Her smile deepens again. "I think that would be fun."

"Thanks for understanding. So." I don't move, shifting my weight and basking in her presence for another minute. "I'll see you Saturday."

"See you, yes."

It's really hard to go. "Mind if I come see you at work?"

"Please." She grins, we both hover and hesitate for a second, then one last quick kiss before she heads inside, leaving me suspended there on the walkway. Inside, the music turns down and both voices raise in happy girl chatter and I leave them to it, hoping for a good review.

The lightness takes me back along the trail for a couple of blocks and I decide to take the bridge loop even though it's longer.

My heart pounds, reliving every single smile and tallying the times I managed to make her laugh, and I wonder what she sees in me. *You're nice and you're tall* is most of what I got from Rowan. And she calls *me* emotionally unavailable.

God, I wish Hunter could meet Olivia.

He never had a real girlfriend. Too on the fringe of social stuff, way into his books, outgoing with friends but shy when it came to a risk like romance. We had fantasies of meeting a girl at a Ren Faire or a con, where our kind of people hang out, but we never made it to one.

My throat closes.

Without warning, the happiness disintegrates, leaving my chest raw. The broken feelings smash together in a mess, like Aunt Gina's art installment. All these vicious fragments of sadness and injustice scattered around for me to walk into, to step on, to cut my heart on and bleed out.

I just want to talk to him.

The warmth and promise and happiness of my time with Olivia slides toward sadness, then warps with disturbing ease into ugly, bitter anger that feels more familiar and more comfortable, and my stride grows longer and heavier.

It isn't fair. It isn't fair I'm here and he's not, that he died for absolutely no reason, that I lost him. That Aunt Gina and Mom and Justine and Jack and the world lost him. And now they have to deal with me.

Don't get sad, Dad advises, on occasion. *Get mad.*

At what? I pause at the bridge and walk out to look at the water in the dark, frosty silence. An ache darts through my head where it hit the car window and my breath hitches.

Who am I supposed to be mad at? Myself, for wanting to see a movie? Hunter, for driving? The ice? The drunk driver? She's in a coma and probably won't wake up. A waste of anger. I got mad at Nan's and now I'm unemployed for the week. Is this what Dad thinks I should be? A boiling pot of anger ready to explode?

"Come on," I whisper at myself, trying to calm down, but now my breath and heart rate are up, ready for battle.

I look at the line of snowmen, trying to recapture the happiness I felt with Olivia. They just make me sad now.

Pathetic. Dad bashes at my brain and he's not even here.

What's wrong with you?

Don't talk about Hunter. It's sad, just don't. . . .

Why could I handle not crying at nine years old, keeping it together for Hunter, and I can't now?

I grasp for the warm happy feelings from my date, but the jagged realization that Hunter never got to see someone smile at him the way Olivia smiled at me severs the thread of my control.

A sob lashes out of my throat and I swing my arm, smashing the snowmen, knocking every single one off the rail into the freezing black water below. For a second it feels viciously good to destroy something, as good as it felt to throw a douchebag out of my diner. Cathartic. Productive.

I stand there, breathing as hard as if I've been doing push-ups, until the anger drains and I'm tired. A soft sound of regret catches my chest at the empty railing.

What's wrong with you?

It's a good thing it's late, and empty, and there is no one around to see me.

What's the catch?

Another sound comes out of me, aching, and I slide down to sit on the bridge.

I need to get out of Clark. Everything here is Hunter, Gage and Hunter, around every corner. People telling me what to do, asking how I'm doing, telling me they miss Hunter and how sorry they are. Or glancing nervously at me from the side of their eye because it's been a year, because I should be over it.

Pretty sure I will never, ever be over it. And I don't know what to do with that.

A couple of texts buzz across my phone. Friends from LWDA, tossing around ideas for my movie night.

I breathe in cold air, exhale, watch my breath turn silver and white. When I try to chime in, my hands shake so badly that I almost drop my phone in the river, so I give up for now.

Melting down alone on the bridge is safe. I cannot let my friends and family see me like this. Like Olivia said, she didn't like seeing her dad upset—there was nothing she could do. There's nothing anyone can do. There's no point showing them, and it would horrify Justine and Mom and Aunt Gina and Jack . . . I can't imagine what Jack would think, seeing me balled up and crying like a six-year-old.

I need to get home. I need to finish the application to Redwood House and find my way out of here. If they hire me, that gives me a deadline to figure everything out.

And I really, really need to figure everything out.

I grab the rail of the bridge and drag myself back to my feet.

THE BUSTLE OF THE HOUSE wakes me. I crashed on the couch after walking Cassidy, and she is curled up with me in the living room.

Aunt Gina and Mom are in the kitchen, laughing. Coffee scent hangs in the air, and as I'm sitting up, a cannonball in the shape of Justine lands on my stomach.

"*Oof*—Justine, come on—"

"Mom said you went on a date!" She laughs hysterically, overly dramatic, while Cassidy looks at us reproachfully from her corner of the couch. I loop an arm around Justine and sit up, digging around in the cushions for my phone.

"Yeah."

She makes a face. "Did you kiss her?"

"None of your business. But yes, I did."

"Ewwww!" She flees into the kitchen and I wonder if she's gotten into the coffee, or if it's just the energy of things happening. Cassidy curls herself into a tighter black ball with an irritated grunt. I tuck an afghan around her and kiss her silver nose before wandering to the kitchen, dragging a hand through my hair.

Aunt Gina is still in sweats and Mom is dressed in a skirt and jacket for a workday, but they're both at the counter, one mixing a batter, one cutting strawberries. I step behind them to assess the piles of fruit, shredded cheeses, and ham.

"Crepes?" My inquiry turns both of their heads and Mom leans over to give me a half hug and a grin.

"You're correct, sir. Go sit down, we're doing the cooking this morning."

I obey as Justine skips around and steals a strawberry. Aunt Gina shoos her away and she retreats to the living room with Cassidy. Eventually the sound of cartoons floats our way.

My throat is sore and my head aches. I wonder if there's such a thing as an anger or sadness hangover.

Mom and Aunt Gina fall quiet, glancing at me sideways.

After a minute, Mom finally cracks. "So? How was your date?"

I rub my face, crawling out of my sleep fog. "Really good."

They're restraining themselves mightily, exchanging looks and managing not to giggle and be nosy. "Very good," Mom says somberly, mirroring my expression and energy.

"Give me a break," I mumble, but it's nice they care. "I just woke up. Um. We went to Belle Vite and it was delicious and she's awesome. I'm going to see her again." I don't mention making dinner here at the house, because one or both of them will lovingly try to microman-age the planning, and I've got it figured out. If Imogen can't watch Justine for a couple hours, she can chill in the living room with a movie.

"Thank you for the report," Mom says, teasing, but looks at me over her shoulder with a warm, genuine smile, and I duck my head. "Do you want savory or sweet?"

"Savory." I sit up, attempting to be present before they ask if I'm okay. "What's the plan today? Where's Jack?"

My phone buzzes on the table. A text from Olivia. A flutter of happiness dissolves some of my morning fog.

Olivia: Walked to work today now that I have a secret route! But . . .

It's a picture of the bridge rail where the snowmen were, now frozen and empty.

Olivia: A tragic massacre :((

Sharp regret and shame lock up my throat. I stare at the picture and her frownies, and even though Mom's answering my questions, I'm not hearing, staring at the phone, heart pounding. All I see is Olivia getting up early, walking to work, eagerly checking the snowmen and finding them destroyed.

I rub my face and look at Mom. "What?"

"The plan is," she repeats slowly, "I'm working. Jack went to pick up a trailer. You're helping to load heavy things into it, then we're having mandatory family dinner."

"Got it." My gaze drops to the phone again, and I respond to Olivia.

Me: Wow. People suck >:(

I suck.

She sends a snowman and a crying emoji and maybe

she's joking, but still. I sit staring at my phone, growing nauseated at the innocent, joyful thing I destroyed, until Aunt Gina slides a stunning golden crepe bulging with smoked ham, Swiss, and sharp cheddar in front of me. The smell makes my mouth water even though my stomach is tight.

"Oh wow." I form a smile for her. "Thanks, this looks great."

She grins and squeezes my shoulder. "Eat up. Lots to do today. And I really appreciate your help."

"Sure." I sit up straighter and dig in, swallowing back bile over the snowman massacre. There has to be a way to make it better.

"Justine!" Aunt Gina calls, making me jump. "Breakfast!"

I pull my phone out again and text the one person I know who will give me advice without being nosy or judgmental.

Me: Hey, what do you do if you accidentally break something that was important to someone?

Fairly confident I'll have a solution soon, I cut into the crepe. "Mom? If I email you a copy of a job application, would you proofread it for me? I want to send it today."

Mom beams, walking over to wrap her arms around my shoulders. "Of course. I'll look at it between my morning appointments. Is this for Redwood House?"

Hearing someone else say it aloud makes it more real. Also scarier. I nod.

Aunt Gina gives a low whistle and Mom pets my hair. "I'm really proud of you."

Justine meanders back in, practicing tap steps across

the floor, takes her plate from Aunt Gina, and sits at the head of the table, kicking my leg idly until I make a face at her.

I check the time. "Aunt Gina, would I have time to run downtown before we start loading stuff?"

"Literally run?" she inquires, teasing. "Or walk?"

"A medium pace," I say dryly. "I want to grab a coffee."

"We have coffee." She points at the pot, and warmth hits my cheeks.

"Um, it's . . ."

My phone buzzes and I lean over it while Aunt Gina cocks an eyebrow. Justine leaves her chair and comes around to peer at my phone.

JackDad: Uh oh what did you break?

I shovel a bite of crepe into my mouth to free up a hand and answer, leaning away from Justine.

Me: Nothing of ours, promise. Just wondering. What would you do, hypothetically?

I don't know how to explain the snowmen thing, so I leave it at that.

JackDad: Fess up, apologize, and replace it with the same thing or something of equal or greater value.

Me: Thanks!

He responds with a thumbs-up and sideways eyes, but doesn't press me further. Which is why I know I can count on him.

"Or did you want a fancy coffee?" Mom asks after I'm done texting.

"No." I slip my phone into my sweatpants pocket. "Just a walk. Some fresh air."

Justine hangs on the back of my chair. "He wants to go

see O-livv-ee-ah." She follows this with two kissy sounds and laughs.

I drop my fork onto my plate and sit back. "Thank you, Justine."

Mom's and Aunt Gina's faces light up, then their mouths purse in unison—they should've been born twins—and Mom glances to the window as if she's not sure. "Well, Jack's not even back with the trailer yet."

Aunt Gina pours batter onto the pan and stirs it out to a thin, round sheet. "And we can't really start without you."

"Thanks, I won't take long."

"Finish your crepe," she says. "You're breaking my heart."

"Is there mustard?"

Mom tosses me Dijon from the fridge, which I apply liberally to the crepe, and the balm of seeing my family happy in the kitchen eases the nausea and regret. I ponder how to repair the damage of the snowmen massacre.

Replace the item with the same thing or something of equal or greater value. I consider going to her apartment and building little snowmen on the stair railing. Seems intrusive. Rebuild them on the bridge? Maybe not. The magic's gone from that now, and someone else might knock them off.

Something that can't melt. Something that isn't subject to the whims of nature or bratty kids or angry people like me.

An idea presents itself as my hunger dies down and the crepe slowly regains flavor, and by the time I'm done eating, I'm sure my idea is genius.

Justine pesters me to come along, but I remind her

we're spending the whole week together, so this is my time. Eventually I escape, shower, and dress to see Olivia. I shoot Mom an email with my application and head out.

It's a low, gray, damp day, with spitting snow-rain. I try not to worry about the road conditions for everyone driving to Seattle tomorrow, and breathe in a gallon of the fresh cold air on my walk.

Downtown is busy with people waiting in line at various restaurants for breakfast, and I make my way straight through the skiers and chattering tourists to my destination: Enchanted Forest Gifts, the most shameless of touristy knickknack shops on the main street. With help from the kid working there, we miraculously find the item I'm hunting for. I have them gift wrap it, and continue on to Mugs.

MOUNTAIN MUGS BUSTLES WITH LATE-MORNING CUSTOMERS, the air saturated with the smell of coffee and baking scones.

Olivia stands behind the counter, drawing a flourish on a lady's cup, and my heart is pounding by the time I move from the door behind the next guy in line. Olivia's gaze lifts, she sees me and blushes, lips pursing, dimples appearing, and finishes the drawing. The lady looks around at me, judges me over her glasses, and appears to find me wanting. She rolls her eyes and moves to the waiting area for her drink.

"Like I said," Olivia says when it's my turn, "I never know when you'll show up."

"Surprise. You look really pretty today." It is a relief to be able to tell her the thing I'm thinking every time she appears in my field of vision.

She's wearing the fuzzy pink sweater from the first time we met and sparkly snowflake earrings. "Thanks. So do you."

I laugh roughly and grimace, pretty sure I look exactly like I slept two hours. "Thank you. I . . ." I feel ridiculous suddenly, with the gift in my pocket, and stall. "I just came to say hi."

"Hm, no coffee? My treat. Monte's Creme Brulatte"—she frames the name in air quotes—"is amazing." She bats her eyelashes at me and the breath leaves my chest even though she's teasing. It's not fair, what she does to me. I wonder if she knows. I should tell her. Maybe it's too much.

I clear my throat instead, looking down at the counter. "Oh sure, that sounds delicious."

"Trust me, you want one." She whips a cup off the stack and draws a snowman on it, and with that, I know the gift in my pocket is actually genius. After glancing to make sure no one's waiting behind me, I lean on the counter and slip the miniature gift bag out of my pocket and set it in front of her.

"And I brought you something."

"No! Oh, come on." But she takes it immediately, thrilled, as if I've handed her a diamond. Which only makes me anxious that she thinks it's jewelry or something. "You're so sweet!"

"It's silly. Just for fun—"

"Can I open it now?" She clutches the little bag to her chest.

"Yeah." I hunch my shoulders, then force myself to relax. "Yes, you can open it."

She grins and picks the tissue out of the bag, brown eyes lifting to mine, then pulls out the snowman ornament with a very satisfying gasp. "Oh, it's so cute—Oh my gosh, you did not!" The ornament spins in her hand, revealing it's a name ornament, the kind you collect from touristy destinations like Clark.

But rather than her name, this one says . . .

"*Gabe?*" She throws her head back with the most amazing, uninhibited laugh I've ever heard. A rush of pure pleasure floods my whole body and I shove my hands into my pockets to keep from grabbing her across the counter and kissing her.

She laughs triumphantly and holds the ornament high while people stare at us, and I'm sure I'm red but I don't care.

"He lives!" Tears of laughter stream down her face, and now I never have to tell her that I am the snowman killer.

"Not too cheesy?"

"It's just cheesy enough." She hops to her toes and leans over until I meet her halfway for a quick kiss.

"I'm glad you like it," I murmur.

She smiles, speaking against my cheek as if we're telling secrets. "It's amazing and I'm keeping it forever." Then she kisses my cheek. I will have to thank Jack for his advice again.

"Gage," Monte says, sliding my latte across the pickup counter and very deliberately not looking at us. The bell jingles as a group of folks in ski boots clomp in.

"I'll see you tomorrow." I lean back as Olivia sets Gabe in a place of honor on a corner of the espresso machine.

"I might call you," she says. "If that's okay. Tomorrow's so far away."

It hits hard how very true that is. "You can call me anytime."

She smiles, and I grab my coffee and head back out and home.

The clouds hang low the rest of the morning while Jack and I work. First we build some rails on the floor of the trailer to keep the glass from sliding around. Then it's carefully hauling big packed sheets and pieces of glass and glass rods and whatever tools Aunt Gina will need to work while they're in Seattle.

She drifts over to supervise as we grasp either side of a massive piece that's almost the length of the trailer. It's encased in cardboard, foam, and packing blankets, but she still hovers as if we're handling an infant. "Be really careful, boys."

"Okay, Gage, you go in and I'll toss it to you," Jack jokes as I back up the ramp.

Aunt Gina crosses her arms, unimpressed. "I literally cannot replace this piece."

Jack grunts with exertion as we angle the glass, glancing sideways at Aunt Gina. "This is more nerve-racking than the time I was transporting a truck of unexploded ordnance from—watch your head."

I duck just in time to avoid the frame of the trailer; my hand slips and Aunt Gina sucks in a breath, but I manage to catch the corner of the piece with my boot. Nobody moves for a second.

"Hey, Gage." Jack grips his side of the glass, nodding one, two, three to lift together. "Did you hear about the glassblower who accidentally inhaled while he was working?"

I grin, following his lead and lifting carefully. "Nope, what happened?"

"He ended up with a pane in his stomach."

I snort, backing slowly up the ramp. Aunt Gina huffs indignantly.

"Don't worry," Jack soothes. "If anything breaks, we'll just call it a smashing success."

"Or," I start, "you could say it's a clear-cut—"

"Please," Aunt Gina says tightly, and I glance at her apologetically, although I'm still trying not to laugh.

"Regina," Jack says evenly. "I promise we've got it. You're scaring Gage."

Finally she realizes she's only making us more nervous and she lightens her voice. "You're sure staring at you doesn't help?"

Jack nudges his glasses up with his wrist and chuckles. "Surprisingly, it does not. Okay, Gage, just—yep, let's slide it from here."

We work on the big pieces while Aunt Gina packs some small ones, black and white shards from the broken sculpture that retained interesting shapes and curves. Then we load it all into the trailer.

Justine helps Aunt Gina for a while, then gets bored and takes Cassidy for a walk—which we only discover after she's been gone for a while—and returns. Dampness settles in the air and I think we're in for a blizzard later. I try not to think about the roads. My family has been driving in the snow longer than I've been alive. Maybe it will clear up by tomorrow.

Jack orders pizza for lunch and Olivia sends me a couple more texts throughout the day, and a couple more people respond to my movie-night invite.

Imogenesis: Sorry, I can't babysit Saturday. I promised Mik some sister time. Everything good?

Me: Really good. I have a date.

Imogenesis: WHO?? :O I leave you alone for five minutes and you're dating? Magic.

I wolf down some pizza.

Me: Her name is Olivia. She works at Mountain Mugs.

There's a minute before Imogen answers, and I eat, starving, feeling good from working and having normal conversations.

Imogenesis: Omg I've seen her she's adorable. Darn. I guess I won't flirt with her ;)

Me: You can, but she's pretty into me.

Imogenesis: :P

Me: She has a cute roommate, though.

Imogenesis: :o Invite them both to movie night ;P

I chuckle, but that is not happening. Invite the girl I've had one date with to the memorial night for Hunter? I'm not sure how well that would go.

By the time the trailer is loaded, it's late afternoon. Jack straps everything down, thumps the straps and pronounces it's not going anywhere, and releases me.

Mom texts to let me know she finished proofreading my application, so I retreat to my room to look it over one more time.

Seems like a good way to launch the weekend. Forward

progress. I fix a couple of typos and start copy-pasting the whole thing into the restaurant's online submission form.

My phone buzzes.

Olivia: Soooo what's this about?

Along with the text is one of the videos of me throwing Blondie out of Nan's. Heat hits my face.

Me: How did you find that?

Olivia: Ummm I might've been stalking you on Instagram. It's on this funny Locals Only page.

I scrub a hand vigorously against my hair, leaning back in my desk chair. Should've known. I should've checked on it, after that first day, but I just don't think about it anymore; Rowan's right about that.

Me: I'll tell you over dinner tomorrow? ():)

Olivia: He insulted your food didn't he.

Me: He did.

She sends two clapping hands and a laughing face and I hope she means that. The longer the video plays and replays, the worse it looks. When I tap through to Instagram, so many people have shared it and added it to their Stories and pages—some with my *username*—it's going to be a nightmare to get down. I untag myself from as many as I can and call it good for now.

Then I focus back on the application, trying to stay in the moment and not think about everything that will happen if I get the job. Or if I don't. I'm not sure which is worse.

"Gage?"

I jump and spin my chair to see Justine peering in my doorway. "Hey. What's up?"

She invites herself into my room and walks over to look

at the computer. "What are you doing?"

"I'm applying for a job."

"You have a job." She cocks her head.

"This is a different—what do you want?" I really try not to be short with her, but we're about to have the whole week and she can't leave me alone for five minutes?

"Can we read more of the book tonight?"

My irritation evens out and a spark of flattery and happiness takes its place. "*The Hobbit*? Yeah, of course." I open an arm and she leans against me. "We'll read some before you go to bed."

"Okay!" She hugs me and I feel like the best man in the whole world. "And tomorrow we'll make a blanket fort and s'mores and watch movies."

"You got it. How about burgers for dinner?" I don't mention Olivia coming over yet, because I don't want Justine's opinion and I want to clear it with Mom and Jack first.

"Yeah!" She twirls once and sees herself out. And I feel like a genuinely good person. Good son, nephew, cousin, managing to hold it together. Cleaning up my own messes. Handling life. I can do this.

Once Justine is gone, I spin my chair back, make sure every box in the application is filled, cross my fingers, and hit send.

I **N THE DARK MORNING AIR,** I dig my shovel into eight
fresh inches of wet snow, clearing the sidewalk and the
alley behind the Tahoe. The scrape of the shovel on snow
and concrete and my breath are the only sounds in the air.

Cassidy trots around me, romping in the new snow like
a puppy. I wish I shared her enthusiasm, but the minute I
stepped outside this morning, anxiousness settled heavy on
my shoulders and hasn't left.

My walk with Cassidy helped. The intense, physical
push of shoveling snow helps. Snow keeps falling, and I
wonder if they'll cancel their trip.

Probably not.

Most people don't cancel their lives because they're
afraid of driving. Just me.

Mom and Aunt Gina made lasagna for our family
dinner last night, so I did a homemade garlic bread, and all

they could talk about was Seattle and getting away for a few days. I wish I felt up to going. I also wish they would stay home. I got the stamp of approval to have Olivia for dinner tonight. Everything's going according to plan and I should feel great.

I feel sick to my stomach.

I grab a broom from the shed and brush snow from the Tahoe, clearing the windows, scraping ice, then shovel a runway behind the rear tires so it's easier to get out and they can pull it around to hitch up the trailer. Then I lean on my shovel, staring at the dark air, the falling snow. It takes real effort to push all the worst scenarios from my mind and the best thing to do is keep busy, so I head inside to start some pancake batter.

It's lighter out by the time everyone wakes up; I have a full pot of coffee on, bacon, eggs. My throat's as tight as if it's the last meal I'll ever make for them.

Get it together. It's a few hours on an interstate.

"Morning!" Mom is dressed in comfy leggings and a sweater for travel, ready for the day, and she hugs me tight. "I peeked outside and it looks like an elf cleared the driveway?"

"Just trying to help," I murmur, turning to engulf her in a hug. "I hope you guys have a great time."

Mom's arms stay around me comfortably, and she rubs my back. "We will." She leans away to look at me, and I must be so transparent because she frowns in worry. "I'll keep you updated."

I push a smile onto my face. "I know."

I say that, meanwhile a reel of possibilities scrolls through my brain—the heavy trailer sliding on ice and dragging them off the road, the Tahoe hitting a deer in the low visibility, or them smashing into a guardrail.

It occurs to me to wonder if I'm old enough to be Justine's legal guardian, along with all sorts of other horrifying questions.

Mom frowns, reaching up to finger-comb my hair. "What's on your mind?"

Before I start, Jack wanders in, glasses off, rubbing his eyes. At least they don't seem like they're in a hurry. Maybe the roads will thaw some before they go.

"Um, nothing," I say to Mom. "Just take it slow? It's really coming down out there."

"Oh, Gage," Mom says, "we'll be so careful, I promise. I'll text you often, okay? If you don't hear from us, it's because we lost signal for a while. Oh, baby. We'll be okay." She hugs me again and I want to scream, like Justine, that I'm not a baby—but I probably look like one, shaking and terrified over a few inches of snow.

It's just that she doesn't know if they'll be okay. Nobody can know that, nobody can promise that. There is so very little we can control.

"Supposed to be clearer after the pass," Jack says, popping his glasses on and heading straight to the coffeepot. "But we'll wait until it's light and warms up a bit."

"Thanks. I mean, yeah." I finally release Mom so I can step away and start on the pancakes.

Aunt Gina and Justine come over for breakfast, Jack gets a fire going in the living room for us to enjoy when they're gone, and with everyone happy and chattering in the kitchen, it takes everything I have not to ask them to stay. I try to immerse myself in the moment.

I can't eat.

It feels like two seconds before the sharp, safe darkness rises to the dull gray of daytime and we're hauling suitcases to the car. I brush off the windows again. On autopilot, I help Jack hitch the trailer.

Justine's hugging everyone. They're loaded up. Mom's hugging me.

They're *leaving*.

I snap out of my cloud and hug her tight.

"I love you," I whisper. "Be careful, okay? Mom . . ."

"We will." She squeezes me. "Thank you for watching Justine. Gage, we'll be very smart, I promise. You enjoy your time."

"I'll try. I mean I will. We will." I force my arms to unlock and Aunt Gina steps in to give me a squeeze.

"I hope you have a fun week. I owe you big-time." She draws back with a smile. There's a ghost of Hunter in her face and my heart jerks, pounding, but if I crumble now, I know they won't go. They won't go, my problem will be their problem, and she won't get to do her show. I can't stop everyone's lives for me.

I scrape myself together. "We will. Knock 'em dead. Send lots of pictures."

She reaches up to cup my cheek with a smile before climbing into the Tahoe with Mom.

Jack steps in, arms wide for a hug. "Low and slow," he reassures me, patting my back. I probably don't have him fooled. "The interstate will be okay, Gage. We'll check in. Okay?"

"Okay," I whisper through gritted teeth. Behind me, Justine is romping around in the snow with Cassidy, singing "Let It Snow" but to the tune of "Let It Go," and I don't know how she's not terrified too. I desperately try not to think about the real possibility that this could be the last time I see them. Who does that? No one normal.

Just in case, I crush Jack in the hug. "Love you, Jack. I really appreciate everything. Just, everything you do. Thanks."

He makes a soft sound. "I love you too, Gage. You're one of the best guys I know." He draws back, gripping me by both arms, seems satisfied with what he sees, and steps away. "See you in a week."

"Yeah." *I hope so.* I'm a mess. Justine smacks into me and I almost crack, but then I just take her hand, and we wave while Mom and Aunt Gina roll down their windows and blow us kisses through the falling snow.

The Tahoe disappears around the corner of the alley. I stand there with snow falling on me until Justine hangs against my hand. "Can I have another pancake? Can we put chocolate chips in it?"

"Yeah." I wrench my gaze from the deep tire tracks in the snow of the alley, take a big breath, and smile for her. "You got it, whatever you want."

She grins and tows me back into the house, with Cassidy on our heels hoping for bacon.

"I'm hungry." Justine pokes my shoulder promptly at noon.

"There's lasagna in the fridge." I'm kicked back on the

couch, self-medicating my anxiety by zoning out to "Food Wishes" on YouTube. I tried reading but only stared at a single page for an hour. Our Lord of the Rings marathon might be a perfect time to try making fondant potatoes, so I watched that video, then let the playlist keep going.

Justine toys with my sleeve until I look at her. "Can you make it?"

"I thought you weren't a baby." I turn up the current video on meatballs, then check for texts from Mom or Aunt Gina. Also a quick email check. I know there's zero chance of a reply from Redwood House about my application, but I can't help checking. I shouldn't have sent it on a Friday.

Justine pouts. "It's better when you make it."

I nudge the pillows up with my elbow and flop back again, exhausted from the emotional morning. "You can do it. Use the toaster oven instead of the microwave. That's what I do."

"Please?"

I rub my forehead and pause the video because I haven't really heard a word. She stands there until I finally relent, roll to my feet, and head into the kitchen to make lunch. Justine is thrilled, eats, and I resume my spot on the couch.

It doesn't take long until she's back.

"I'm bored."

"Only boring people get bored," I say without looking up. It's one of Aunt Gina's maxims.

Justine scoffs and twirls around. "I want to go skiing."

I close YouTube and lower my phone, grasping for why I volunteered to do this. "Well, you'll have to see if any of your friends are skiing. You know I can't take you."

She pouts again. A full-on lip-sticking-out pout, then

sticks her tongue out at me. "I don't have their numbers. Mom does. What if I take the bus? There's a stop at the grocery store and it goes up the mountain and then I can ride it home."

"Not by yourself." With a sigh, I sit up. Probably time to do something productive anyway. "I will try to get you up the hill today or tomorrow."

"Today!"

"Justine."

"Gage," she mimics me sternly.

I rub my face, then text Aunt Gina to get some phone numbers for Justine's friends. As I'm texting her, a message comes from Jack, and relief calms my mood back to magnanimous. Justine's really not asking that much.

True to Mom's word, they have kept us updated on their progress, even sent pictures of the highway west of Snoqualmie, which is wet but mostly clear with patches of blue sky above. Jack has sent a picture of their lunch—his is a burger.

JackDad: They put arugula on it. >:{

Me: Sorry for your pain.

He sends a GIF of a guy flipping a table, so I give him a thumbs-up.

Aunt Gina sends me a bunch of contacts to get in touch with Justine's friends' parents, apologizing she didn't think of it sooner.

"Okay, who do you want to try? Bailey?"

"No," Justine says, offended. "She's mean." She plops next to me on the couch and grabs for my phone, so I hold it up out of her reach.

"Why did your mom say she's your friend if she's

mean?" I reach my other hand high to start a group text and explain the situation and see if Justine can get in on any skiing in the next couple of days.

"Mom doesn't know. At Shelby's birthday party, though, Bailey was saying how silly her hair looked because she cut it short, and . . ." She keeps talking, but I can't keep track of all the girls' names, and the details of the scandal go in one ear and out the other. Still talking, she clambers around me onto the back of the couch, standing to try to reach the phone—then topples onto my shoulders so I have to grab her to keep both of us from crashing into the coffee table.

"Okay, you *do* need something to do." I lurch up with her clinging to my back like a monkey. "Let's make your blanket fort. Olivia's coming over for dinner and you can hang out and watch a movie if you don't bug us."

She lights up. "Okay."

It occurs to me, with her hanging around my neck, she'll be sitting with us at dinner. Her and her loud mouth. I squeeze her wrist gently. "And, uh . . . look, I just met her, and I don't want to talk to her about Hunter yet, so if you could . . . just don't bring him up, okay?"

She's quiet for a second and guilt lances me. I sound like Dad. Like Rowan. But I try to picture bringing up Hunter over dinner—or at all—and my heart skips.

"Okay?" I ask.

"Okay," she agrees. "And we'll make s'mores, right?"

"Burgers and s'mores." Relief flutters in my chest. Of course she's fine. "That's the plan."

The plan must be acceptable because she drops from my shoulders and sprints away to start gathering raw materials for our fort.

Hunter and I were practiced fort builders. Tents, blankets—then constructing lean-tos and shelters out of pine boughs in the woods—and, on rare occasion, a tarp. Ranger style. I haven't done it in the house in years, though, not since I was Justine's age.

By the time we're done, there is a Pinterest-worthy arrangement of sheets draped from the fireplace mantel down to the couch, with supporting walls of cushions on one side and the coffee table turned ninety degrees on the other to hold snacks. One blanket-wall can be draped up to see the TV, with another side open to the fireplace.

We drag extra blankets and pillows from the linen closet to line the floor, steal a few twinkle lights from the Christmas decorations to light up the inside, and Justine is content there decorating with more pillows, giving me a chance to tidy. A sweep of the living room, kitchen, bathroom, and my bedroom.

Just in case.

A few texts float through the LWDA group about movie night and I run food ideas by everyone. Bryson shoots me a text with a selfie of him and Mia on the ski lift making faces at me, and I grin.

Mom calls in the afternoon and talks a lot about the drive and the weather and I know it's her not-subtle way of reassuring me. They send pictures of the hotel in Seattle, Aunt Gina's friends' studio, the gallery. Music floats from the blanket fort; Justine is listening to one of Hunter's playlists.

You've got a good life, bud. Dad's right. I need to stay focused on the right things. That shouldn't be too hard tonight.

AT SIX O'CLOCK, THE CRUNCH of snow under tires out front announces Olivia's arrival, along with a soft *boof* from Cassidy, who is curled up in the blanket fort.

I feel pretty good. My outfit is Rowan-inspired because I'm not too proud to admit she has a great sense of style and I was at a loss staring at my closet until I went with an old staple she calls "mountain casual": plaid flannel over a maroon T-shirt, sleeves half-rolled, and my one good pair of jeans.

I had to endure Justine's teasing when I came down groomed and dressed for a date, and now she jumps up with a shriek to answer the door.

"Nope, hang on." I snag her around the middle and kneel. "Listen." She meets my eyes, grinning. "Olivia is really nice, and I like her, and I'm glad you're here and it's going to be fun. But can you promise to be polite and wonderful and all the things you promised you'd be when I said I would watch you this week?"

She lays her head back and rolls her eyes. "Yes."

"And you'll be cool and entertain yourself and give us some time alone?"

She scrunches her face. "Yes."

"Thanks, buddy." I give her a quick hug.

She slings her arms around my neck, then draws back, wrinkling her nose. "What do you smell like?"

I pull back. "Aftershave? What's wrong?" She snickers and I frown. "Are you messing with me?"

She covers a giggle while I stand and smooth my shirt, then head to answer the front door. Whatever.

My heart rate is already up and a warm but pleasant nervousness in my chest blossoms at the sight of Olivia. The snow quit for a while in the afternoon and now it's back, burying the world, and she trots up the sidewalk in a pretty white peacoat and the knitted beanie I've seen before. She's carrying a bakery box.

"This is so pretty!" She tips her face up to the snow as I usher her in.

"Glad you like it. I called in some favors."

She laughs and I try to remember why I was nervous. Though I wonder about Justine's comment. Is my after-shave really too strong? Great.

"Here." Olivia offers me the box shyly. "I thought I should bring dessert. Don't get too excited—it's not from the bakery. I made them. That's why I took longer."

"It's even better because it's homemade," I assure her. My heart skips because she baked something for us. Wow. I stare at the box of cookies, then at her, then get my brain together, tuck the box in my arm, and help her with her coat only to discover she's wearing a gorgeous gray sweaterdress that absolutely flatters her soft round curves. I flick my eyes back up to her face, cheeks hot. "You look beautiful."

"You too." She grins, blushing.

I'm about to lean in and kiss her cheek when I remember Justine is standing there, watching us, hands clasped behind her back. Cassidy wanders in, ears perked, tail wagging, and thrusts her face into Olivia's thigh. The welcoming committee.

I clear my throat. "And, uh . . . that's Cassidy."

"Oh, hello." Olivia ruffles Cassidy's ears. "Hello, ma'am. Yes, what a good girl."

"And, Olivia, this is my cousin Justine. Justine, this is Olivia."

"Hi," Justine says, and grins. "Come see our fort!"

"I would love to." Olivia lifts her eyes to me, and I am physically incapable of movement. So I'm lucky she leans up to kiss my cheek, then pauses, taking a breath. "Wow," she whispers. "You smell so good."

Then she's gone with Justine, Cassidy trotting behind them, and I'm breathless in the entryway with a box of cookies, trying to remember my own name.

I fall in behind the girls as Justine gives the grand tour, and Olivia is either really polite or genuinely delighted by everything. If I'd realized my own house was as enchanting as Olivia thinks it is, I would have tried to host more girls here. But maybe it's because she's never seen winter. She loves the fort. She loves the fireplace. Some of our Christmas decorations are still up and she loves those. By the time we gather in the kitchen so I can make dinner, she's convinced I've transported her into a Hallmark card.

It's an illusion I hope to maintain for the duration of the evening.

I task Justine with choosing and chopping crisp lettuce leaves while Olivia chills at the table with a mug of hot cider, staring at the snow inching its way up the kitchen window. I've made this kind of cheeseburger literally thousands of times, but I'm afraid, somehow, I'm going to mess it up, so I'm going slower than usual.

Her phone buzzes and all of us jump. Then again. A call. "Oh," she says. "It's my dad. Do you mind?"

"Of course not, go for it." I smear butter across the hamburger buns and rest them butter-side down in a hot pan. That's one secret; grilling the buns with butter for an extra rich, crisp texture. Olivia slips out of the kitchen with her phone and Justine looks up at me.

"She's really nice," she whispers.

"I know," I whisper back. "Thanks for helping."

She grins conspiratorially as Olivia's voice murmurs from the living room. I focus on my burger. Onions. Mustard. My hands do everything on autopilot.

Olivia returns as I'm sliding patties into the pan. Her eyes are down, cheeks pink. I leave the stove and stand close as she resumes her seat and hesitantly touches her hair.

"Is everything okay? If you need to talk to him more . . ."

"Oh, no. It's fine." She breathes deep through her nose and smiles at me, which tightens my heart. I want to tell her I understand, that she can talk to me if she wants. "Sorry."

"Don't be sorry."

She fiddles with her phone. "Could, um . . . Can I have a hug?" She releases a breath like a laugh and looks up at me, and I sink in close to wrap my arms around her in silence. She rests her head right against my heart. Emotion tangles there and we take a deep breath together, quiet.

Justine comes over and hesitantly offers her a plate with pickle slices on it. "My mom made these. You should try one."

Olivia laughs and sniffles, giving me a squeeze and grabbing a napkin from the silver reindeer holder on the table to wipe under her eyes. "I guess it does run in the family."

"What's wrong?" Justine asks, before I can tell her not to be nosy.

"Well," Olivia says quietly, "my grandmother died a few months ago and my dad is still sad sometimes."

I wonder what it's like to say something like that so calmly, without breaking down. I wonder if I'll ever be able to. Hesitantly, I rub her back reassuringly and she leans against me.

"I'm sorry," Justine says, and sets the plate of pickles on the table before fidgeting.

For half a second my heart pounds harder, afraid Justine is going to bring up Hunter. I realize I'm staring at her, brow furrowed, and look away.

Olivia tries a pickle and her eyebrows lift and she smiles to Justine, then up at me. "Thank you. Thanks, both of you. I'm okay now." She makes a rallying noise and grabs her phone. "Here's something funny we did at the coffee shop today." Her playful smile is back and I don't know if she's putting up a front for us or if it comes in waves, like Hunter, but I am determined to make the rest of her evening perfect. "It's a quiz to find out what kind of bread you are."

Justine laughs. "Me first!"

Olivia smiles over Justine's head at me, then back to her phone. "Okay."

Justine abandons her post as sous chef to do the quiz and I focus on the cheeseburgers, relief swelling that Olivia's okay—or acting okay?—and it didn't break me open to see her sad. I liked hugging her. Feeling like a bastion, a source of strength. Maybe that's what Dad means when he says a man protects his family. If so, that is definitely who I want to be.

"All right." Olivia begins the quiz. "Do you prefer to be alone, with a small group of friends, or at a big party with lots of new people?"

"A party," Justine says very seriously.

"Mm-hmm. What is your favorite color?"

"Orange." They carry on and by the time I set out the burgers, with a side of sour cream and chive-seasoned fries, we have determined Justine's bread type.

"You are challah," Olivia announces. "Ooo. You enjoy family traditions and the company of others, you are inspiring but down-to-earth, unique, worldly, and adaptable."

"Wow," Justine says, then shoves a handful of fries into her mouth. "Do Gage!"

"Let's eat first," I say, because a cold burger is not going to make a good impression.

Olivia sets her phone aside. "Good plan."

I make sure everyone has something to drink before I sit, and I try not to stare at Olivia as she takes a bite.

Olivia savors her bite, eyes wide. "Yes. I see. This is amazing. It's like if McDonald's was, like . . . homemade and good."

I laugh. "Thanks."

She presses her fingers to her lips. "I mean—that's a compliment!"

"I take it as one. They're the most successful restaurant franchise in the world."

"Really?"

"Really."

She peers at me, takes another bite of her burger, closes her eyes in satisfaction, then lifts her phone to google my trivia. "Wow, you're right."

"'Do a few things really well,'" I quote Andrus.

"They do lots of things," she says.

"Yes, but they do a *few* things"—I aim a french fry at her, and we're both smiling—"really well."

"So do you," she says, lifting her burger.

I consider countering with how I can do lots of things really well, but maybe that sounds conceited. Maybe she sees it in my face because she drops her lashes low with a tiny smile, and my heartbeat skips up to a faster pace.

"Okay, do the bread quiz," Justine demands, bored with our flirting over McDonald's facts. Olivia nudges her foot against mine and I try not to laugh.

"Oh yes, let's."

"You don't have to," I say. Olivia lifts her shining brown eyes to me and I will take every quiz she asks.

"Ahem." She sits up, lifts a fry, and begins. "Small group of friends, being alone, or a big party with new people?"

"Small group of friends."

"Favorite color?"

"Blue."

"Mountains, beach, forest, city or town, or farmland?"

I ponder, then chuckle. "How does this tell me what bread I am? Forest, I guess."

She gives me a stern look. "You have to answer seriously, or the results won't be accurate."

"I would hate to have my bread-personality be inaccurate."

Olivia taps her foot against mine again and grins. We run through the rest of the questions while Justine watches, intent, as if all my inner secrets will suddenly be revealed, and we arrive at the final conclusion.

"You are . . ." Olivia purses her lips, eyes flicking to mine. She holds up a finger, clearing her throat against laughter. "A biscuit."

"What?"

"A buttermilk biscuit." She turns the phone to show me the result, a picture of a perfect golden biscuit with a pat of melting butter on top.

Justine erupts into laughter, sliding down in her chair, while Olivia reads the description.

"The original family favorite"—I grab for the phone and Olivia scoots her chair out of reach, reading, breathless with laughter—"you are a basic heartland staple, comforting, charmingly flaky, but still warm and reliable, with a crisp outer layer and a warm center." She finally dissolves into giggles.

"I would rather be a gnocchi. What did you get when you took it?"

"I got kouign-amann."

"*What?*"

"What's kun-ya-man?" Justine wants to know.

"It's a European pastry." I scowl between them and

cross my arms. "She got challah and you got kouign amann and I got *biscuit*? This is rigged."

"At least you didn't get pretzel. That's what Monte got. Twisted and salty." She and Justine start laughing again. I finally crack and laugh too. Biscuit indeed. I wonder what Hunter would've gotten, and a quick ache snarls in my chest. Maybe I'll take the quiz for him later.

Conversation with Olivia continues to be easy and fun; we swap stories about our best and worst customers, I tell her how to distinguish locals from part-timers and tourists. She reveals her family's been to San Francisco too, so we try to figure out if we went to any of the same places. Justine pipes up now and then and they talk as if they've known each other for years. I was afraid Justine would be weird and shy, but she opens right up.

Although it's a bit of a struggle to get her to transfer to the living room for a movie, to give us some alone time.

"You promised." I gently herd her out of the kitchen after we clean up dinner.

"You said we could do s'mores."

"And we will. Later. We just ate."

"Later when?" She plants her heels in the archway separating the kitchen from the living room and I don't want to shove her—but it's tempting.

"After your movie."

She hmms as if she's in charge, and the irritation in my chest threatens to warp into anger and kill the mood. "Do I have to call your mom? You promised me, Justine. Just chill out for a while. What do you want to watch?"

She breaks away from me to stomp into the living room and sulk in our beautiful blanket fort. Olivia politely ignores the interaction and heats up more cider. Since Justine's not speaking to me, I pick a movie for her on Netflix, stoke the fire, and head back into the kitchen.

Olivia steps forward with her sweet smile and offers me a mug of cider. We hang in the kitchen so she can watch the snowflakes fall outside. We talk about her road trip here from Florida with her mom, and compare her experience of half homeschool, half multiple high schools to mine— same school, same town forever, watching my friends grow up around me.

Songs from Justine's movie infiltrate our pauses, with Justine singing along at a distracting volume I'm sure is intentional, until Olivia smiles and touches my arm. "Can I see your room?"

I know better than to read too much into that, but still, my pulse skips ahead. "Probably our best bet for quiet." Also, I don't know if Justine's going to break our promise about Hunter if she's mad at me. Time to escape.

"Mm-hmm," Olivia agrees.

I glance in the living room on our way to the stairs and Justine has settled in with her drawings and the movie, finally.

In my room, Olivia sips her cider while I turn on the lamp, infinitely glad I cleaned earlier.

"It's very you," she sums up.

"What's 'me'?" I draw the shade so Hunter's window is not in my peripheral the whole time.

"Hm." She looks at my posters, books, the pictures on my dresser and pinned to the board over my desk—family, Imogen, Justine, me, and Dad. Hunter. I remember, in that moment, she knows. Aiden told her. But she doesn't know that's him; maybe she won't ask. "Cozy. Safe." She picks up the anthology of sci-fi stories on my bedside table and waves it with a grin. "Nerdy."

"Cozy" and "safe" don't sound super manly, but the way she's looking at me, I'll take it. "Don't forget biscuity."

"A biscuity nerd," she agrees, and bites her lip, setting my brain on a very specific trajectory.

"As long as you like it." I have a drink of my own cider, warm, spicy, and soothing.

She grins, setting the book back exactly how she found it. "I like everything so far."

I smile to cover my sudden uncertainty, and sit on the bed, motioning for her to take the old but comfy chair by my bookshelf. She considers, then comes and sits next to me instead. I keep my hands around my cider mug and try to remember the last time I had a pulse this fast and wasn't panicking. Oh right. With her.

A chilly fear that this pleasant nervousness could contort into anxiety is new, though. I take a deep breath, counting backward, focusing on this moment.

"Is this okay?" she asks softly, watching my eyes. I can smell her. Flowers and oranges, sunshine.

"Yeah, of course." I realize she's misreading what I'm feeling. I clear my throat and edge up on the bed, tucking a leg up and trying not to look toward my window. "It's perfect."

"What's the job application on your desk?" She sips her cider, watching me over the rim of the mug, and I release a breath, running a hand roughly through my hair. We didn't cover Redwood House in our earlier conversation.

"It's this restaurant—in San Francisco, actually.

My favorite chef owns it and they're hiring for starter positions this summer."

"Michael Andrus?"

I sit up. "Yeah. I guess I've mentioned him?"

She's smiling. That shiny, secret smile where I'm going nuts wanting to know what she's thinking. "A couple times."

"Sorry."

She smacks my knee. "Stop saying sorry."

"Sorry." I grin.

"Stop it," she murmurs, hesitates, and kisses me, short and soft. My eyes close.

"I'm so, so sorry."

She leans over to set her mug on the dresser, then, watching my face, scoots closer. Too many things are happening in my brain and I try to focus on her face and her warm body all snug and close in that impossibly soft dress. She touches my hand, takes my mug from me, and sets it aside too.

Then she wraps her hands around mine and watches my face. After a minute of me sitting there, thrilled and silent and uncertain, she tips her face up. "I really want to kiss you some more, Gage."

"Oh good," I mumble. "Me too. I mean, I want to kiss *you*, not—"

She touches my lower lip, then we both move close but at the wrong angle, and she sits back with a laugh. I rally and lean in close to cup her jaw, our mouths press, and she makes a soft sound that clicks a light in my brain. For a second I compare even though I shouldn't—but kissing her is not like kissing Rowan, at least from what I remember. It always felt like Rowan was judging me, or wanted me to do something differently but wouldn't ask.

Meanwhile, Olivia is having fun and seems completely relaxed. She smiles against my mouth, teasing me, playful and curious. At first it's light, brief touches of her mouth before she presses closer, lips parting, opening the kiss, asking and offering more. I brush a hand over her hair, fingers catching in her curls, and cradle her face in both hands. She rubs my neck, my chest, warmth flushes my whole body and sinks low, but even that's okay. Better than okay. It's so good. I haven't felt any of this in so long. Too tired. Too sad. Too angry.

But this is so sweet, and vital, and now. I feel alive and that maybe it's even okay for me to *be* alive. To have this, to enjoy it.

Wind shudders against my window and the lamp flickers, once. Olivia snuggles closer, dips a kiss to my neck, and breathes deeply against my skin. Sparks shower my brain and my body and I wrap both arms around her, pulling us down to snuggle close on the bed. She squeaks in surprise but falls with me, hands climbing up my neck to my hair.

"Is this okay?" I murmur against her ear.

"Yes," she breathes, kissing my chin, but pushes a hand to my chest to pause me. "It's good. I mean . . . this feels really good, but I don't want to go further right now." She bites her lip, petting my shirt uncertainly.

"We don't have to do anything else. This is perfect— thanks for telling me." I rest my hand over hers on my chest, reorganizing my body's heated, eager expectations. "I just like being close."

"I like it too," she says softly, relieved, and I rub my

thumb against her hand reassuringly. "Are you sure? Um . . ." She shifts slightly.

It occurs to me we're pressed close and she is definitely aware of my hard-on.

A different kind of self-conscious heat swamps my body and I scoot back. "Oh. Yeah." I clear my throat, then of all things, a laugh sneaks out. "It's okay. Sorry—"

"Don't." She hits my arm lightly, then curls her hand in mine, playing with my fingers. "As long as it's . . . I mean, it's not uncomfortable for you?"

"I've never been more comfortable in my life." I kiss her cheek, now suspecting she has about as much experience as I do, which is to say, not much. I tip my head back to meet her eyes again. "Don't worry about him."

"*Him?*" She snickers, but stays cuddled close, and there's a wisp of embarrassment but then I'm laughing too.

"It—yeah, him. Me. Just don't worry about me. I'm fine. Perfect." My brain skitters between worry and laughter until we've both dissolved into the latter. "Everything is perfect."

"Can we still kiss?" She picks at my shirt, just before my wave of happiness crashes inexplicably toward an indistinct sadness. All the emotions, woven together. I shove it back.

"Yes, please."

"Oh good," she echoes me from earlier, and kisses me eagerly again. Flowers and oranges envelop me.

"What's that smell?" I ask softly, warmth pulsing in my ears.

"I smell?" she teases, fingers curled against my stomach. Then she unfastens a couple of the buttons on my flannel and slides her hand inside it, between that layer and my T-shirt.

"Yes, you . . ." I try to remember my question, but everything narrows to her hand for a second, rubbing my side. "You smell really good. What's that flower?"

She kisses my chin. "Hibiscus." She kisses my neck. "And orange." She kisses my mouth. "And secret stuff."

"Wow," I whisper. And that's all the words I have left.

For a few more glorious moments my whole world is Olivia's hands exploring me, Olivia's lips on mine, the scent of oranges and my new favorite flower, hibiscus. Now that we've established where we're stopping tonight, she's even more relaxed, giving, and receptive. Her leg nudges around me, trusting me with her closeness. I'm getting hot, but I don't want to take off the flannel in case she thinks I'm trying to go further than she wants. It still feels good.

It's all so good.

For the first time in a long time, I exist one hundred percent in this moment, in my body tangled against hers, right now. It feels safe, as if I've never been hurt and might never be hurt again. I can feel good and happy for a while.

She seems to be feeling good and happy as well, with bubbling laughs and soft sounds driving me pleasurably out of my mind and into my body as we melt together in a soft, sustainable rhythm of touches and hungry kisses.

My door creaks.

Justine gasps—

I lurch up, dropping poor Olivia to the pillow with a peep of surprise, while I yank a corner of the blanket over my lap.

"Jesus, Justine! *Knock!*" My harsh shout startles

everyone, including me, and I suck a breath, closing my eyes for a second.

When I open them, Justine's still standing there, staring.

"What's up?" I run both hands down my face, scrambling mentally, everything trying to click back into not-horny alignment. "I'm sorry. Sorry for shouting—you surprised me. What do you need?"

Justine grips the doorknob, swinging my door with a smirky know-it-all look on her face I suspect is a cover for discomfort. "I'm telling!"

Olivia has buried her face in my pillow to keep from laughing, but she rests a hand on my back, fingers closing around my shirt. I should have locked the door. I shove my irritation, frustration, and embarrassment to their own compartments in my brain.

"You're telling who, what? We weren't doing anything wrong. What do you want?"

She looks from Olivia to me, and then at her own feet, and I know I'm right: she's just as embarrassed as I am. "Netflix stopped working."

"You know how to restart the router—"

My lamp pops off, dropping us into abrupt, inky blackness.

For half a second it's silent and dark.

"It's okay," I say. "It's just a—"

Justine screams delighted bloody murder, and at least I don't have to worry about my erection anymore.

"Blackout," I finish unnecessarily.

THE BLACKOUT CONCLUDES THE PRIVATE, romantic portion of our evening.

We reconvene downstairs, light candles, and all three of us huddle in the blanket fort by the fireplace for a few rounds of checkers, then Olivia and Justine get out some paper and draw.

Then s'mores, as promised. As the girls gather ingredients, I step out onto the porch to check the weather. The air is damp, snowing and windy. The wind, more than snow and ice, is probably what caused the outage. Streetlights are out as far as I can see on this side of the river. All the houses are dark, or candlelit and dim, and everything is violet and black and cold as if it's the last night of the world.

The eerie silence of wind and snow in the neighborhood sends a pleasant shiver down my spine and I hurry back to the invincible shelter of our fort.

"This is the best blackout I have ever experienced," Olivia declares, turning her marshmallow over the fire. Then she leans against me and it's suddenly the best blackout I've ever experienced as well.

I'm slow and methodical with my marshmallow so it toasts evenly to tawny, crispy gold with a gooey center, while Justine chars hers to a crisp. She laughs and hands it to me to blow out.

"Hey, Justine, go get the cookies Olivia brought, please."

Olivia glances at me sideways. "Are you about to do something genius?"

"Yes I am."

Justine fetches the bakery box, and instead of graham crackers, we sandwich the marshmallows and chocolate between the cookies for a transcendent s'mores experience. I have to compliment Olivia on successfully soft-baking her chocolate chip cookies. A lot of people get them too crunchy. She also used dark chocolate chips and I wonder if it's too soon to be falling in love. Probably.

Cassidy lies on her belly between Justine and me, her nose resting on her paws, mournfully watching us devour s'mores, tail tapping a slow, hopeful wag.

When Justine finally yawns, I seize on it. "Hey. Time for bed."

She groans. "Can I stay here? I want to sleep in the fort."

"Of course. Go get your toothbrush and stuff." I hand her one of the flashlights we've gathered in the fort.

She rolls onto her back, arms flopping, smacking my knee. "I don't want to go to sleep!"

"You don't have to go to sleep." I nudge her with

my knee, wondering if she'll ever do one thing without arm-wrestling over it. "But you have to go to bed."

She tsks, but crawls out of the fort and trots away with the flashlight to fetch sleepover gear from her house.

Olivia shifts as if she's going to get up. "I should probably start back."

"What?" I rest a hand on her knee as a quick, cold sweat springs out on my back. Instant, as if a mountain lion appeared in the house. "The streetlights are out. The traffic lights are probably toast too and there's like eight feet of new snow. Why don't you stay here?"

She leans in close, peering into my eyes—then kisses my nose. "Eight feet, huh."

"I just . . ." I clear my throat, breath tight as all the fear that hit me this morning watching my folks leave crawls back over my skin. So not only can I not get in a car, I can't handle *other* people getting in cars? When does this end? Is there a single corner of my life safe from this?

Olivia's watching me, worried, and I motion to the windows. "It's bad out there."

She wraps her hands around mine. "I'm a really good driver. I drove all the way from Florida."

"Please don't," I finally say point-blank, gaze darting to the fire. "I don't feel good about it. Please." My voice cracks and I wonder how pathetic I must look, as if I'm begging her not to dive off a cliff instead of drive five minutes somewhere. "I promise I don't have an ulterior motive, we have a guest room, you can——"

"Okay, Gage," she says, and touches my hair, my cheek. "I'll stay. It's okay. I don't really want to go anyway."

In that moment, I remember again she knows about

Hunter. Aiden told her. We've avoided Hunter, but she still knows. I wonder if she knows it was a car accident, if that's why she's so understanding. And now my fear and my weakness are served up for her to see. I lean in, eyes low, and kiss her cheek.

"Thank you. Thanks. Uh, I might have a shirt or something you can sleep in, if that's not weird." I strive to take control of the situation again. An emergency weather situation. It's not just me. It's not safe. It's dark. Her car is half buried in snow and she's from the literal Sunshine State.

"Actually." Her sweet, unruffled voice brings me back, along with leaning way over to force her brown eyes back into my line of sight. "Guess what?"

"What?" I exhale.

"I have emergency pajamas."

That clears my head because it's not a phrase you ever expect to hear, and a smile worms above the fear. "What?"

She pets my hair again and it helps. It's soothing and reassures me that she's not completely turned off by my fear and stuttering, or if she is, she's keeping it to herself. "I told you, Mom and I drove here from Florida. She insisted I have an emergency duffel with a road kit, snacks, water, light, blankets. And pajamas."

"Wow. Your mom's awesome. Where are your keys? I'll grab it for you." I can do that. If I'm insisting she stay, I can at least brave the snow and get her things for her. She smiles.

"In my coat pocket. And the duffel's in the trunk." The trunk. I can handle the trunk; I can handle not getting in the car. I nod and she smiles at me, then starts looking around for something. "I should text Alonya and let her know I'm staying here."

We dig through the pillows and blankets until I find her phone and hand it over, and she leans back against me while she texts. Her roommate responds and she laughs, holding it up for me to read.

Olivia: Power is out here and there's so much snow! I'm staying the night, all safe, don't worry about me. :))

Alonya Roomie: U sure? If ur in trouble I will come get you, send blank text if u need help.

"Good roomie," I approve, which makes her smile.

"Yes, she is. Let's send her a picture to reassure her." She cozies her back up against my chest and holds the phone up for a selfie.

"Hang on, let me fix my hair—"

She laughs, laying her head back to look up at me. "Why? You're perfect."

"Oh." An unexpected emotion lodges in my throat. I'm so trained to Rowan's selfies, even two years later. Perfect hair, angle, light. Perfect mask.

Olivia leans back again, tilting her phone until the dog and the fire are also in the frame, and she's beaming, so I smile too. And she sends it off without a single adjustment or filter.

After a minute, her roommate texts back.

Alonya Roomie: Omg jealous :< that looks so cozy.

With heart-eyes.

Olivia remains snuggled against me and texts her back and forth for a minute. I hesitate, then kiss her hair. "Will you send me that picture?"

"Mm-hmm."

"I'm going to get your emergency pajamas."

"Thank you." She sits up and starts cleaning up the

s'mores before Cassidy can get into stuff.

Justine is back by the time I return with the duffel and she's in her pajamas. Olivia takes her bag and changes in the bathroom, and I feel like the odd man out, still fully dressed when she emerges in matching lavender plaid flannels, so I change into some sweats for sleeping.

Justine and Olivia are huddled by the fire in the blanket fort. I kneel to add a log and stir up the embers so it's stuffily warm, and am about to offer to show Olivia to the guest room when Justine thrusts Hunter's copy of *The Hobbit* into my hands. For a second it feels odd that she took it out of his room. But it's okay. He would've loved this whole night. It's good. A good time for the book. I manage not to hug it protectively against my chest.

Justine points at it as if I need direction. "Will you read some?"

My gaze flicks to Olivia and she hugs her knees to her chest, face bright with curiosity.

"We're, uh . . . reading *The Hobbit* together." I run my thumb over the embossed title lettering, and think of Hunter, camping, reading by the fire.

"Can I stay or is it family time?"

"Stay!" Justine says, and I can't argue without feeling like a jerk, even though Olivia checks in with me with a look.

"Please stay." I take the book and pull a candle closer on the coffee table so I can see. Justine scoots in to lean against me and pulls out Hunter's phone, making my heart skip, to turn on the playlist. Olivia mirrors her on my other side, and I manage to get over my stage fright and pick up where we left off, with Gollum and Bilbo.

After a minute of "Riddles in the Dark," Justine lifts her head with a frown. "You're not doing the voices."

Heat burns my cheeks as Olivia burrows her face against my arm with a gleeful noise, then peers up at me. "Um, yes. Please do the voices."

So I get over myself and do my best Gollum and Bilbo, reading by the fire. Eventually we get tired of sitting and rearrange ourselves against a mound of pillows. Justine curls against me on the right, Cassidy bunched next to her, head on my leg, and Olivia on the left, her head on my shoulder and a hand on my chest.

I held it together all night, and they are safe, fed, warm, and entertained.

I feel like the king of the whole damn world.

We read until the fire burns low and they're asleep. I mark the spot we stopped and read on alone, fighting sleep out of habit even though everything feels calm and safe.

My brain crawls toward fatigue anyway, clinging to images from the book. But somewhere in the middle of the spiders and the Mirkwood, we're all piling into the Tahoe with Jack, Mom, and Aunt Gina.

And Hunter.

I'm so happy to see him, I start crying, laughing and hugging him, gushing to him about the date and the blackout and trying to introduce him to Olivia, but Dad's pushing me into the car. No one hears my warning about the snow and the roads. They can't go out in this weather. Nobody's listening. I can't tell who's driving.

Then it's me, hands white-knuckled on the wheel.

Black air and ice stretch before us and headlights sear

across the windshield.

The seat belt slashes tight across my chest and I'm screaming for Hunter to get out of the car.

I can't breathe. Sobs rack my chest.

The car spins across the road, blue and red lights flash, and Hunter's staring at me, blood sliding down his temple.

That empty, rhythmic clicking of the turn signal bores into my head—

—until I spasm awake with a wet, choked gasp.

A blanket is snagged across my neck and I jerk it down, sucking a breath.

There's way too many arms and legs going on, a dizzying array of twinkle lights overhead. The fire has burned to embers. The power's back on.

And I'm roasting, clammy with sweat.

I wrestle free of Olivia and Justine and the dog and crawl from the fort while they utter surprised, sleepy sounds of protest. My skin is cold but my shirt's soaked in sweat and I can't catch a breath or orient myself because of all the blankets and crap filling the living room, and I almost eat it on the corner of the coffee table. The world swings around me and I grab the mantel, sucking a breath, trying to place myself.

"Gage?" Olivia calls from the fort, worried.

"I'm—bad dream." My voice breaks and I wave a dismissive hand and stumble away to the kitchen. I lean over the sink, the cold horror of the dream quivering through every muscle in my body, and swallow back bile. My head aches, real or phantom, I'm not sure.

It sounds like they're getting up, coming out of the fort.

Stay in there, oh God, no, no, stay, please stay in there....

"I'm fine!" My voice barely leaves my throat, fluttery and scratched.

I fumble in my sweats pocket for my phone, pulling up an earlier text from Mom again. A cheery photo of them safe in front of their hotel in Seattle. They're safe. Everyone's safe. I'm safe. I drop the phone to the counter with a clatter and grip the sink, head bowed, then turn on the faucet and splash icy water onto my face.

"I'm fine." I manage to raise my voice, but suddenly there's a soft hand on my back and I startle with a choked sound. I didn't hear Olivia come in. I can't turn around.

She stands close. I feel her, warming the air between us, her hand on my back. Smaller steps are Justine, walking into the kitchen.

"I'm fine," I growl again, mortified. "Please . . . I'm okay. Please leave me alone."

"Gage," Olivia whispers. "Can I do anything? It's okay."

Is it?

"I'm . . . I'm going to my own room." I grind the words out through my teeth. "Sorry I woke you guys up. Justine——" My voice warbles and I hate it, hate it. Nowhere is the guy who made the blanket fort, the dinner, took care of them in a blackout, the man of the house. Just a pitiful mess they have to worry about, with a pounding skull and tears sliding down my face. "Can you show Olivia the guest room? Please?"

Olivia's hand closes on my shirt, pressing against the small of my back. I don't move, both hands gripping the sink. I'm strong. I'm stone. All of my willpower is focused on not curling into a ball on the floor.

Finally, she lets go of my shirt.

Finally, they go. I release a sound and retreat upstairs to my room, shut the door, and lock it.

MY MORNING WALK WITH CASSIDY IS A TRUDGE THROUGH knee-deep snow and a dark, transformed marshmallow planet. Not a single soul has walked the neighborhood before us and it's Sunday, so it's doubtful the plows will get to our streets before noon. It gets the blood flowing. Sets me back on track. I attempt some push-ups in the breezeway while Cassidy wags and licks my face every time I come up as if it's the best game in the world.

Hot shower, ended with a shock of cold. Shave. Clothes. That takes a minute because I know Olivia will see me and I need to reframe her impression again after the pathetic meltdown in the middle of the night. The good jeans and a soft, sort of fitted long-sleeve I think is too tight but Aunt Gina always says is "so handsome!" when I wear it. I'll trust her.

I can do this.

Olivia sent me the picture of us, but I almost don't recognize myself in it because I'm so happy. I look at the cool black-and-white photo Rowan took of me and try to channel that guy again.

By the time Olivia ventures down from the guest room, my sleeves are rolled to knead dough, and sausage is browning in a pan for gravy.

"Wow," Olivia murmurs. She's still in her pajamas, adorable and sleepy, her curls tamed by a fuzzy headband.

It seems like an intimate, trusting way to see her and I feel overdressed. But not really. It helps to regain that feeling of being on top of the world and in control.

"What's for breakfast?" She doesn't come closer to me, smiling but reserved. Disappointment and failure tighten my neck and shoulders. I knew it. I knew seeing me like that would change things.

"Biscuits." I press mentally forward, trudging through just like I did the drifts of snow. I grin over my shoulder. Nothing to see here. "What else?"

She laughs, and the air lightens. "Aw, no kouign-amann?" She steps closer, hesitant.

"I don't think there's enough butter in the whole neighborhood to make that." I want to go to her, to have that golden warmth again from huddling in the fort, reading, kissing, but she looks so hesitant.

Maybe I look hesitant too. Everything is broken because of my nightmare.

Finally she smiles, looking away toward the window. "Do you mind if I make some coffee? I'm hooked after working at Mugs."

"Yes, that sounds great. Everything's in the drawer by the coffeepot." We stand there a second, then she moves, so I move, roll out the dough, and start cutting biscuits, then stir the sausage.

Olivia putters through the kitchen once the coffee's started, pausing at the fridge to look at some of Justine's drawings, gifted to Mom, and family photos we've printed. Jack has them arranged by size and shape, with the favorite printed the largest in the middle. All of us are gathered on a cluster of boulders near the river, the camping trip on our sixteenth birthday, everyone surrounding Hunter and his brand-new sword. Even Dad is in that one, grinning. He arranged his whole schedule that July so he could be home for it.

Olivia touches the corner of that photo, smiling.

"Your family is really close." It isn't a question. Maybe she's trying to find a way in, to ask, to talk, but I can't. I'm certain she doesn't want to see me crying over the gravy. I can't look over at the photo again.

"Yeah," I confirm, blending a small dish of seasoning for the gravy—salt, black pepper, crushed red pepper flakes. A hint of rosemary and one shake of garlic salt. *Moody*, Rowan's cool observation bounds through my head.

The gurgle and hiss of the percolator and the nutty, charred cocoa scent of brewing coffee fill the kitchen along with sausage.

Olivia drifts closer, her gaze low. She watches my hands as I blend the spices, then cut butter into the pan. I stir it all to let the flour taste cook off, then pour in milk.

"You should start a YouTube channel," she murmurs, finally a spark of the warm, safe teasing back in her voice, and splays her hand as if she's reading off a marquee. "ASMR: Cute Boys Making Breakfast. I could literally watch this all day."

"You could," I say quietly, stirring the gravy. "You can stay as long as you want."

"Thank you." She touches my side. "This is a nice shirt."

A smile slips through my worry and I chalk a point for Aunt Gina. "Thank you."

I grasp at her compliments, swallowing my fears that

everything has changed.

"Gage," she says, and nothing else until I look at her. Her expression is determined. "This is the kind of thing my dad does. Closing up and pretending nothing's wrong." She fidgets with the fabric of my shirt but seems intent on keeping eye contact, brows knit. "I know we haven't known each other that long, but I really like you, and Aiden told me about your cousin and the accident and I understand if you don't want to talk to me about it, but if you do . . . I know I can't fix anything, but I can listen. Or at least, if you don't want to talk, you don't have to pretend nothing's wrong."

She says it all fast, as if she's been thinking about it. And she's so sweet, and so gentle.

But she's the one new thing in my life that doesn't involve Hunter. Except now it does. I clear my throat, and whatever she sees in my face tightens her expression and her eyes glass up as if *she* might cry, and that I cannot handle.

"Thank you." I mean it.

"Sure," she says, eyes dropping, fingers curled in my shirt.

I add, low and careful, "It's just—no, I don't really want to talk about it." She nods, once, and I continue quickly, "It's not you. It . . . it hurts and talking about it hasn't helped, so I would rather not. Not right now. It's not you."

My chest tightens at even sharing that. And it's a fib. I haven't really talked about it at all, to anyone, because I'm certain it isn't going to help. A couple of weeks after the accident, Mom and Jack asked if I wanted to talk to a therapist—which Dad thought was a terrible idea, and I agreed. I still do. It seems useless. It won't undo the accident.

It won't bring Hunter back. It won't do anything but rip me open to relive it again and cry and slog through the pain—in front of a stranger. My hand tightens on the handle of the pan as I suppress the urge to fling it across the room.

"Okay," Olivia whispers, then, still seeming determined, hugs me sideways around the waist and rests her head on my arm. And she stays there, watching me stir the gravy. "I had a really, really fun time last night."

I don't know how she knew I desperately needed to hear that, but relief lifts a hundred pounds from my shoulders. "I did too."

What's the catch?

I guess she's finding out.

After a minute, seeing I'm focused on food, she pulls away to pour coffee. "Do you want some?"

"Sure, thanks, with some sugar." I grab another pan. "How do you want your eggs?"

"Poached," she says impishly.

"You got it."

She claps her hands with a laugh. "Oh my gosh, I was joking. I was trying to pick something that was hard." When I look over my shoulder, she's still smiling at me, willing to ignore last night, willing to step out of the broken mess with me for now. "Just whatever's easy."

I would make her a personal frittata for more smiles like that. "Nope, poached it is. It'll be good. Like biscuits and gravy Benedict."

We've woken Justine. She wanders in, looking between us, then curls up in a chair with her knees to her chest, while Cassidy wanders in behind and takes her place under the table.

"Morning!" I head to Justine for a hug, trying to be upbeat, but she twitches away. "You want some juice?"

"No."

"No thank you," I say automatically, and she scowls at me. "What's wrong?" I poke her foot, then kneel next to her while Olivia focuses intently on spooning sugar into our coffee mugs.

"Nothing." Her voice is that deep, flat mimic of mine, and I pull back.

"Hey. Don't be rude."

She turns her face against her knees and shrugs. For a minute I'm at a loss. I lighten my tone.

"Come on, buddy, what do you want to do today? A couple of your friends' moms texted me, if you want to go skiing. Or do you want to grocery shop for the movie night with me?"

"Don't call me buddy," she mutters.

"Fine," I say, parroting her attitude. "How about muddy?"

"No." She squeezes her arms around her knees.

"Nutty? Nutty buddy?" I nudge her leg and she scrunches into a tighter ball in the chair. "Fuddy-duddy?"

"No!" She's trying not to giggle. Thank God.

"Tinkerbell?"

That does it. "Nooo! Stop it." Her limbs flail open in exasperation at my silliness and relief blossoms in my chest. Olivia ventures close to set my coffee on the table. Justine looks at the mug. "Can I have coffee too?"

"Sure." I stand up and ruffle her bed head. "Knock yourself out."

Her hazel eyes widen. "Really?"

"No, not really, you dork. How about hot chocolate?"

"Yes." Whatever mood she was in seems to have dissipated. "Please."

Breakfast is more pleasant after Justine chills out, but worry sits sharp in my heart. She's mad at me or disappointed, and I can't blame her. I can't imagine how it feels to see me like she did last night. *That little girl needs you.*

The eggs come together nicely even though I'm really not an expert in poaching, and Olivia is sweet and complimentary. The biscuits are perfect and apparently the gravy is the best either of them has ever tasted. I joke that's because it's made with love, and Olivia looks at me as if she can't decide whether I'm a dork or too good to be true.

I guess we know the answer to the second option.

Justine scrolls through pictures on Hunter's phone while we eat, and I don't have the heart to tell her to put it away while we're at the table.

Then, abruptly, she shakes the phone and smacks it against the table.

"Whoa, hey!" I touch her wrist but don't dare try to take the phone from her. "What's wrong?"

"It turned off!" Her face is red. I know the feeling. It doesn't take much to break the dam. "It's broken. Did I break it? I didn't do anything."

"It probably needs to charge." I hold out my hand for the phone. "Hey. We had it on a long time last night. Have you charged it at all?"

She shakes her head and, to my surprise, hands it over to me, sniffling. I rise with the phone and plug it in at the charging hub on the counter, while she follows and watches, gripping my shirt as if I'm performing life-saving surgery. "Look, it's fine. It's just . . . the battery's worn down." I just can't say, *It's dead.* "It'll be back on in like five minutes. It's fine, Justine, you didn't break anything."

A text buzzes through on my phone and I tug it from my pocket. "Hey, your mom's making new glass pieces! Look, they're really neat." I kneel and we page through the pictures Mom sent of Aunt Gina working in her friend's studio. "Do you want to send them a picture of the blanket fort before we clean it up?"

"Okay!" My angel cousin is back.

"Here." I hand over my phone. "You know how to use the camera?"

She rolls her eyes and takes the phone to the living room. Olivia rises from the table and steps in close to me.

"Wow," she murmurs. "You're like her hero. That's so sweet."

A derisive noise escapes my throat. Hunter's her hero; I'm a weak substitution. "She puts up with me."

"If you say so."

Something in me rises to say, "Hunter was her brother. My cousin, who . . ."

"Oh," she says, looking toward the living room, then to me.

"So," I finish roughly, "I try to be there for her, you know."

"And she's there for you," Olivia says, with her tiny smile, a thought that never occurred to me. Justine is young and vulnerable and I am here to protect her. Not the other way around.

"Sure," I say anyway, smiling crookedly.

Olivia looks grateful that I shared something. She steps in front of me and wraps her arms around me, and a glimmer of the safe, vital, golden warmth glows back to life in my chest. "What's the movie night you're shopping for?"

Warning taps my brain. I shove it down. "Oh. Tomorrow I'm having some friends over to watch Lord of the Rings, but it's . . ." My breath tightens. "It's like a memorial thing, for Hunter."

"That sounds really neat," she says, and there is nothing, absolutely nothing in her tone fishing for an invite.

Yet, as half my brain cries a warning, my mouth is saying, "Do you want to come? It's going to be fun. I'm making a bunch of food. It's chill. I mean, it'll be a lot of people, like ten or fifteen friends, if that's too much . . ."

She pulls back to look at me and I know it's a terrible idea for her to come. His favorite movies, our movies, our friends, all the memories, Justine—the entire evening is already going to be a battle and now she's smiling, shit—

"Oh wow. I would love that. I would love to meet your friends. But it's not private? I totally understand if it is. Are you sure?"

She means it, I know she does. This is my chance to say, *You're right. I'm not ready. It's private. I'm mourning.*

I stare into her sincere, frowning, hopeful face, and touch her cheek. "I'm sure."

"Monday I work the later shift," she says. "Unless I can trade with someone. Will you still be going after nine?"

"Extended editions," I say.

She grins, petting my shirt, searching my face, and I lean in for a kiss.

Justine wanders back in and she's on FaceTime with Mom. I know because I hear Mom saying, "Oh, biscuits and gravy! I wish we were there. Can I talk to Gage, honey?"

Olivia's eyes widen and she ducks away as if to hide as Justine hands me the phone.

"Hey, Mom. Seattle's good? Really cool pictures."

"Everything is wonderful." She looks it. Bright-eyed and refreshed. I'm glad they went and I try not to think about them driving back in a week. "Justine tells me there was a blizzard and you have a guest."

Warmth flushes my cheeks and I motion Olivia over since it is Mom's house and she deserves to know who's in it. "Mom, this is Olivia. Olivia, my mom—"

"Liz," Mom says warmly, dark eyes flicking Olivia up and down with a smile.

"It's nice to meet you," Olivia says, relaxed and sweet as if we're all sitting down at breakfast together. "You have a beautiful home."

"Thank you, it's nice to meet you, sweetie. Gage, I assume you were a gentleman."

"Yep." I rub my face, mortified, while Olivia presses a hand to her mouth. "I had her do the dishes and sweep the floors and she's heading out to shovel the walk in a bit, just like you taught me."

Mom wags a finger at me, but she's grinning.

Jack hollers from the background. "Thanks for holding down the fort, Gage! Hon, breakfast bus is leaving." Keys jingle.

Mom laughs. "Okay, I'm going to run, honey. Have a fun day."

"Okay, Mom. Call you later—hi, Jack!"

"Okay. Love you." She looks so happy to see me happy. That's what I want her thinking all week. All is well. "Bye, Justine!"

"Bye!" she calls from the stove, where she's eating a spoonful of gravy.

I tip the phone so it's just me and Mom. "Love you too."

We hang up and Olivia dissolves into giggles. "Such a gentleman. Your mom seems nice."

"Yeah. Maybe we can . . ." I pause, not wanting to be weird and pushy.

"Maybe I can meet the rest of them when they get back?" she finishes for me. "That would be fun."

I don't know how she manages to make intimidating things sound light and fun, but I smile. "If you want to."

"If you want me to," she teases, leaning up, and there's no doubt I'm supposed to kiss her now, which I do, and touch her soft headband, while Justine makes a disgusted sound behind us.

I turn and point at her. "You have too much energy. You're going skiing one way or another. Go get dressed."

Justine hops away from the stove and flees, giggling and making kissing sounds. A text buzzes. Staying snugly close to Olivia, I lift my phone.

Imogenesis: Just checking in, you stopped answering in the LWDA group message. All's well? Your family got to Seattle okay?

Me: All good :)) Was ignoring my phone last night.

I glance to Olivia. "Mind if I send our picture to a friend?"

"Nope. Send it to your mom if you want." She grins and retrieves her coffee cup, and I send the picture Olivia took last night to Imogen.

Imogenesis: AAAAHH CUTIEEEEES!! Omg you look so happy.

She sends two lines of heart-eyes and crying emojis.

Imogenesis: She looks so nice!

Me: She's amazing.

I look over my phone at Olivia, who sips her coffee, then peeks at the text and grins.

Me: I invited her to the movie night.

Imogenesis: OOooooooo. Better get back in the message. Everyone thinks we should start earlier but that's up to you. Some people are working during the day or at night and that way people can drop in when they can make it??

I roll my shoulders, bracing myself for a day of planning, shopping, and fielding texts. A to-do list unfurls in my brain—clean, deconstruct the blanket fort, get in touch with Justine's friends and arrange skiing, shovel the sidewalk, groceries . . . I cram any threat of stress, sadness, Hunter, or the accident to the back of my brain and lock it down.

It's going to be great.

I realize I'm standing there staring at my phone while Olivia watches me over the rim of her mug.

"Hey," I murmur.

"Hey." She lifts her chin.

"I don't suppose you want to help me put together a party today?"

The private, dimpled smile. "Funnily enough, that is exactly what I wanted to do today."

FRAGRANT STEAM BILLOWS FROM THE slow cooker when I lift the lid to check my meatballs. The oven beeps, letting me know my timer's up for keeping grilled cheeses warm, and my phone dings—time to start the mulled cider. It feels like I'm cooking at Nan's, keeping five things going at once.

The sense of purpose, timing dishes, and tracking everything keeps me on my feet, head in the game, moving forward.

"That smells out of this world," Imogen says from the sink, scrubbing the pan I used to make inside-out grilled cheeses so they'd be ready when people show up.

She invited herself over early to help. Now that it's almost noon, we're expecting people for the official start time. She's wearing Rohirrim cosplay-lite, looking like a true daughter of Rohan with her platinum hair in several braids, a rust-colored cotton tunic belted at the waist, and gilded bracers on her wrists.

I opted against dressing up because I don't want to get food on my stuff, and it's too close to something I would do with Hunter.

That will be a thin line to walk all day.

"I hope it's good," I mutter, stirring the meatballs. "I should have stuck with tried-and-true recipes."

"You need to chill," she says, laughing. "Anyone else would've ordered pizza and called it good."

"Not for this."

Her expression sobers. "Should I ask how you're doing?"

"Good." I press the lid back to the meatballs and set up the big stewpot to start the mulled cider.

"Gage." She dries her hands and walks over while I twist the cork off the apple cider; Mom treated us to super-quality bottles from a local orchard.

"Mm?" I empty the bottle into the pot. I felt great this morning. Happy to see my friends, thrilled that Justine's bouncing off the walls, and psyched for the challenge of making a metric ton of food and watching movies all day.

Now, as the clock ticks toward start time, seeing Imogen in her Éowyn-inspired stuff, a knot curls in my stomach and my pulse presses tight in my neck. *Don't screw this up. Don't make anyone worry about you.*

"You tell us if you need anything," she says.

I need Hunter.

I chuckle wryly, tugging the cork out of the second bottle, and pour. "What, like to leave for a while and cry?"

"Yes," she says, rubbing my back. "Like that."

I grab a knife to slice an orange, and it catches the stove light ever so briefly. I think of Hunter's sixteenth birthday, the campfire, him drawing his shining new sword dramatically by the fire to see how the gold light played over the blade.

I cut the orange crossways so the slices look like golden flowers, and drop them into the pot, then cinnamon sticks. Imogen's still standing close. She is almost my height and impossible to ignore. I take a bite of orange, tart and sweet, to ground myself, and smile at her, nudging her with an elbow.

"I'll let you know."

"Okay." She wraps her arm around my middle and rests her head on my shoulder. For a second, I so desperately need the hug that I relent and turn to wrap my arms around her.

"Thanks for coming," I murmur, and she squeezes me tight. "For helping, and everything."

"There was no question." She tightens her arms and tries to lift me with a grunt, making us both laugh. "You know I just wanted to sample the food before everyone else."

"Nobody loves me," I say mournfully.

"I do," she says matter-of-factly, leaning back. Her big blue eyes are so frank, searching me. "I miss you. With school and everything. It's nice to hang out."

"I miss you too." Guilt whisks through me. "It's just . . ."

She waits, but I can't say it. I can't say it's hard to hang out with her because Hunter's not there. She hugs me again instead. "I get it," she whispers.

Relief dissolves my breath. I wrap her in my arms again

and we share a sigh. Maybe she doesn't want to break down either, because she pats my back with playful firmness and pulls away to finish the dishes.

I follow her example, rallying. I have a good life. My house is about to be full of friends, food, my favorite movies. If only I could shake the feeling that something crouches beyond all that. The shadow, Hunter. Ready to ambush me. Maybe if I stay on guard, if I'm prepared, I can keep a lid on it.

My phone buzzes. Imogen releases me. "Will you get the movie queued up?"

"Yes, my liege!" Happy to be of use or maybe seeing my mood has lifted, Imogen heads to the living room, calling for Justine to help her put on finishing touches. Yesterday, with Olivia's help and her artistic eye, we decorated the living room in pine boughs, hunted down birch bark, and spent an hour cutting paper snowflakes. Not that snow is particularly relevant to the Lord of the Rings, but it completes the enchanted forest look.

Meanwhile, my phone. I've been so absorbed in food I've missed several texts. Mom and Jack, wishing me luck on movie night, Dad saying he's home through the week if I need anything, Bryson checking what drinks to bring, and the latest, from Olivia.

Olivia: Soooo slow at work right now I wish I was there :D Can't wait. Monte said he might be able to let me go early if it stays this quiet tonight. What are you cooking?

Me: Wish you were here too. Thanks for everything yesterday. :) Right now, meatballs, mulled cider, then I'll start on the braised chicken. Should be baking lembas by the time you get here.

Olivia: Aaaahhhh :)))

She was unfazed about walking to the grocery store with me on Sunday, maybe because the plows still hadn't come and it seemed reasonable. Also, a good chance to really enjoy the snow. We shopped, got coffee, came back and decorated the house, and even got in some more make-out time while Justine was skiing.

Olivia: I took a LotR quiz for who I would be, and got "hobbit," lol. I was hoping for something more glamorous.

I chuckle and sprinkle cloves and star anise into the cider before answering.

Me: Hobbits saved Middle-earth.

Olivia: Omg <3 <3

Olivia: Hey look it's you:

She sends a GIF of Samwise, saying *po-tay-toes*, and the dark cloud lifts from me briefly. I would want to get Wizard or Ranger or something cool on the quiz, but after a glance around my busy kitchen, I'm pretty sure I'd get hobbit too.

There's a knock at the door. Cassidy barks, trotting in from the living room.

Justine flies into the kitchen screaming, "Someone's here!"

"Oh my God, Justine, please chill out." I wonder if she's going to maintain this level of energy and volume all day, and brace myself. It started with her jumping on me at four thirty this morning, awake and stoked as if it's Christmas.

A weird, reverse Christmas.

Imogen trails Justine and Cassidy who, having given her warning, now wags her tail expectantly. They open the door to Mia, who is decked in full elven queen regalia—warm silver-and-white brocade, complete with pointed ear tips molded to her real ones, gold powder dusted over her cheekbones, jewels winking at the corners of her eyes, and a delicate woven silver circlet over glossy black ringlets. I'm certain she hand-sewed every inch of that costume herself.

"*Wow,*" Justine breathes, gaping as if Galadriel herself has walked into the house.

"Thank you." Mia beams at her, then at us. "Well met!" She lifts a hand to show off she is also wearing Nenya, the Ring of Water.

Imogen fans herself. "I might faint."

"You can bow," Mia says magnanimously.

"Wait till Bryson sees you," Imogen says.

"He can bow too." They both dissolve into laughs and hug each other.

I rinse orange stickiness from my hands and dry them before coming forward to get my hug. "You look incredible."

"This old thing?" she teases, and hugs me tight. "I think it's great you're having this party. I had to do my part."

"And you did."

"Here." She hands me a grocery sack filled with paper plates, napkins, and plasticware. "Nobody wants to do dishes all day."

"Genius."

"And this is from Mom. She says hi." She offers a Tupperware with a small, round chocolate-frosted cake, and a lump clots my throat at her thoughtfulness.

"Tell her thanks."

Justine is still staring, then turns on her heel and runs

out the door toward her own house. Imogen and Mia look at me curiously and I lift a hand. "No idea."

Mia folds her hands together elegantly. "What can I do?"

I point to the living room. "Uh, you can go sit on the couch and relax, and not get any food on that amazing dress."

She laughs, but the work is stunning. Professional. I'm not at all surprised she got the job with the theater. I set everything she brought on the kitchen table.

"I'll answer the door." Mia ignores my instructions to relax as another car pulls up.

"I'm carrying the first round of food to the living room," Imogen says.

Thinking of Mia and the theater reminds me—since it's finally Monday, I pull my phone out to check for any response to my job application.

I have two new emails. One is spam. . . .

"Thanks, guys," I manage absently.

The other email is from Redwood House.

Adrenaline slicks up my chest and my thoughts blur. This is it, oh God, this . . .

Re: Application for summer position
Dear Mr. Bryant,
    We reviewed your application with interest. However—

Chaos and noise erupt at the front door as Bryson arrives with a couple other friends behind, stomping snow, laughing, removing coats. Rowan's brother, Ash, came after all, and he's like the male version of her—striking, black hair, blue eyes; he lifts his chin to me in greeting and I try to grin, distracted. A few others trail in—nerd friends, and LWDA members, people Hunter scooped up from loneliness and brought into the pack.

They're all bearing multipack drinks and bags of chips, and I look over in time to see Bryson's face when he beholds Mia.

"Holy shit," he whispers, and she laughs in delight. "I feel like I should kneel or something."

"Feel free," she motions, and he starts to bend a knee, until Ash grumbles.

"Can we move the courting displays out of the doorway?"

My gaze drops back to the email and that word, *However*—

Bryson is suddenly close and grabs me in a hug. There are few people in the world capable of lifting me off the ground and he is one of them, for half a second, with a grunt. Normally I'd laugh, but impatience sizzles in my brain and I shrug him off.

"Just a second—"

"Sorry, sorry, bro." He grins. "How can I help?"

"I need to check this message. Uh, you can . . ." I turn, trying to remember what I was just in the middle of. Mulled cider. That's done. Meatballs are in. Imogen put the grilled cheese and a charcuterie out. Email. Bryson. I rub my forehead. "There's a cooler in the living room. You can put drinks in there, or just on the porch. Thanks."

"You got it, man. Hey." He grips my shoulder and I force my attention to his jovial face. "It's going to be great. It's really cool of you to do this. And thanks again for the cooking lesson." He grins toward Mia. "Worth it."

"Sure thing. Yeah. I'll be right back." Mia and Imogen usher people in, handling coats, taking charge. I let them, and retreat to the hall to read the email.

Dear Mr. Bryant,

We reviewed your application with interest. However, when HR performed a standard perusal of your public social media activity to make sure you were a cultural fit, we were concerned with the following content.

It's a link to the video.

The awful video of me throwing Blondie out of Nan's. I click through to Instagram. I'm still tagged all over, in multiple posts, different shots. It looks bad. Really bad. There's no way it doesn't look bad. Even in context, it's not great. Bashing out the door, wrestling a smaller guy until he swings at me and I throw him to the ground. One video even has the police cruiser turning the corner in the background.

Nausea warms my throat and heat pounds my face. Trembling, I read on.

We would appreciate any context you can give your actions, or if we've made a mistake and this is not in fact you!

Once again, we were very interested in your application, but we strive to form a cohesive team who respects our core values of professionalism and service. We look forward to your response.

> *Cordially,*
> *Gillian Andrus*
> *Hiring Manager*
> *Redwood House, San Francisco*

Gillian Andrus. My hero's daughter has seen actual footage of one of my worst moments. I wonder if she sent it to him: *Hey, Pops, how about this guy? I don't know about cooking, but do you need any bouncers? Lol.*

I feel like an absolute clown, a complete joke. A small-town fry cook with delusions of grandeur. Are they allowed to look at my social media? I guess it's public. I did do that, *at work*, so I guess they can ask about it.

Disappointment and anger skitter up my chest.

I'm one heartbeat away from smacking the phone against something or smashing a fist to the wall, when there's a collective "Ooo!" from the front door, followed by Justine making happy sounds and greeting people.

I toss my phone onto the kitchen counter on the way to the door. I can't even think about what I'm supposed to do about it, if there's anything to be done. Everyone has clustered around Justine in the entryway, even Cassidy, whining and wagging her tail.

Inspired by Mia's and Imogen's costumes, Justine has thrown her hair into a loose braid, put glitter on her cheeks . . . and she is wearing a shimmery gray elven cloak. His cloak.

Hunter's cloak.

My hand spasms; a tight ache snags my jaw. She's folded it up so it doesn't drag on the ground at least, wrapped and pinned it with one of the emerald leaves of Lorien that Aunt Gina got us both for Christmas one year.

A high whine pierces my head and I shake it, rubbing my temple. "Justine," I say tightly.

Take it off! my brain is screaming. *It's not yours, take it OFF!*

She spins to see me, beaming, eyes lit up, spreads the cloak, and curtsies.

I swallow my scream. Swallow my unnecessary horror that she is wearing her own brother's things, and my sense that something sacred is shattered. It's my problem. Not her problem. There's something wrong with me, to be upset she's wearing it.

Still. She took it from his room. We haven't taken anything from his room but the book. She wore it. No one's worn it since he wore it.

"You look great." It's not me, not my voice. I have retreated and something else is speaking for me. Just words that come out. The right words, the right mood, a solid mask of support to keep things light and keep that smile on her face. "Try not to get food on it."

"Gage?" Imogen asks with a frown, but I smile and lift a hand.

It's only eleven hours. I can do this.

"Let's start the movie."

I SLIDE A BATCH OF SHORTBREAD COOKIES INTO THE OVEN AND return to the living room for the last bit of *Fellowship*.

Justine has been in turns entranced and unable to sit still. So horrified by the Balrog and Gandalf's death, she cried into my chest . . . but then bounced up to stare at Lothlórien. I lock everything down.

Through most of it, all I can think of is Hunter and how he would spout the running commentary—*did you know that's the only thing Legolas says to Frodo in the whole series—did you know Viggo really dodged that knife, did you know they used a huge prop ring for close-up shots, Peter Jackson desperately wanted Daniel Day Lewis to play Aragorn....*

Did you know . . .

We are all entranced in the final moments. Justine stands in the middle of the room, staring during the battle, Boromir's death. When they send Boromir over the falls, Hunter's voice springs to life again and his words are coming out of my mouth.

"Did you notice Aragorn is wearing Boromir's wrist guards after his death?" My throat tightens. "To . . . to make it feel like he was still part of the Fellowship."

"Really?" Bryson asks. He is sitting on the floor near Mia, who lounges beautifully on the couch.

"Yeah, he's not wearing them in the boat," Imogen says.

"I have a confession," Bryson says. "I've never actually seen these movies."

"What?" Mia shrieks, and the rest of the group *shh*s them sharply. Mia stares at Bryson in horror, as if she's just met him. A corner of my brain wants to laugh.

It freezes in my chest. Hunter should be here.

Bryson climbs onto the couch to murmur in Mia's ear, and whatever he says seems to calm her down, and she leans comfortably back in his arms. Maybe the fact he's been completely engrossed the whole time is proof enough they can still date. I lift my gaze to the movie.

"The Breaking of the Fellowship" music swells. My phone dings to alert me to the cookies just in time, and I shove from the couch and back to the kitchen.

I lay out "Afternoon Tea": shortbread cookies, the chocolate-frosted yellow cake from Mia's mom, whipped cream, and some of Aunt Gina's raspberry jam for the cookies. Then I put the teapot on the stove in case anyone wants actual tea. It's a pretty enamel pot that looks like a peach, which Hunter got Mom for a birthday. There's no escaping him.

From the living room Aragorn declares, "We will not abandon Merry and Pippin to torment and death," and I retreat to the bathroom to splash some cold water on my face.

Everything is going great.

"May It Be" floats from the living room along with the sounds of people stretching and heading to the kitchen, and exclaiming over the pretty spread. I have to go back in. I know I do.

Eight more hours.

Hunter's awed know-it-all voice: *Did you know Viggo broke two toes when he kicked that helmet?*

We know! Laughing and throwing popcorn at him. I try to remember the last time we watched the movies together. Maybe my seventeenth birthday. Wow.

My throat clenches and I flip instantly from everything's going great to this being the worst idea I've ever had.

I shouldn't have done it.

My heartbeat quickens; warmth rushes my skin. I can't do it. I can't do this. I wonder if anyone would notice if I disappeared to my room. Imogen said it's fine.

Everyone *says* it's fine, but is it? It's not who I want

to be. I want to show up, to be the host, to honor Hunter, to let everyone be together and safe in my house without worrying about me or seeing me collapse.

Maybe I could fake sick instead.

But Olivia's coming later. A headache snarls against my skull.

Someone knocks and I jump, straightening from just slumping over the sink.

"Gage?" Imogen peeks around the door as I splash more water on my face. "Do you want us to wait for you to start the next one?"

A low buzzing drones in my ears. I have no idea how long I've been standing in here. The entire credits of the movie have rolled. Did I just lose time? Is that a thing?

"No. No, uh, it's fine." I grab some aspirin from the cabinet. "I'll be out in a minute. Too much rich food." I grin at her in the mirror and try not to look at myself, because I don't look good.

Imogen meets my eyes for a moment. She doesn't ask if I'm okay, just shuts the door with a soft "All right."

The dramatic, dark opening music of *Two Towers* fills the house, the notes searing while the viewer soars over snowy mountains. I take the aspirin, patch myself back together, dry my face.

As I step out of the bathroom, Justine flings herself around the corner, still in Hunter's cloak, although Mia rewove her hair into a more intricate style during the Fellowship's time in Rivendell. "Did Gandalf live?"

I rub my eyes, fighting irritation. I should be glad she's into it. "I don't know, you have to watch. Did you get some meatballs?"

"I'm not hungry."

"Okay, but you've been eating cookies and stuff all day. You need some protein."

"'One small cookie is enough to fill the stomach of a grown man,'" Justine quotes Legolas and my heart splits into thirds—I want to laugh because she's a mini Hunter; I want to cry; I want to shout at her. I build a wall around all of it.

"Just, like, one meatball please?"

"I don't like them." She all but disappears into Hunter's cloak, arms wrapped tightly. "I want lembas bread."

"We're having it later." I can't believe we're standing in the dark hallway having this conversation. I should've let Aunt Gina pay me. She knew.

"You're missing it!" Mia calls from the living room.

Justine squeaks and runs from me and it's unclear if she's going to eat any real food or not. I'm over it. I wander back to the living room and sit on the couch, and Justine snuggles up to me sweetly, as if she hasn't been acting like a pain in the neck all day.

Did you know—

I pull out my phone and stare at the email from Redwood House, racking my brain for a solution. There probably isn't one.

"This is delicious," Bryson says, holding up his cookies. "Thanks for all this work, Gage."

Mia gestures to the room, the decorations, the food, in agreement. "This is really beautiful."

"Hunter would have loved it," Imogen says, watching me, as if to remind me why we're doing this. Justine snuggles closer to me but doesn't manage a thank-you.

I rein in my emotions; she's ten, she's thinking about Hunter too, her veins are currently flowing with sugar and apple cider. Still. If it weren't for her, I could be reading by myself right now. Or making soup for one. Or sleeping.

A murmur of agreement fills the room.

I lift my eyes and see everyone smiling at me. More have drifted in since we started the movie. Happy, fed. Some in costume, some in pajamas because I said people could stay if they were too tired to drive or if the weather got bad, even though it's been mild and sunny all day.

A text drops my gaze to the phone.

Olivia: Still hinting to get out of here early :)) Let me know if you want a coffee. I hope everything's going well.

I look back at my friends, forming a smile. "Thanks for coming. Uh." I feel like they expect something. I expect something. I didn't say anything when everyone got here; we just dove into the movies. I should say something. "It really means a lot and . . . I know that this would've been special for Hunter. Even though he would've ruined it by talking through the whole thing."

Justine giggles and burrows under the cloak. Imogen chokes a laugh and raises her mug.

That's it. That's all I have. That's all I can manage to say at this memorial for my dead cousin. I can't even talk about his favorite parts of the movie or scrounge up any poignant memories or even say out loud how much I love him.

Pathetic.

Everyone follows Imogen's example and raises their mugs of tea and cider in a silent toast anyway.

"We love you, man," Bryson says. And they raise their

cups again to *me*, and I duck my head, sucking a breath.

"Thanks." It takes everything, everything, all the fibers of muscle and my dwindling willpower to stay on that couch, my arm numb and heavy around Justine's shoulders, and turn my attention to the movie.

Seven more hours.

FOUR MORE HOURS.

The scent of braised rosemary chicken, lemon, and potatoes fills the kitchen. I pull the cast-iron skillet that's stuffed with chicken thighs out of the oven and turn the oven off.

It feels like I've been awake for a week.

After a sunny, warmish day that melted off a lot of the snow, it's finally dark again, cold outside and cozy in the house. We've lit candles and let the fire die down because it's too hot with me cooking and ten people lounging in the living room. A few drifted in and out, either too much movie for them, working evening shifts, or only wanted to say hi.

Making the food was a wise choice. I could have prepared things ahead of time, but I knew I would need something to keep me distracted.

It's kept me on my feet all day and I had to consult my recipes and be on top of the timing. The early wake-up call from Justine, the email from Redwood House, and the strain of keeping my brain together every time dramatic music swells are breaking me down. I focus on the chicken, mind a ham and lentil soup for later, and bake soda bread to keep me level. It's mostly working.

While people can eat whenever they want, in true Lord of the Rings marathon tradition, every serving of food has its name—elevenses, even though we started at noon, luncheon, afternoon tea, and now "Dinner!"

A chorus of *shhhhh* answers me from the living room.

"Fine," I mutter. "Eat it cold." Then I smirk at myself. Moody.

But I'm just tired. Olivia texted she probably won't be able to get out early after all, and that soured my mood more than I expected, even though one more person smiling at me might be the straw that breaks my back.

Justine trots into the kitchen, steals a single potato wedge from the pan, and trots out again, saying, "Po-taaayyyy-toes . . ." and giggling.

There was a time, nine hours ago, when that would've been cute. "Hey, get some chicken, too." I'm all out of *please*.

She ignores me. Or didn't hear me. I'll pretend she didn't hear me, but I know she's just showing off for everyone, enjoying the movies and the attention and apparently having me as her personal footman all day.

I guess that's good, a night of no-holds-barred fun. This should be one of the funnest days of my life. I've always wanted to do something like this with a bunch of people—the movie marathon, the food, even dressing up. So did Hunter.

My bite of chicken lodges in my throat and I cough and spit it out, squeezing my eyes shut.

"I'm sorry," I whisper, staring at the counter. "I'm sorry we didn't do it when you were here." My voice warbles. I can't believe I'm now muttering to myself, to my dead cousin, alone in the kitchen. "I'm sorry," I whisper again, as if he's going to hear me and say, *Don't worry about it.*

Realizing someone could walk in any second and not wanting everything to grind to a halt because of me, I grab a clean towel, soak it with freezing water, and press it to my face.

Just a few more hours.

The food has turned out amazing, everyone is being awesome, quiet for the movies, kind. Except Justine, who's being . . . I guess she's being ten. I ratchet down on my frustration and wander back into the living room in time to see Elrond visiting Aragorn at Dunharrow.

The living room is dark except for a few flickering candles and the twinkle lights woven into pine boughs on the mantel. Justine has settled in next to Imogen, eating more cookies and now cake. I've probably permanently corrupted her system with sugar and apple cider and hot chocolate. Aunt Gina will never forgive me. I cross my arms and lean against the archway.

The music drifts and swells as Elrond unveils the sword.

Justine gasps in true surprise and wonder. "It's Andúril!"

Everyone stifles giggles. Justine is in awe. Hunter

would be so proud. I shut my eyes against tears when I should be laughing too.

I retreat to the kitchen. A couple people sneak in and out for a plate of chicken, murmuring compliments, and back to the movie. I make a small plate for Justine, steel myself, and head into the living room.

"Justine, you need to eat three bites. . . ." I glance around at everyone, but she's not in there. "Guys? Where's Justine?"

Bryson looks around, and Imogen points toward the door. "She said she had to get something."

As if Imogen's gesture summoned her, Justine bursts back in the main entryway, glowing with excitement and carrying . . . Andúril.

Ice plunges down my throat.

"Oh," I say weakly. "Let's not—Justine . . ." But I haven't used my voice all day, not really, not effectively. I don't know why I expect it to work now.

She pads into the living room and holds out the sword in its handsome black scabbard, to a collective wave of admiration from my friends.

"Whoa," Bryson says, and Justine offers it to him.

"Hey," I try again, my throat cracking, bricks crumbling from the walls I've built around my heart all day. "Careful . . ." My jaw tightens and locks.

Bryson tugs the blade halfway free in the firelight, and my hands spasm and clench, crumpling the paper plate, chicken and potatoes.

"Guys," I manage, loud enough for them to finally hear me. Imogen frowns, standing, as if she might come to me. Something in my posture makes her hesitate. Her gaze drops to my hands, crushing the plate and the food.

"Look at the letters!" Justine ignores me, encouraging Bryson to fully draw the sword.

"Runes," Imogen corrects. "Gage?"

"Uh." I scrounge for some volume as the thing uncoils inside me, the simmering red thing that threw a guy to the ground and smashed a line of innocent snowmen and . . . *No, no, not here* . . . I raise my voice to a normal volume, finally, every word mechanical and gentle. "Justine, maybe, can we put it away? Please? It's Hunter's and—"

"No!" Justine finally looks at me, hands on her hips, head tipped in stubborn challenge. "I want to show them."

My face feels hard, stone, brows drawing together, jaw clenched, everything is too, too hot. "I said put it away."

"No! You're not my mom and can't make me. It's not yours!"

"It's not *yours*, either."

Bryson glances between us, wary.

Justine frowns.

Then she sticks out her tongue and turns her back to me.

Molten anger blazes up my chest, scorching the last of my compassion to ash.

"*JUSTINE.*" My shout makes everyone jump and it feels so good to unleash. "I said put it away! I've let you have your way all day!" I can't grab the words back, the anger; my voice roars and cracks. "I did this for *you*. I didn't even want to do this. Any of it!" I throw the plate of chicken to the floor, rage coursing cold and hot through my body. "I wanted to be alone. I did all this for you!"

I fling my arm wide to indicate the movies, the food, the decorations. "Why can't you do one thing I ask without acting like a little *brat*?"

Justine stares at me. Bryson slowly sets the sword onto the floor.

My breath shudders, hoarse, my head aches, the room lurches around me.

"Gage," Imogen breathes. Trembling, my gaze darts from her to Mia, Bryson, my other friends, but they're staring at the floor. And finally to Justine again. Her eyes are huge and she looks suddenly tiny in Hunter's cloak, frozen. Scared.

Scared of me.

No, no, no . . . My anger dissolves, my ally, my strength, leaving me shaking.

Red clouds Justine's face and her chin trembles.

"Justine," I whisper, remorse washing my body, draining me. I lift a hand and step forward. She flinches back. "I'm s—"

She breaks into tears. Then she wrestles herself out of Hunter's cloak, throws it at me, and flees past me out the door.

"PLEASE, JUSTINE." I KNOCK ON HER BEDROOM DOOR. "I'M sorry. That wasn't okay. That wasn't your fault. I'm so sorry. Please come out."

She's sobbing. I want to go drown myself in the lake.

"Please? Unlock the door. I brought you some dinner.

I'm really, really sorry. I shouldn't have yelled." I knock again and try the handle, but it's still locked.

"Leave me alone!"

"Justine—"

"Go away! I hate you!"

Cold lodges in my chest, my throat, locking it shut. I nod at her door.

I hate me too.

I slide down to sit against the door, draw my knees to my chest, and fold my arms, resting my head on them. A creak on the wood floor alerts me to company and I look up as Imogen approaches down the hall. I bury my face again.

"Give her some time," she says. "She's hurt and embarrassed."

"I know." I stare at the tray of food I brought, as if it could fix everything, or anything. As if she would want to eat now, after I humiliated her and myself. I resist the urge to throw this plate of food too.

"This is probably a silly question," Imogen says, "but can I do anything?"

"Back up time by five minutes," I mutter.

She comes forward and sits next to me on the floor. "She was being kind of a brat," she murmurs wryly.

I heave a breath. "I don't care. She didn't deserve that."

Imogen's quiet. "No. Do you want to talk?"

"Not really." I ignore her resigned sigh. "Did everyone leave?"

Imogen's mouth quirks and she presses her shoulder to mine. "Well, yeah. Most of them. You said you wanted to be alone. Nobody wants to stress you out. Do you want us to stay or go?"

Disappointment in myself drags my shoulders. I look at the plate of food again, the chicken, in particular. I got the skin just right, crispy brown and pretty, speckled with herbs. "I don't care." That's the truth. I simply don't have the energy to make that decision. "I guess I should apologize to everyone."

"I think you should come back, at least." She moves around to crouch in front of me. "And chill out. Maybe sit down for five minutes, and let Justine chill out for a while. Let her cry it out. I promise she'll come back."

I'm not so sure. I know my family. I guess I've pushed her enough tonight, though, and there's a big part of me that does want to give up and have a break.

"Give her some breathing room. Maybe she'll eat if there's nobody staring at her." Imogen smiles and raises her voice for Justine's benefit. "Because the food is really good."

The other side of the door is quieter now, punctuated by sniffles and hiccups that break my heart into smaller and smaller pieces until I'm afraid I won't ever be able to put it back together again.

"Come on." Imogen stands, offering her hand. "They need us at Pelennor Fields."

I don't feel good about leaving Justine alone, but it's probably just regret, and wishing she would accept my apology. I can't blame her, though. I take Imogen's hand and haul myself up, and she traps me in a hug.

"You're okay," she whispers. "This was a hard day. I'm sorry I wasn't paying attention."

I close my eyes, standing heavy and useless in her hug.

"It's okay. It's not your job to watch me."

She pulls back with a pinched expression, brow furrowed. "It is, though. You're my pack." A smile nudges her mouth. "What did Hunter say? 'I *am* my brother's keeper'?"

"Yeah. Something like that." I manage a smile, rub my face, and wrap an arm around her, pausing to lean toward the door. "Justine, we're right next door, okay? I'm really, really sorry and I hope you come back."

She doesn't answer.

As Imogen said, almost everyone has left. Everyone but Mia and Bryson. I don't blame them, but shame heats my face.

Bryson stands when I come in and hands me the sword. "I'm really sorry, I didn't know—"

"Stop." I take the sword in one hand and grip his shoulder. "It's okay. I was just—it surprised me."

"You think?" He chuckles, eyebrows lifting, and rubs the back of his neck. "Is Justine okay?"

"She's upset." I glance over my shoulder, hand tightening on the sword. "I'll check on her in a bit."

"Are you okay?" Mia asks point-blank from the couch. "If this is too much, we can go."

"You can stay," I say quietly.

"But do you *want* us to stay?" she clarifies. I know what they're still thinking of. *I didn't even want to do this. Any of it. I wanted to be alone.* My own words.

"Yes. I want you to stay and I'm sorry."

Her eyebrows creep up in the candlelight.

"I mean it." I do. I don't want anyone to leave things like that. "I promise. I want you guys here. I'm really sorry for my outburst."

Bryson squeezes my shoulder, Imogen hugs me from behind, and we settle in on the couch. I should feel calmer, but I don't. Almost everyone left. I ruined the whole night. I can't be happy, I can't melt down and cry, I can't be angry, because it destroys things I love. It feels like I can't be anything.

And I don't know what to do about that.

A text buzzes through.

Mom: Hope your movie night is great so far! We're so proud of you and Gina says thanks again.

Guilt burns hot in my throat. I might vomit. I try to think how to fix this thing I've broken, but I just sit there and stare at the movie I've seen a hundred times, the heroic words and characters, the good shining above all, facing down the evil trying to consume the world.

When you're a kid, reading books about sword-wielding heroes performing great acts of valor, all you feel is longing, like you want to do those things. It's hard to move that into the real world, to understand what it really means, in the end. Here, in this place.

They don't tell you your act of valor might be hugging your cousin while he cries because his dad is driving away for the last time and neither of you really understands why.

Or it might be the moment you realize you have to keep living after that cousin dies nine years later. Or when you finally force yourself to walk away from the riverbank where you spread his ashes. You just have to.

You have to sleep. You have to wake up. Every time, it feels like a field of war, but you don't feel like a hero.

Instead of battling a demon from the underworld, you

get up every morning and keep contributing to the world, even when your heart is broken because the person you love most in the world is no longer in it. That's it. The battle. It's not fighting soulless orcs and trolls with a cool sword. It's showing up. It's showering. It's dragging yourself through the end of the school year, doing homework that feels empty and pointless, doing your job, smiling when you want to scream, walking forward when you can't see beyond the blinding dark. When you can't even imagine the dawn.

Sometimes the battle is just putting food in your mouth, which takes all the strength you have left.

It's taking care of someone who looks up to you and trusts you, when you can't even take care of yourself.

You're like her hero.

I've slumped down into the couch, hugging Hunter's sword to my chest.

Justine's not coming back on her own. I know it.

I have to fix this. *We clean up our own messes in this house.*

Silently, I take myself and the sword into the kitchen. Nobody says a word about it.

Making lembas bread is fairly simple, and I embellish the recipe by grinding some almonds to press into the dough, so at least it's not all butter and sugar. Once I have some freshly baked and ready, I take a plate over for Justine.

The house is dark all the way up to her room. Her tray of food is untouched outside the door.

"Justine? I made the lembas if you want to try it." I tap her door and it opens slightly, so I push it all the way but don't invite myself in. Her room's dark and I wonder if she cried herself to sleep. "Hey?"

I turn on the light.

She's not in her bed. Not at the desk. Not anywhere.

The room is empty.

My pulse skips. "Justine?" I leave the plate of lembas bread with the other tray, and stride through the house, pushing open doors and turning on lights.

"Justine? Hey! I'm really sorry for shouting." I shove into Aunt Gina's bedroom and check the closet, under the bed, even out the window. "You win. This isn't funny, please come out." Down the hall, Hunter's room, the kitchen . . .

"JUSTINE!"

I know every corner of this house and I look in every single one. If she were hiding, she would be laughing by now, unable to keep it together after scaring me. The house is empty. She's not here.

She has to be here.

She's definitely not here. My pulse hammers in my neck.

Maybe she snuck past me, back to my house. I head outside, hanging a right to check Aunt Gina's studio, just in case, then the yard. Empty. My logical mind is losing to a rising tide of panic and I try to breathe it down. She might've just gone for a walk. The neighborhood is safe. She's probably fine.

Nothing feels fine.

I charge back into the living room in my house and turn on the lights, startling everyone all over again. "Guys! Did Justine come back? Did anyone see her?"

They shake their heads, checking in with each other. Imogen and Mia stand, looking around as if Justine might be under one of the pillows.

"No?" Mia says. "What happened?"

"She's not in her room. Not in the house." I press my thumb and forefinger to my eyes. "She's gone. I—I don't . . ."

Bryson's in front of me suddenly, his big hands on my shoulders. "Hey. We'll help you look. It's okay, man."

It's not okay. Nothing about this is okay. I lost my temper and screamed at her and now she's gone who knows where. This is not how a man treats his family, I know that.

I knew I shouldn't have left her alone.

I stare at Bryson's calm, determined face, my jaw locked open while I try to breathe and fail to make any of my thoughts into words.

"Dude." He tips his head close, calm and firm, as if he knows eye contact is the only thing holding me together. "Take a deep breath. It's going to be okay. There's only so many places she can go."

Right. Only so many places.

So, so many places.

Mia and Imogen have already thrown on coats to go outside to look, to ask neighbors. Cassidy pushes herself up and trots outside to bark once, helpfully.

"She probably went for a walk," Bryson says, still holding me by the arms. I'm afraid if he lets go, I'll collapse. "Let's go outside and look."

"Okay."

I take my phone, we bundle up, and I scrawl a note for Justine, explaining where we are, in case she comes back.

The neighbors haven't seen her. As far as I can tell, she's not hiding somewhere. I force myself to keep walking, looking, beyond houses to the walking trails and the patches of forest. Maybe she wanted to run away and be a lady of Lothlórien, who knows.

I'm halfway to downtown when the sense creeps up on me, as my friends text what streets they're on and who they've talked to, that Justine is, somehow, completely gone.

I stare at the frosted trees, the thick blanket of snow off the trail, and try to comprehend the true magnitude of my failure in this moment.

"I'm sorry," I whisper, my breath silver in the air. I tip my head back to breathe in the silent cold, and between broken clouds, a handful of stars blaze.

My phone vibrates. Oh God, maybe someone found her. I yank off a glove to wrestle the phone from my pocket, but pause when I see the screen. For a second it doesn't make any sense. It's not a text, it's a call.

From Hunter.

HEART POUNDING, I ANSWER. "HELLO?"

"Hello?" a vaguely familiar boy's voice echoes.

For a second I'm so confused and scared that there is nothing reasonable in my head about what's happening.

"Gage?"

"Yes." I clench a fist in my hair and squeeze until my scalp stings, trying to ground myself in physical pain. "Who is this?"

"It's Colby."

"Colby?" A breath spasms in my chest.

"Yeah, Colby, Colby Harting? From——"

"I know who you are." I stare at the snow-packed trail as logical reality clicks back into place. "Why do you have that phone? Where's Justine?"

"She's here. She didn't know how to turn on the data to call, so, anyway—here."

The soft scuffle of a handover. Then Justine's voice, scratchy and meek. "Gage?"

"Oh my God, Justine." Weak with relief, I sink to a crouch in the middle of the path, rubbing my forehead. "Where are you?"

"A gas station."

"Where?"

"Spruce Falls."

My hand drops from my face and I stare blankly at the trees. "Spruce Falls?" The words make no sense. "How?"

"I took the bus. From the stop at the grocery store."

A soft hysteria swirls around my fading panic now that I know she's alive and somewhere. I want to ask a hundred questions, starting with what kind of bus driver let her wander onto the bus by herself. But I know Justine. She charmed her way on with a story and they bought it hook, line, and sinker.

"So can you take the bus back?"

"No. Colby said that's the last one." Her voice drops to a whisper. "I'm sorry." She's crying.

"Justine," I say quickly, firmly. "Stay there. I'll—I'll get you. Okay? Stay there, promise?"

"I promise."

"Like, a real, true promise. You have to stay right there this time and wait."

"I will."

For a second we're both quiet. I clear my throat and say again, "I'm going to get you. I'm not mad. It's all okay. All right? Just stay there. Can I talk to Colby again?"

"Okay," she mumbles. "I'm sorry."

"I know. It's okay. I promise."

She hands over the phone again.

"Hello?" Colby says uncertainly.

"Hey." I stand and turn toward my house, walking fast. "Can you do me a huge favor?"

"Like what?"

"Can you tell me what gas station you're at, like, where you are, and can you stay with Justine until I get there?"

"Uh, sure."

"You're awesome, man. It won't be long."

He gives the address for the gas station and we hang up. I pause at the end of the trail that leads back onto the sidewalk of the neighborhood, mind scrambling. I said I would get her.

I said *I* would get her. A hoarse noise leaves my throat. I could still walk it. Frosty air and the empty road loom and warp around me. Could I walk it? I could walk it. It's almost—only—not quite ten miles. That would only take . . . but then Justine would have to walk *back* with me.

"Come on," I breathe and press both hands to my face. This is absurd. I have to drive. It will be fine. The snow melted. The road is plowed, wet, but decent.

We clean up our own messes in this house.

I close my eyes, visualize myself at the wheel. Cool, calm . . .

My heart spikes and sweat fills my palms inside my gloves. I tug them off, trying to count, trying to think.

I need help. My friends know I don't get in cars, but not about the panic attacks. Not really. And I've dumped enough on them tonight. I can't ask them to do this. I need someone who already knows, someone who knows I can't break down in front of everyone, in front of Justine, when she's already upset.

I jerk my phone up again and tap my contacts.

After four rings, he answers.

"Hey, bud!"

"Dad!" My voice catches. "Hi, are you still in town?"

"You bet. How's it going? Don't you have your party thing tonight?"

"Yeah. Um." My throat tightens and I clear it roughly. "I need your help."

He chuckles. "Oh yeah? You need me to grab you guys some beer or something?"

A short, rough laugh catches my chest. "No, thanks. Uh, look, Justine and I had a fight and she ran off—"

"Is anyone hurt?" His voice hardens, steel and protective. Relief swells in me. He can help. "Is she okay?"

"We're okay." My voice starts to break and I suck in a hard breath as tears swarm my eyes. "She's in Spruce Falls. Do you think—could you pick her up and bring her back? I can't—"

"She's okay?"

"Yes." I release a breath. He sounds calm. Almost wry. I'm overreacting. She's a few miles away and she's okay and she's even with someone. I don't feel remotely better, because this should be an easy fix and it's not. "We're all okay. I just can't—you know I can't drive—"

"Hey." His voice sharpens. "Hey, are you crying? Calm down, Gage."

I take a deep breath, grab a fistful of snow and press it to my throat. "I'm calm."

"You're both okay. You know where she is. Don't you

have a bunch of friends there?"

A slow understanding crawls cold up my back. "Yeah . . ."

"With cars?"

"Yeah," I say through my teeth.

"Can't they help?"

"Dad," I whisper. "I can't ask them."

He makes a noise of disbelief. "Bud—"

"Please. Dad, I can't. I can't—*you* said I need to keep it together and not . . . I can't panic in front of them, in front of Justine. I've already freaked her out enough tonight."

I can't, I can't ask one of them to go pick up my cousin for me who I ran off because I couldn't keep it together. Shame and anger simmer in my stomach, shortening my breath.

"So don't."

I stand in the cold, in silent disbelief. "I can't control it, Dad."

"Have you tried?"

"Yes!" I snap, shaking the phone. "Yes, Dad, I've tried! I need your help, please—"

"Listen, bud." His voice is slow and firm. "Remember when you and me and Hunter went swimming off the docks, and you were afraid of the deep part, so I tossed you in?"

"Vividly," I mutter.

"Well, you got over it, didn't you?"

"Dad, please . . ." My voice splinters, pathetic, weak, and he can hear it.

"This is like that." He sounds so calm. My breath

heaves through me, threatening tears or panic or another angry rampage. "You're a strong, smart, grown-ass man, Gage. You've got this."

He hangs up.

I stand there, phone pressed to my ear.

He hung up.

Rage and disbelief explode in my head. He hung up on me. A single, harsh, angry laugh of amazement gets out, and I fight the urge to punch a tree. Trembling, I pocket my phone instead. No. Then I'd just be dealing with all this *and* broken knuckles, probably.

He hung up on me. I can't dwell. I know I can't. Justine is waiting and I don't know how long she'll stay or what the gas station is like and how long Colby will hang out.

He hung up. When I was begging for help, when I finally asked for help.

Who else could help? Who else can I call?

Meaghan and Tank, maybe—they would understand. But I don't have their number. I would have to call Jack. Then he would know. They would all know how I let everything unravel and that I'm not okay, an incapable mess; they're a state away, trying to have a vacation, they can't help . . . no. It has to be me.

Hands trembling, I text my friends to call off the search, and stride back to the house.

It has to be me.

Heart hammering, sweating, I lunge up the porch into the main entry and grab Mom's keys from their hook. I turn back to the door and almost plow into Mia, who's coming up the porch steps, followed by Imogen and Bryson.

"Whoa! Wait!" Mia plants her hands on my chest. "What are you doing?"

I point east. "She's in Spruce Falls. I'm going to get her."

They stare at me.

Bryson lifts both hands peacefully, coming around Mia, eyes on the keys in my hand. "Gage. Bro. Let one of us—"

"I got it."

Mia blocks the door and crosses her arms. "You are not driving."

Imogen comes forward, closing one strong hand over mine, over the keys. "Let us help. Please. Please?"

My gaze darts over all of them. My head is shaking slowly, no, no.

"I ran her off," I say through gritted teeth. A strong, grown-ass man. "I have to get her. She's expecting me. It has to be me."

"That's fine," Imogen says. "But let one of us drive."

They're so concerned. So gentle. So calm. This is not a big deal to any of them. Justine is ten miles away.

"Gage," Bryson says, gentle in a way I've never heard before. "It's okay."

Is it?

As I struggle and fail to hold back tears, it finally occurs to me, unfurling with slow, shocking clarity, I am less afraid of getting in that car, less afraid of a wreck, less afraid of my panic, than I am of letting any of them see it. In that moment, I would literally rather die than let them see me cry.

The breath leaves me.

Dad.

Not them. Dad. Dad, angry, horrified, shaking me, telling me to calm down.

That can't be right, it can't be, it just can't—I can't let them see this. I can't fall apart.

I can't . . .

I can't do this anymore.

There's a moment, and I feel it, like letting go of a rope over a chasm, when I give up.

I have to.

At this point, if I don't let these tears continue down my face, I'll give myself a heart attack. They've already seen me go full Hulk; they might as well see me cry. Giving up feels kind of good. Whatever happens now happens, and if everyone disowns me because I can't keep it together, fine. I'll figure it out then.

"I—I just . . . I . . . When I'm in the car, I—" My throat closes as if I'm having an allergic reaction—it's so much, I can't do this to them, I can't dump this all on them, they don't need that—

"You have panic attacks," Bryson says matter-of-factly.

My eyes snap open. "What?"

"You have panic attacks. You had one when I offered you a ride in the truck. Right?" He lifts a hand, and when I don't move, he comes forward to grip my shoulder. Imogen stays close and rests a grounding hand on my back, and Mia looks so worried and stern, like she wants to hug and smack me at the same time.

I watch Bryson warily, silent, embarrassment sliding coolly through my body. He knew. They all knew. Of course they did, because they've been watching me like I watch them, for pain, for weakness.

And I pushed them away.

"My mom has them," Bryson explains when I say nothing. "Like, if someone slams a door, because of Dad. We'll go get Justine. Everyone understands. Don't you get it? It's *okay*."

It's not okay. "I have to go too," I croak.

"Is that a good idea?" Mia asks. "Gage, you don't have to do that to yourself."

"I have to go," I say again. "I told Justine I was coming." I suck another hoarse breath. "I can do it. As long as you guys don't mind seeing me . . . uh, freak out. I don't know."

Bryson squeezes my shoulder.

"Gage," Imogen says with gentle irony, "I think we've all been worried that you haven't freaked out more often. Is that what it is? You don't want us to see?" She motions me up and down and she looks so sad and regretful, as if they did something wrong, and not me. "You didn't think we would understand?"

I look at her. Mia, in her beautiful gown with a puffy winter coat thrown over top. Bryson, unfazed. Whatever's left in me crumbles and I choke on a sob.

"I'm sorry . . . I—I didn't want you to worry, I didn't . . ."

Imogen unfolds her arms, touches my elbow, and gently works Mom's car keys out of my hand to hang them back up.

Bryson takes me by both shoulders. "I can help you. I help my mom when she panics. You just have to let me. You have to stop lying to us." He squeezes my shoulders and I look up. His blond brows are knitted. "Listen. You and Hunter saved my life. You literally saved my life, when he invited me to LWDA. Now I'm telling you, you can't do this anymore, man. You have to trust us. You've seen us cry and get angry and all that crap. You can't ask us to open up and ask for help while you pretend you're okay. Because you're not, and we all know it. So say it."

I huff a sound, rubbing my eyes. "I'm . . . I'm not okay."

"And?" Bryson urges. "Lone wolves . . ."

"Lone wolves . . ." I clear my throat. "Lone wolves die alone."

"Yeah," he says.

I didn't see it. I thought I was being strong and right, and doing right by my family. I didn't see how it was all wrong. How I'd wandered into the dark woods of my own soul by myself. How alone I was. How I was dying, a small piece every day, alone.

I nod, slowly, eyes on the floor. "Okay. I want to go. I can do this. I might be a mess, but I just need help. Or I need to . . . to move through it. As long as you don't mind—"

"Bro." Bryson claps my shoulders firmly and I look up to his big, bright grin. He presses his palm to my chest. "You have my sword."

A laugh chokes my throat.

Imogen raises a fist with a grin. "And my bow."

Mia lifts her own keys on one finger. "And my Subaru."

WHILE MIA WARMS UP HER CAR, I GATHER A COUPLE OF things to bring to Justine as a peace offering, including Hunter's cloak, wrapped around another surprise.

Hands trembling, I force myself to text Olivia so she doesn't show up to an empty house.

Me: Hey, the night just got exciting. Justine ran off and we have to go get her. I'll explain when you get here. Side door is unlocked, please come in, we'll be back soon.

She doesn't text back. Maybe she's busy. Or helping to close.

Or doesn't want to get involved in my drama. Maybe I should have told her not to come.

Too late now. I have to go.

Imogen and Bryson flank me to the car.

Mia's Outback smells like pine. That helps. They let me take my time, standing at the door of the back seat, Bryson's hand on my shoulder. I thought I might be too wrung out for the panic to strike, but it's there, a warning drone in my ears, my body on high alert for danger that doesn't exist. Or does it? We can't know.

I shove my way into the middle of the seat, hunch over myself, and Imogen and Bryson stuff themselves in on either side of me. My breath is too fast. My heart rate climbs, and for a second it feels like the car is spinning when we aren't even moving. I grab both front seats for balance and hang my head.

Bryson's big hand comes around the side of my face, steering my head so I have to look at him. His left hand rests on my other cheek. Imogen's hand presses against my back.

"You're okay," Bryson says firmly, quiet. My eyes drop. I'm not okay. "Gage. Look at me."

I look at him. No one's upset. No one's laughing. Imogen rubs my back and Mia waits until I say it's okay to go, I guess.

"Say fifty," Bryson says.

"Fifty," I mumble, locking my attention on him.

"Forty-nine."

"Forty-nine." I take a breath, pulse in my ears, and squeeze my eyes shut.

"Gage."

I look at him. We count backward together. When we hit thirty and I'm well focused on the numbers, he tips his head toward Mia, and she shifts the car into reverse, but doesn't move yet. Imogen's arms come around my shoulders. At twenty, the car rolls slowly, backing up—my throat locks, I feel out of control. I look to Mia as sweat soaks my back.

"Mia—"

"I'll go as slow as you want," she says, warm and calm.

"Gage." Back to Bryson. I can't remember numbers or where we were. I stammer, then dissolve into tears. I couldn't hold back now even if I tried, and the car is going exactly two miles an hour.

Numbers aren't working.

"Okay, Gage," Bryson says when I stop counting. "Think about something else. Like, visualize. It's ten seconds left in the fourth quarter, third down with ten yards to go. How would—"

"Not football," I mutter.

"Food," suggests Imogen.

"Right." Bryson steers my face up to meet his eyes. "Let's do *Chopped*. You've seen my mom's garden. It's August and you have to make something from what you find. Squash, tomatoes, zucchini."

I can see it. A summer garden bursting with vegetables.

"Eggplant?"

"Sure," Bryson says, smiling lopsidedly.

"Ratatouille."

"Okay, another one." He starts listing ingredients, but I'm remembering watching that movie with Hunter and how he tried to convince Justine that a rat was actually doing all my cooking.

I heave and swallow hard as all the grief I've been holding back blends with the panic and threatens to burst out in a horrible combination of vomit and tears and incoherent sounds.

I'm here, I'm safe, I'm here—it fractures and I curl over myself.

Imogen hugs me from the side and Bryson tugs me up gently so I can breathe better.

"Repeat after me," Imogen murmurs. "Gage. 'All that is gold does not glitter.'"

My face is wet and hot with sweat, tears, shame, but they're both holding me, not repulsed, holding me together. I swallow bile as Mia turns out of the neighborhood.

The road is clear and safe. I know this. Logically, I know this.

I might be sick.

"'All that is gold,'" Imogen prompts again. "'Does not—'"

"'Does not glitter,'" I blurt, forcing the words, then laugh weakly, edging on hysteria as Mia flicks on her turn signal. *Tck tck* . . . The headlights, the streetlamps moving by, make my stomach turn. "I have to close my eyes, guys. I can't . . ."

"Do whatever you need to," Bryson says. "Imogen, keep going."

We haltingly say "The Riddle of Strider" together and the words are like a massage on my brain. Bryson's fingers press my temples, his big hands cradling my face, as he probably does for his mom, keeping me there, in my body, instead of spiraling back to the accident.

I almost choke on my gratitude.

Imogen starts the riddle again, and by the end we're speaking in unison.

"'Renewed shall be blade that was broken

The crownless again shall be king.'"

She doesn't let up. We say it again. *Deep roots are not reached by the frost. . . .*

We quote from Star Wars. *Situation normal. This is the way.*

We mumble "Misty Mountains Cold." Bryson tries to sing it, having never heard it, and I laugh.

We return to counting and I don't care anymore that they can see me. I need them to see me; I need to see them and know they still love me, that it's okay. That I haven't lost their respect, that I'm not a burden, that I'm still in the pack. That I'm broken and they still love me.

Maybe I can be broken, like Narsil, and still reforge myself into something worthy and new.

I'm crying, laughing, terrified, and we're halfway to Spruce Falls. Cars pass us as Mia continues slowly.

It's both the best and worst fifteen minutes of my entire life so far.

The car stops.

The whole world spins to a stop.

"We made it!" Mia announces.

My breath drains. I thought it would never end, that I would fall, like Gandalf in Moria, forever.

"You did it," Bryson says, giving me a shake. "Dude! Say you did it."

"I did it," I whisper. And break into a crying laugh. Pathetic. I don't care. I did it. "We did it. You did it."

Imogen is crying, laughing, rubbing my shoulders. Bryson hugs me before he climbs out of the car and I haul myself out after him, letting the cold air hit my face.

"Here." Mia comes up to me, offering a tissue. I crush her in a hug.

"Thank you for driving. Oh my God, Mia. Thank you so much. I'm sorry I was—"

"Stop." She hugs me tightly. "Thank you for letting me."

The gas station door chimes and we look over as Justine and Colby come out. Justine pauses, watching me hesitantly, and I lower myself to one knee, opening an arm.

"Good evening." I try for lordly formality, but my voice is raw and tired. I hold out Hunter's rolled cloak for her. I'm wearing mine, pinned with a leaf and everything. "I'm looking for a hobbit to share in an adventure."

She covers her mouth, tearstained cheeks bunching in a smile, and runs to me, burying herself in the circle of my arm. I hug her silently, lifting my eyes to Colby with a nod. He shrugs, brow furrowed.

"You rode in a car!" Justine cries.

"Yeah. I did. Hey, listen." She leans back, while I continue to offer Hunter's cloak. "You know what I gave Hunter for his birthday, but do you remember what he gave me?"

She shakes her head. My sixteenth birthday was the same camping trip, a day after his.

"Here." I hand her the bundle and she realizes there's something wrapped in the cloak, and unrolls it carefully. Then she gasps as she withdraws another sheathed but unmistakable sword.

"Sting," she whispers, eyes round.

I hold back a proud laugh. "Yeah. You can take it out."

She tugs the hilt, to see the metal of the blade.

"Huh," I say. "That's weird."

"What?"

"It should be glowing blue."

Justine looks around, then frowns at me, suspicious. "Why?"

I lean forward, knee digging into the packed snow, and meet her eyes squarely. "Because you've been acting like a goblin, and I turned into a horrible ugly old orc."

She giggles and pushes my shoulder. Then she sniffles. "I'm sorry. I thought you wanted to do the movie—"

"I did," I say. "I just did too much, and I didn't let anyone help. I'm really sorry. But you also weren't listening to me, so can we try again?" She nods, and I hug her close for a second before standing up. I wrap Hunter's cloak around her shoulders and pin it again. "Go get in the car, okay? I'll be right there."

She trots to the car and Imogen meets her there with a hug. "You scared us!"

Meanwhile, I turn and walk to Colby. He looks me up and down, cloak and all. "You guys are weird."

A weary grin finds my face. "Yeah, I know. Thanks for helping her." I hold out my hand and he thinks a second before he takes it, and I shake firmly. "I owe you a burger or something."

"You don't owe me." He steps back, sliding his hands into his pockets.

"Are you okay here?" I glance around the gas station with a shiver as the cold seeps through my layers. "Do you need a ride or something?"

He shakes his head, looking up the road. "My brother's coming soon—I used your phone to call him, sorry." He looks up at me and I smile reassuringly. "Thanks."

"Sure thing." For a second I hesitate, wondering if he's lying, but I can't exactly drag him to the car. So I turn to leave.

"Andy gave me a job."

I turn back, smiling again in surprise. "Oh yeah?"

Colby shrugs and smiles back and it hits me that the only other time I've seen him smile is when he saw me spill mustard. That feels like a year ago. "Just a couple hours a week, in the afternoon, busing and stuff. And only on the weekends when I start school again. But he said since I'm at Nan's all the time anyway, I might as well do something. And that if you trusted me, I must be okay."

I smile faintly, then laugh, because I can picture the conversation, and I walk back to Colby to shake his hand again. His grip is firmer this time. "Guess I'll see you at work, then."

His smile broadens and for the first time there's a glimmer of confidence. "See you."

We rearrange ourselves in the car with Imogen up front, me in the middle, Bryson and Justine on either side of me. I'm not ready to sit by a window. I don't know when or if I ever will be.

Mia has kept the car idling and glances over her shoulder at me inquiringly.

"One second," I murmur, and lean close to Justine to prepare her. "This is hard for me. I don't want to scare you or for you to think I'm hurt or something. I-it's just . . . I might cry, or I might breathe really fast, but it's okay and I'm okay. Bryson's going to help me. I just want you to understand."

Imogen leans around the front seat and touches Justine's shoulder, adding simply, "It's called a panic attack."

Justine looks at Imogen, taking it all in, then wraps her arms around me. "I want to help too. Mom says it's okay to cry."

I close my eyes, nod once, and reach out to touch Mia's shoulder.

"You good?" she asks.

"Good as I'm going to get," I murmur, baring my teeth in a grimace, eyes closed. Justine squeezes me tight and Bryson grips my shoulder, and we pull back out onto the road.

Most of the ride has me panting softly, silent, because I'm too wrecked, hunched over with Bryson, counting down to give my brain some focus. Justine sings to me, petting my back like she does to Cassidy when she wakes up with a howling bad dream. Bryson rubs my shoulders.

Soft golden light from the streetlamps of Clark rolls across us and I shut my eyes.

Justine shouldn't have to do this for me. I should be the one to comfort her.

Pathetic.

My face scrunches as Dad elbows his way back into my brain.

That can't be right. It just can't. Nobody else is saying that.

I had hoped it would be easier than last time, but it isn't. It's just different. Raw, tiring, disorienting. What's different is not trying to hide it, moving through it, sinking into fear and panic but climbing back up, always up, toward the love of the people surrounding me.

"We're here," Mia says. I might pass out. "Everybody good?"

"You did it!" Justine cries, squeezing me so hard, I grunt. She isn't horrified. She is so genuinely proud of me. "You're so brave!"

I crumble again and turn to hug her. "Thanks," I whisper.

Finally we all untangle ourselves and lurch out of the car.

"Wooo!" Bryson smacks my back, then thrusts both fists into the air. "Quest accomplished!"

"Good lord," Mia murmurs.

"Good lady." Bryson points at her, and she laughs, batting at him as he scoops her close to kiss her.

"You've turned him into a nerd," Imogen says in approval.

"Pretty sure it was there the whole time," I say. Justine huddles in close under my arm, hugging Sting to her chest.

I did it. I got her. I got in a car. We're home.

The only thing that keeps me from face-planting in the snow in relief is looking up as my front door opens and seeing Olivia step out onto the porch.

"Olivia!" Justine runs to her since they're old buddies now, I guess. "I ran away and Gage came to get me and he hasn't been in a car in forever, and he let me see this sword. Look, it's Sting!"

"Wow!" Olivia leans forward to see Sting, but she's watching me. I must look like a train wreck. For the first time, I don't care. Coming home to see her there, in a pretty wool dress with her curls in Rivendell-style twists with little flowers woven in and the candlelight behind her melts some of my lingering fear. She lifts her hand in a hesitant greeting, but turns her attention to Justine, who is still talking, explaining about Sting and the bus and all.

I pause to hug my friends, thanking all three, but they're just so proud of me, and urge me to get back in the house. Imogen pats me on the shoulder. "Oh my gosh, go see her. I can't stand it."

I head up the steps and Olivia looks me over, brows knitting in worry. "I got your text. Do you want me to leave?"

"No," I whisper before I can hold back. I swallow hard. "No, I don't. I want you here. It's—it's really good to see you. You look beautiful. It's just been . . . a night, sorry." It all tumbles out like my tears did; the relief and happiness and embarrassment pour out because I just don't have the strength to hold things in right now. "Please stay."

I expect her to back away, repulsed by too much emotion or my tearstained face.

She touches my shirt, petting my chest lightly. "Thank you," she says, soft as a snowflake, and my heart cracks.

Thank you. As if it's a favor I'm letting her in, not a burden. Maybe it's not. I think of hugging her when she was upset, how it felt, how she trusted me. Maybe I need to trust her.

I gaze at her and I finally understand the phrase "a sight for sore eyes." The ambient light of the streetlamp catches on her necklace. It's the Evenstar pendant. Like everything else that evening, it makes me want to cry and I don't even know which emotion it is.

I touch the necklace, as inarticulate as the first time I saw her, and she smiles, shyly. "Oh, um. My mom gave it to me forever ago. I thought it would be appropriate."

"It is. I'm really glad you're here. I'm sorry it's . . ." I pinch the bridge of my nose. "This is awkward."

She pulls my hand from my face. "It's not awkward," she murmurs, her clear, earnest brown eyes locked on mine. "It's life."

I close my eyes for a second. I know we're blocking the door and my friends are staring and I'm a tearstained, sweaty, disheveled mess. But I want Olivia to see me, my hurt, and know she can still want to be around me. "Right." I smile weakly. "Can I have a hug?"

Her face lights up and she grips my cloak to tug me close and wrap her arms around me. "Anytime."

"Can we move the party back inside?" Mia asks. "The fabrics of Lothlórien are not weatherproof."

It has started to snow, and I'm making everyone stand out in it. Olivia laughs, grabs my hand, and pulls me inside, and everyone introduces themselves to her as we shrug off our coats and shoes. They're warm, laughing, familiar, like this is just another day, and relief settles in my chest. On autopilot, I head toward the kitchen, but Bryson squares into my space, blocking me.

"Bro. You're done. Go sit down." He points to the living room.

"Justine needs to eat something," I argue.

"I'm on it." He frowns at me. "Dude, I'm exhausted looking at you. Go watch the rest of the movie. I'm begging you."

I turn and everyone's sort of suspended there. The movie is paused. They're waiting to see what I want to do. Justine is standing on the pile of pillows in the living room, hugging Sting.

"You want us to go?" Imogen asks. "Or finish the movie?"

I scoff, running a hand through my hair, while Olivia steps close and slides her fingers through my other hand.

"A day may come," I begin roughly, and slow grins start over their faces, in unison, "when the courage to finish the movies fails us." Imogen snickers. I raise my head. "When we forsake our friends and break all bonds of fellowship . . ." I grab Sting from Justine, draw it, and brandish it high. "But it is not this day!"

They laugh and cheer. Bryson howls, since this is a victory for LWDA, too. No lone wolves here.

I collapse in a heap on the couch, and we back up the movie to a mutually agreeable point. Bryson takes over service and Justine even eats some actual food.

One mug of rich, hot cider soothes everything and puts me down for the count. I fade in and out of the movie, Justine's exclamations, Olivia petting my hair. I twitch awake once, anxious over a possible nightmare—but it occurs to me that it's okay. Heart pounding, I lie there and let myself fall back asleep, knowing if I come awake crying or gasping or scared, my friends aren't here to judge me. They're here to love me.

For the first time in a year I feel safe. Not safe from danger, but safe to expose my heart, my hurt, my fear. I've forgotten what that felt like. I sink into it, grasping hard to this feeling so I'll recognize it every time.

I'm here. I'm safe.

THE RUMBLE OF A TRUCK wakes me, diesel wafting through my open window. My throat is sore, my head aches, my eyes are scratchy and dry. I don't even remember going up to my room. Maybe they dragged me.

Bryson is passed out on an air mattress next to my bed like a guard dog and I step over him carefully, pausing to pull the afghan up over his shoulder as cold air trickles through my window.

I head downstairs and through the living room, which is littered with half-eaten bowls of popcorn, plates and empty mugs sitting everywhere. Justine is curled up on the couch with Cassidy, Mia and Imogen are back-to-back on the pillow pile on the floor in pajamas, and Olivia is curled in Jack's oversized armchair.

I peer out the front door, blinded by new snow and morning sun. Late-morning sun. I have no idea what time it is and I'm pretty sure I only fell asleep an hour ago. Diesel fills the air and I watch Dad blearily as he strides up the sidewalk, carrying a box of doughnuts.

"Wow." He grins at me. "Long night?"

"Hey. What's up." I try to keep my expression smooth as I step out onto the porch because it feels like getting angry gives him some power. Somehow last night I changed from clothes to a T-shirt and sweatpants to sleep in, and the icy snow on the porch feels good on my bare feet. I try to feel something about Dad other than sheer, exhausting disappointment.

"Thought I'd check on you guys. Looks like you have everything under control?"

"Yeah. I do." I cross my arms, shivering as the cold hits me.

"Justine's okay?"

"Yep."

He frowns at me, as if he's truly confused why I'm not thrilled to see him there with doughnuts. "Well, I brought these."

"Thanks." I consider, but I do have guests and I don't think I'm up for cooking, so I take the box. "Thanks for checking in."

He shifts his weight, motioning to the door. "Can I come in?"

I don't move. "No, I don't think so."

His eyebrows shoot up, then he nods a couple times like he's got me figured. "You're mad at me about last night."

My gaze drops to my feet, now numb. I feel ten years old again. "I mean. Not mad—actually, yeah. I am mad." I glare up at him. I'm *not* ten years old. And I've bit back enough words with him. "You hung up on me, Dad. I don't know why you couldn't just help me."

He sighs and rests a hand on the railing. "You handled it, didn't you?"

"Eventually. It's just . . ." I clear my throat, grabbing for surety. "You're always telling me about what a man needs to do for his family, and when I called you for help, you didn't—"

"Hey." He aims a finger in my face. "That's different. I knew you could handle it."

"Thanks. I guess." I breathe through the anger, the disappointment, trying to relax my glare.

He stands there, scowling at me, realizing I'm really, truly not going to invite him inside. Then he chuckles and shakes his head, rubbing his jaw. "Look, bud. I know your generation's more touchy-feely than mine—"

"I don't think that's fair," I murmur, irritation and injustice sizzling in my chest. I consider setting the doughnuts aside so I don't end up throwing them in his face. It'd be a waste of good pastry.

I'm just so sick of being angry. I try to be something else, searching his face, the familiar hard lines of him, remember all that he's done for me and for Hunter. I try to understand him, instead of being angry that he doesn't understand me.

It comes to me that he lost Hunter too. That he could've lost me.

And for a brief, sharp moment, I get it.

It's not Mom, Aunt Gina, or Justine who he thinks couldn't handle seeing me freak out, couldn't handle seeing me in pain, seeing me cry. It's him. He can't handle it.

He's charging through it the only way he knows how, and he's been forcing me to do the same. He'd rather see me angry, hurting, holding it in, than deal with it all.

I swallow a hardness in my throat.

"Well, whatever it is"—he waves a hand between us—"we're different. And I'm trying to help you be ready for the world. Someone's not always going to be there to call, Gage."

"Obviously," I say quietly. "You're just . . . This has been really hard for me, and I—"

"It's been hard for everyone—"

"*Dad.*" I stop him, closing a fist. Then force it to relax. That's not me. I don't want it to be me. My whole body trembles as if I might cry again. Whatever. Maybe that would get through to him. Standing up to the guys in the diner is nothing compared to this, to my dad. "I know it's hard for everyone. Okay? I know. But this—all this stuff you're saying, no one else is . . . It's not helping."

He stares at me, and something I don't recognize shadows his face. Maybe regret, maybe pain. I don't know. Because he's hiding it. Because maybe I don't really know him at all, and I don't know how to do this. But I know for sure I don't really trust him, not with my heart, not the way I trusted my friends last night. My chest aches.

"Look." He rubs his forehead, breaking our stare before I can understand anything. Or before he can. "Hard knocks is how my granddad raised my dad, and how he raised me, and it's what I know. And I turned out fine."

I look at the box of doughnuts, take a deep breath, and lift my eyes to his again. "Did you?"

His expression relaxes in pure surprise. Then his cheeks

redden and his hand tightens on the railing. I feel like I'm not looking at my dad, but at a path I was headed down.

Just when I think he's on the verge of something new, he laughs.

He *laughs.*

It dawns on me what Rowan meant by "emotionally unavailable."

"Yeah," he says easily. "I did. And so did you." He takes the last two steps up the porch, hands raised in peace. Then he offers one for a handshake as if I'm a fellow trucker, not his son in mourning. "You handled last night, and I'm proud of you. Sorry, but I'm old-school."

I set the doughnuts on the rail, herding my thoughts.

In one way he's right. I had to open up to my friends, to ask for help, to finally crack, and that was a good thing. Who knows how long I would've gone on that way? Maybe forever. Maybe I would've ended up just like him. So in that way, he did do me a favor.

My emotions spin until they roll to a stop on the one I think is stronger than pain, stronger than sorrow, stronger, even, than my anger.

I take his hand and pull him into a hug. He makes a noise of surprise, but I don't let go.

"Sorry," I say quietly, thinking how I want to leave things if this ends up being our last moment together. "But I'm new school."

He's stiff and uncomfortable in my arms and I think the last time we were this close and intimate was when I was four years old and he showed me how to cast a fishing pole.

"I love you," I say, very quietly, as if I'm a kid again and unafraid of telling him. Then a deep shaky breath, and my voice drops to my chest. "But I'm not you. And I'm doing my best."

He shifts his weight, silent. One arm comes slowly around me, pats my shoulder, and I'll take that as a win. I can't leave things on a bad note anymore, not with anyone, not after losing Hunter. And I feel like maybe Dad needs a hug more than anyone, that he truly believes he was doing his best by me—but maybe his best is not right for me. So if he's going to try to make me more like him, maybe I can try to make him more like me, too, and we'll figure it out somewhere in the middle.

And if we can't, I'll cross that bridge then.

"Okay, bud," he murmurs. "Love you too." Triumph floods my chest before he pats my back again, as a hint. I release him and he pulls back, looks me over and smiles halfway, shakes his head and turns quickly to go, voice rough. "Take care. Say hi to your mom."

"I will. See you soon." During that whole encounter, my heart rate stayed level, and that feels like a sign it was the right way to be. My way, not his.

I head inside with the box of doughnuts and start some coffee. The house rouses slowly to the smell and I pile the doughnuts on a platter, breathing in deeply the maple sugar and chocolate, and set out the last of the paper plates and some mugs. Imogen wanders in, wearing her Washington State hoodie and sweatpants, and Mia after her. She's in a cozy purple sleep shirt and shorts with her hair bound in a silk wrap, a hint of elven sparkle still dusting her cheeks.

"Morning, ladies." I grin. Mia holds up a hand and heads straight to the coffeepot. "Got it."

Imogen comes close for a hug. "How are you?"

I think about it for a second instead of answering *good*, which is a step. "Better," I murmur. "I don't know." I laugh weakly, rubbing my face. "Right now I'm good."

"I feel you." She squeezes me around the shoulders while Mia sits at the table with her mug. I don't disturb her until she's had some coffee.

We eat doughnuts. Bryson and Justine meander in, and lastly Olivia, and I wonder if I look worse now than I did last night. I hadn't thought about seeing her, forgot to shower or dress or do anything. She doesn't seem to mind, but casts me a warm, shy smile across the table. Maybe it's not even that she doesn't mind; maybe she *prefers* seeing me disarmed. Maybe it feels like trust. I mull that over.

"So," Mia says at last, with some apple fritter and coffee in her system. "It didn't seem appropriate last night with everything, but some of us put together a video of Hunter. If you want." She sips her coffee. "As part of the memorial."

"Oh," I murmur, heart quickening. Right. Last night was supposed to be about Hunter. "Sure. Yeah, I'd love to watch it."

We exchange a look around the table and by silent agreement, everyone rises, Bryson grabs the doughnuts, and we head into the living room. Mia retrieves her phone and sets it up to cast to the TV.

With a deep breath, I settle on the couch and Justine curls up next to me, Imogen close on the other side.

The first photo is his goofy, grinning face that looks like a screenshot from Snapchat, with his hand up in a peace sign, his birth and death date, and under that, *We love you.*

I don't even make it past that first picture before my throat clenches and my eyes well up, and I wrap both arms around Justine. She pets my arm, and I let her.

They've set it to his favorite music, a montage of Hunter—skiing, hanging upside down from a tree aiming a bow, all of us in a group during an LWDA meeting at the bowling alley. Shots of us as kids. Pictures from football games after we became friends with Bryson, short videos, camping under summer trees.

Tears slide down my face, but I'm also laughing at some of the pictures. I had those things with him. Nothing can take that away. We won't make new memories, but I have that.

The shadow, the loss of him that prowls at the edges and haunts me, begins to evaporate and reveals something warm, safe, and true. He will always be with me, part of me, and that's a good thing.

"You guys," I whisper. So many of the pictures involve me, too. Justine asks questions, where was that picture, where was that video, who's that . . .

Then everything fades to black for a second, and the light, familiar opening notes from "The Last Goodbye" by Billy Boyd float through the living room.

My heart fractures and I curl forward, pressing my face to my hands. Hunter's pictures, his moments, his laugh, his voice fills the living room, set to one of our favorite songs. The clash of metal as we spar carefully with our beautiful, expensive swords. Little clips of our lives, his life, everything he was, everything he gave. Everything he meant to me.

Everyone is clustered around me and Justine. I know

they lost Hunter too, that I should offer some comfort, but I can't. I have nothing; the regret and sorrow and gratitude that I had the privilege of knowing him racks my body. I cry and I laugh and I melt into my friends, here, now.

The music fades.

Bryson is sitting on the floor by my feet, Mia near him, Olivia next to Justine, and Imogen hugging me from the side, all pressed in against me as if everyone is keeping me from flying to pieces. They probably are.

"Hey," Hunter's voice murmurs from the screen. I look up. I know this video, from his Instagram, something he sent out to LWDA. His bright hazel eyes meet mine through the screen. "You're awesome and don't forget it." He points at the screen. "You're not alone. Peace."

He grins, and the screen fades to black. I stare at it, nodding slowly, my brain scrambling as I struggle not to do what I normally do, which would be to hide. I stretch my arms to engulf my friends instead.

"Thank you," I whisper. "That was beautiful. That was perfect."

"Good," Mia says, and I know how lucky I am to have them.

And maybe how lucky they are to have me.

"Remember that first football game you came to?" Bryson asks.

"When you ran fifty yards against Sandpoint?" I nudge him with my bare foot. "Everyone remembers it."

He smirks over his shoulder, turning a doughnut in his hands. "Well, I remember when everyone was shouting and Hunter jumped up and yelled 'Goooal!' like it was a soccer game."

"Oh my God," Imogen says. "I forgot about that!"

Justine laughs even though I don't think she knows much about either sport, and I hug her.

"Me too," I say. It's vague. Rowan was there, so I wasn't paying as much attention to Hunter, and for a second, murky despair washes over me that there are things I don't remember, moments I didn't know were going to be precious and important. Bryson is smiling mistily, and the despair fades. Maybe that's his memory. Maybe that's okay. I have so many of my own.

I look at my coffee mug. "Did I ever tell you guys about when my dad took us to Boat Box Hot Springs for the first time and we drove him nuts pretending it was a troll's stewpot?"

"No," Imogen says, grabbing a doughnut. "But you definitely should."

ANDY ACCEPTS MY CALL-IN SICK TODAY BUT SAYS HE COULD really use my help the rest of the week. I knew it. My friends hang out for the morning, helping me clean up. We share more Hunter stories until exhaustion swamps me. Instead of trying to push through, I tell them.

They understand, and I bid everyone goodbye, one at a time, at the door.

Mia leans into me for a long hug, no words.

"Thank you for everything," I say quietly. "For just . . . the costume and for driving and being there for me."

She gives me a squeeze and leans back, looking me over. "We take turns, you know? Thanks for hosting." Her smile is small and wry, but she means it. I laugh and Bryson moves in, and he offers a prolonged hug too.

"You're okay," he says, half a question, half a statement.

"Yeah." We clap each other's shoulders and I step back. "I need to tell you something."

"Anything, bro." He watches me closely and I run a hand through my hair.

"You don't cook rice the same way you cook spaghetti."

His blond brows knit together. "What?"

Mia bursts out laughing behind him. "You what? I thought there was something funny."

He looks between us, betrayed. "You said you loved it."

"I did," Mia says, closing her hand on his wrist. "But I mostly loved that you had paid attention to what I said."

"Oh," he says, looking redeemed.

I pat Bryson's arm. "Next Wednesday, Warhammer. We'll make rice."

He hangs his head and laughs in defeat, and we bump fists.

Imogen marches up to me and we engulf each other in a hug. I heave a sigh of relief. "Thanks for . . . for seeing me."

She chokes a quiet laugh against my chest. "Anytime. Call me, okay?"

I clear my throat. "I will. We'll hang out. This week. Before you go back to school."

She looks me over in misty-eyed satisfaction, pats my arms, and turns to follow Bryson and Mia out.

Olivia lingers for a moment after everyone has gone;

even Justine went to her own house to shower and change clothes.

"Thanks for letting me stay," she says as I help her into her coat. I'm still in my rumpled sleep clothes.

"Thanks for staying. I know this was kind of a mess."

She turns to face me, cupping my face in both hands. Her brow furrows, brown eyes peering into my heart until I break and smile, and she smiles. "I'm a mess sometimes too."

"Sure, but not like——"

She leans up and kisses my lips. I close my eyes, and she holds there until she seems sure I'm not going to argue anymore.

"Hunter seems like he was a wonderful person," she says carefully. It feels surprisingly good, not painful, to hear her say his name, to share him with her instead of being afraid to. "And I think I would be more worried if you weren't sad. It shows how much you cared about him. Does that make sense?"

I think of my dad, refusing to show weakness in any form, and nod. But maybe my sadness isn't weak. Maybe it's a mirror of my love.

"Yeah, it does. Thank you." I rouse out of my own head and close my arms around her, trying to be alive and here for this moment. For a second it's all cozy warmth and relief, then guilt strikes me. "I have a confession," I mumble.

"Okay?"

I heave a breath, tightening my arms. I'm so glad she's a hugger. "I killed the snowmen."

A soft pause, then she draws back. "What?"

I scrub a rough hand against my hair. "On the bridge. The first night we went out. I got sad and angry and I knocked all the snowmen off the bridge. I'm sorry. It—it wasn't about you or us. I was thinking about Hunter and it just came out. I felt horrible and I didn't want to tell you."

Her lips purse and twist and her dimples deepen, so I don't know if she's sad or about to laugh. "Oh, Gage," she murmurs, hugging me close again. "Thanks for telling me."

She doesn't say *it's okay*, which is oddly comforting, because I don't feel like it is. I don't want to destroy things when I'm angry. "Thanks for understanding."

"Mm-hmm." She burrows against my chest. "We'll just have to build a bunch of new ones."

"I would love to," I say honestly.

She hesitates, then smiles. "I have to get to work. You should come by, if you feel like it."

"Okay."

"*If*," she stresses, watching my eyes, "you feel like it. That was a lot." She motions to the living room and I nod, then lean close to kiss her again. Then she goes.

I stand for a minute, decide not to watch her drive off, then give up and flop back onto the couch. Sunlight streams through the windows and I stare at the ceiling, then lift my phone and tap a contact.

He answers after one ring. "Morning!"

"Hi, Jack. Morning. How are you guys?"

"Boy, I miss you," he says. "These women are running me ragged."

I chuckle and drape my free arm over my eyes. "I bet. I miss you guys too."

"How was the movie night?"

I swallow hard. "Um."

A pause. "Is everything okay?"

God, I wonder when I'm ever going to run out of tears, and in that instant I know I trust Jack in a way I may never get to trust my dad.

"No," I whisper, voice breaking. "I mean, yes, we're all fine. Everything's okay. I—I just—I . . . When you guys get home, I need to talk to you about some stuff."

He's quiet, then his voice is warm and firm. "Absolutely. Do you want to talk now?"

I can barely gather my next syllable. Trying to explain last night and everything else over the phone seems insurmountable. "I don't think I can. We're okay though," I stress. "I have . . . There's some stuff. I think . . ." I rub my eyes, shutting my dad's voice out of my head. "I think I need some help."

"All right." A vast, gentle pause before he adds, "Thanks for telling me."

"Thanks for listening."

It's quiet for a second. "Call if you need anything, Gage. Okay? Anything. This is what I do, remember?"

"Yeah." I sit up slowly. "I will. I'm okay right now. I am. You guys have a fun day."

"Okay." I hear his smile. "Take it easy."

"I will." The door opens and I look up as Justine returns, dressed and ready for the day, while I feel like a lump of moldy bread. "Gotta go, a gremlin just walked in. Tell Mom and Aunt Gina hi."

"Will do."

I toss my phone onto the couch as Justine comes over,

and her face scrunches. "You need a shower."

I think of last night, all the cooking, then running around after her, panicking, and nod. "Thanks. Figure out what you want to do today."

"I have dance later."

I push myself up, finding my bearings. Maybe it's silly to some, but I think of the Fellowship after losing Gandalf, losing Boromir, splitting, and carrying on. I might not be bearing a ring of power to its destruction to save the world, but I have my own duties.

"You got it," I say to Justine, and head upstairs to start another day.

SNOW DUSTS AROUND JACK AND me as we trek the sidewalk toward the wooded trail. He's quiet, letting me have my thoughts. I'm quiet, gathering them.

The rest of the week flew and was somehow packed but easier at the same time. Easier, because I wasn't hauling such a massive burden alone.

I worked shorter shifts because of Justine, and finally believed Andy when he told me it was okay, that I could take it a little easy this week. On Wednesday, Justine went to a sleepover at a friend's house and I got a night off, which I kept for myself—and did absolutely nothing important. When I missed Hunter, I cried, then hung out in his room. I slept. I botched a new recipe and actually laughed at myself. It was amazing.

Thursday afternoon, Mia and Bryson came over to bake something with me. Mia didn't ask if I needed anything;

she just called and said she had a cookie recipe and could they come over. We're never going to let Bryson's rice attempt be forgotten, and Mia supervised every teaspoon and cup of flour and I never thought baking cookies could be so funny. I didn't realize how much I just needed people to do things instead of asking if I needed anything, if I'm okay. They know.

Over warm snickerdoodles, Mia shared more details about the Idaho Shakespeare job and it filled my heart to watch her light up. There is so much room in my heart now, I think I might've glowed with happiness too, and I was finally able to tell her how inspiring she is. Somehow by the end of the afternoon Bryson talked me into working on my panic together so we can road-trip down and see one of her college shows this spring. He's putting in his application for the fall semester, and while the thought of everyone scattering is bittersweet, it's not bad. It's good, to see everyone moving on and up. It makes me think maybe I'm ready too.

That's the good stuff. That's who I want to be—here, now, for my friends. And I'm starting to realize I don't have to hide the hard stuff to be that. That actually, I can't hide from them and be there for them at the same time.

On Friday, Imogen and I had breakfast together, then hiked to the spot on the river where we spread Hunter's ashes last year. I meant to just go for a minute, but we ended up having a solid cry together, then stayed for almost an hour, talking about Hunter and her college classes and everything else. I told her about the Redwood House thing so she could get angry on my behalf and tell me how ridiculous they're being. I still haven't answered their email.

We sat in the snow on the riverbank, back-to-back

under the bare winter trees, and it felt like we were really together again for the first time in a year.

The air is clearing again, and even though it's scary to show people my heart, they're holding it carefully, keeping me safe.

Friday, Justine landed another sleepover and my friends and I went bowling on what I suspect was actually a triple-date. Olivia and I, Bryson, Mia, Imogen, and a girl named Julia who came over from Washington to ski—and to see Imogen. I think she's not quite ready to introduce her as a girlfriend, but Mia and I conferred while getting nachos and she thinks I'm right, but we didn't want to push Imogen. Julia definitely passes muster though: an anthropology major who has, indeed, seen all of the Lord of the Rings movies.

At Nan's, things felt easier again. Almost too easy, like I'm feeling restless, finally, itching for more of a challenge. Maybe I am a big fish. Colby told me he'd check out the next LWDA meeting and he's coming out of his shell and clicking with a couple of the other kids, and Mikaela is happy to no longer be the youngest.

We're all figuring it out.

Late Saturday night, Aunt Gina called to tell us about the show. Justine and I were up finishing *The Hobbit* and the folks FaceTimed with us because they just couldn't wait, Aunt Gina trying to tell the story while Mom broke in proudly and tearfully with details.

Aunt Gina's was one of the most popular pieces. One old man walked the glass path three times until he broke down crying and a young couple rushed to help him, and he said he'd lost his sister just two months ago. Another woman shared with Mom that her wife's father had died of cancer, that they'd come as a family to every gallery opening together but almost hadn't that night. And they were so glad they did. She felt like her father-in-law was there, with them. An old air force guy found Jack and they talked most of the evening. Strangers spoke quietly, shared with Gina, with Mom and Jack, hugged, laughed with these people that they'd never met but who they *knew*, through grief. Children, parents, friends, grandparents, all different, all holding a common, painful thread.

As people walked through the shattered glass and began to understand what the shards represented, the whole evening opened into a collective, understanding trust, and for a little while, everyone realized they weren't alone. The gallery owner said she'd never seen anything like it, and someone from the *Seattle Times* even interviewed Aunt Gina.

Justine was so proud and I think she felt bad for not going. But I told her I'd needed her here, I was glad. And that was true.

They left Seattle early to get home today, and arrived safely this afternoon. Justine and I confessed about the movie night and everything that had happened before everyone was even unpacked. I just couldn't keep it in anymore. Instead of being disappointed, it looked like Mom felt horrible that they weren't here to help, and from the look on Aunt Gina's face, Justine might get a retroactive grounding. But mostly, they were impressed I got in a car and handled it. I guess I did. With a lot of help.

When I started to break down, Jack said he needed to stretch his legs after the drive and invited me on a walk.

"I want you to know," he says, bringing me back to the

moment, the trail, "if something like that happens again, I mean if you need help, you can always call us. Even if you're embarrassed. Even if you think we'll be mad or disappointed. I would rather you call."

"I know." *Lone wolves die alone.* I hunch my shoulders, then force them to relax. "I'll know next time. I haven't been handling things very well."

"Well." He frowns and wipes snow from his glasses. "I agree. But neither have we, really, your mom and I."

I glance at him in surprise, heart thudding.

He smiles sidelong at me. "We were trying to let you move through it in your own way. But I didn't realize how much you were keeping in, because you've always talked to us. It isn't good for you, Gage, and it's turning you into someone you're not. If you don't want to talk to us about it, let's find someone else."

"Like a therapist?" I grimace. I can just hear my dad laugh.

"Yes," Jack says easily. "Like a therapist. Like the therapist I saw when I got back from Afghanistan, or your aunt, when Hunter died. It's what people do. If you had a broken bone, would you try to fix it yourself?"

"Maybe," I joke weakly, and he elbows me.

"You would not."

"I get it," I mutter. We turn down along the river path, enveloped by the scent of frozen water and pine. "What about the . . . the panic attacks?"

"That's something to work on," he says carefully. "Sometimes they get better and sometimes they don't, and that's not really something you can control." He taps his head. "But there are things you can do to help—medication, sometimes, and new treatments coming out all the time."

I rub my eyes as this gets worse and worse. "Medication?"

"Or other methods," he says. "I see you trying, Gage, and I'm proud of you. But sometimes we don't have the tools. You think I haven't seen this before?"

"No, I know. I just . . . I feel like if I were stronger, I could—"

"Whoa." He stops me in the middle of the trail. "It has nothing to do with how strong you are."

I look away and shrug, brow furrowing.

Jack moves in front of me, gripping both arms. "Remember Chase?"

Vividly. Jumping up in the middle of the living room, panicked. Breaking down on the porch. "Yeah," I say.

"He was a Navy SEAL. Purple Heart. Silver Star for valor. Do you know how many of those they give out? Not many. And he has panic attacks, nightmares, and anger. Just like you. Do you think he's not strong?"

"He was in *combat*," I stress, frustrated.

"Well." Jack clears his throat. "The brain doesn't really differentiate—"

"I just see everyone else moving on. Or doing better. I don't—"

"Gage. Stop." His sharp, hard first sergeant voice. "I need to say something, and I need you to listen to me."

"Okay." I duck my head, bracing for him to tell me to calm down.

"You were in the car."

I look up, meeting his eyes, watching snowflakes land on his glasses. "What?"

He squeezes my arms. "You keep comparing yourself to everyone else, but you were in the car. Ground zero. You were in the wreck. You were injured. You were there when Hunter died. Don't you think you're going to have to deal with all that in a different way than anyone else? Do you really, honestly think you're supposed to be over it in some magical amount of time? That this is something you can control or suck up and walk off?"

"I—I don't know. Yes?"

"No." His mouth tightens, disappointment flashes over his face, and he pulls me into a rough hug. "I'm sorry. I thought time would help, and you kept saying you were okay. But that stops now. We're going to get you through this. Together."

I just wrap my arms around him there in the middle of the trail.

"You have to be honest with us, though."

I nod once, my normal impulse to clamp down on my emotion welling up at the same time the emotion does. A hundred things occur to me and are washed away by relief, remorse, and gratitude, and two words fight to the top. "Thanks, Jack," I whisper.

"Yep," he murmurs, gives me a squeeze, and backs off a step. "Can I ask you something?"

"Yeah." My gaze drops to our feet until he speaks again.

"Is there a reason you felt like you couldn't talk to us?"

You can't do that meltdown shit you did to me.

I fold my arms over my stomach and shrug, glancing to the snow-covered aspens off the trail. "It was . . . I was embarrassed?" A bunch of words line up for me, excuses, lies, covers. I realize how much I've been lying. To Jack, to everyone, to myself. I don't want to throw my dad under the bus, but at the same time, I just can't lie anymore. "I . . . The first time I had a panic attack, my dad said . . . he told me to keep it together. That Mom and everyone needed me." I clear my throat, the words all clogged up in my mouth and heart because I've been holding them for so long. Jack grips my arm again. Listening. "I was just trying to be strong for everyone," I whisper, staring at our boots in the snow.

"You were," Jack says, his voice edged and quiet. "You are. But you don't have to be all the time." He squeezes my arm. "We want to be strong for you, too. Us, your friends, your Lone Wolves group, right?"

I glance up and see his mouth tight, red in his cheeks. Anger is a rare expression for him, but I know it's directed at my dad, not me.

"I know. Just . . . it was embarrassing. Crying and panicking. I thought I could . . . You said helping others can be part of healing, so I was trying to do that."

"And you did. Gage, look at me." He levels his eyes at me, then lifts his chin, and I mirror him unconsciously. "You've done so much for everyone. Service is part of healing, but it's not the only part, and it comes later. Let us take care of you, too."

The same thing my friends said. I try to shove Dad from my brain.

Jack's reading me closely. "I want to say one more thing."

"Okay."

He takes a deep breath, like he's been thinking about this and how to phrase it tactfully. "You're going to get a lot of advice in your life, and you're going to see a lot of different ways of doing things. A lot of different ways of being a good man, a strong man. And at the end of the day, you get to decide what that means to you." Pride and remorse twist together in my chest and I suck a breath against tears, watching him. "And whether it's me or your dad or Andy or some hotshot chef someday, it's okay to tell someone to back off. Okay?"

I duck my head. "Yeah. I did. I told my dad, I mean."

A proud, surprised smile flickers over his face. "Good, then." He almost pulls away, then he presses a hand to my chest, as if he wants to push the next words straight to my heart. "You're already a good man, Gage. A strong and compassionate and kind man, and I'm glad to know you. Your mother and I are so excited to see what you keep doing with your life." I stare at his face as he smiles up at me. "And I'm just . . ." His voice breaks and he pats my chest, mouth in a tight smile. "So proud of you."

My jaw moves and I finally grip his arm in return. "Thanks, Jack."

We stare at each other. Then he cracks a grin through tears and backs away to tug off his glasses and wipe his eyes, gesturing. "There, see? Happens to the best of us."

I grab him in a hug. "You are the best of us."

He laughs, hugging tight before pulling back.

We let the fresh cold air and snow swirl down on us. He rolls his shoulders and, seeing I'm saturated with advice and emotion, motions up the path. "Mind if we still walk? I really did need to stretch."

"Yeah, I'd like to." I'm not ready to face Mom with all this yet. It'll be another tide of guilt and regret that I didn't talk to her, and I'm exhausted. I just want to walk with the cold wind on my face.

Snow clumps in the naked aspen branches and my gaze lifts to a bunch of crows peering down at us as Jack says, "Justine is something, huh?"

I laugh roughly. "Yeah. Wait'll she gets her driver's license."

"Yep." He motions forward. "She'll just call Gina from Yellowstone some morning all, hey, I took the car, see you guys in a week!"

I laugh, Jack pats my back fondly, and it's easy quiet for another minute, my heart calming.

"Hey, uh . . . can I ask you about one more thing?" I take my phone out and pull up the email from Redwood House.

"Yep." Jack wipes his glasses again and takes the phone, eyebrows crooking up as he reads, then he chuckles and hands it back. "We'll sort that out. A nice letter explaining, a couple extra character references." He motions like it's no big deal. "Heck, Tank and I will write a reference about your volunteer work for Wounded Warrior Project."

"What volunteer work?"

He grins up at me. "Cooking for my peer group."

I chuckle and rub my forehead as a weight comes off my back. He's usually right about this kind of stuff. A different kind of relief, a new understanding glimmers when I realize it's okay if I don't get the job, after all. It was never actually my way out, my way forward.

This was.

I roll my shoulders and crack a knuckle absently. "Awesome, thanks."

"Honestly, I don't know why they wouldn't want a guy who can throw down now and then. It might keep the customers in line." He grins.

Embarrassment mingled with pride heats my face. "Hopefully all I'll have to throw down there is some really good dough."

"Hopefully you'll *make* some really good dough." He rubs his fingers together.

I groan, but rise to the challenge. "Hey, Jack."

"Yeah?"

"What does bread bring to his first date?"

"I don't know, what?"

"Lots of flours."

He snorts, lifting a hand. "But did you hear why the other loaf of bread was upset?"

"Nope."

"His plans went a-rye."

I groan.

"You started it." He gestures widely. "Don't challenge the master unless you're prepared to battle."

It's quiet a minute. A couple of ambitious folks in bright matching hoodies jog by us, breaths puffing, and wave. I lift a hand, then glance at Jack. "What did the biscuit say to his sad friend?"

His mouth tightens. "I do not know."

"Don't worry." I sling my arm around his shoulders. "Tomorrow will be butter."

He laughs. I tell him about the bread quiz and he thinks that will be a great family activity over dinner, then he asks about Olivia as the sky lightens, and a hint of sunlight glows through the falling snow.

EPILOGUE

"He is weary now, and grieved . . . But these evils can be amended, so strong and gay a spirit is in him. His grief he will not forget; but it will not darken his heart, it will teach him wisdom."

—J.R.R. Tolkien,
The Return of the King

MY HAND CLENCHES THE PAINT roller as I slide a warm jade color over the wall in Hunter's room.

It's not erasing, I remind myself. It's transforming. A whole new chapter in the story of this room. In Hunter's story, in ours. The idea is the only right one, but it still took us a couple of months to move on it, packing away a few clothes here, schoolbooks there, finally able to let some things go so the room can evolve to its new form.

Aunt Gina finishes taping off the base molding, then comes over and wraps an arm around my middle from the side. Spring rain patters against the window.

"Thanks for helping," she says.

I pause, pulling the roller from the wall. "Of course."

She smiles in approval at the color. "I think he would like it."

"Definitely."

A knock on the doorjamb makes us both turn as Justine tows Olivia in, chattering.

"... going to paint it green, except for one wall, which is this stick-on tree mural so it looks like a forest, and Uncle Jack is going to build shelves and it'll be a library for our house!"

"Wow," Olivia says, meeting my eyes across the room. "That sounds amazing."

I've already told Olivia about the library, but she doesn't shut Justine down. We're going to hang Hunter's sword and display his figurines and frame some pictures, and keep all the copies of his books, which we now lovingly refer to as "the sacred texts," and have a couple comfy places to sit and read.

"It was *my* idea," Justine says. She wades through the plastic and the construction materials for the bookshelves to hug Aunt Gina, and I navigate over to Olivia, handing off my roller to Justine.

"Hi," she says. It's almost April, when her contract with Wild Range is up.

I touch her elbow and we step out into the hall. "Hi. You're early."

"Yeah." She offers me a coffee. "It was totally dead and Aiden let me go." She picks at my shirt with a shy smile.

"Shoulder season." I take the coffee, leaning close to kiss her cheek, breathing her in. Orange and hibiscus and secret stuff. I wonder if Rowan can make me that smell out of her oils. She seems happy to do favors if it involves her work. We've been polishing my online image to drown out the diner incident, flooding my Instagram with food pictures and "on-brand" things to drive off any lingering negativity from January. My "Boys Making Breakfast" reels get thousands of views—especially when I include Bryson. It's actually fun if I don't read the comments.

Olivia glances down the hall. "I didn't think you would mind if I came on over."

"Of course I don't mind. Now you can learn how to make our famous chicken corn chowder."

"If it's as good as the chili you brought to Bryson's Super Bowl party, I'm in."

"It's better. He's coming soon too, so we can practice." I don't have to explain; she knows. Practice getting in and out of the car. Staying calm, getting used to it. We're working up to drive down to Boise to see the last play of Mia's semester.

Olivia touches my shirt. "When's Imogen getting home?"

"In time for dinner. I convinced Mia to drive up for the weekend too, so it'll be a party." I slip my hand into hers, weaving our fingers together, and she grins slowly. "The paint should dry by then, so we can add details."

When I told my friends about the library idea, everyone wanted to contribute. Imogen volunteered to paint the LWDA wolf-and-star logo on the wall, Mia offered books and help displaying a couple of Hunter's costumes in shadowboxes, and Olivia wanted to help with the painting too. Little details, leaves, birds, flowers. Bryson is helping Jack build shelves and the others are chipping in on cozy chairs, a few plants. A room filled with love.

Olivia smiles shyly. "I'd be honored to paint something in Hunter's library."

Her tender honesty cleaves straight through my chest,

along with all the other emotions of clearing and remaking the room, and all the emotions about her. "I wish he had met you. But I know he would have loved you and he would definitely want your art on his wall."

She smiles deeply, watching my eyes. "Thank you, Gage. I, um . . ." Her eyes drop and her voice catches. "I've really loved this time with you and your family."

"Me too. Us too." I clear my throat. Life just keeps coming at you, I guess.

She tucks in closer. "I . . . Well, we can talk about it later. I might've been looking into jobs in San Francisco. There's this one art camp for kids that needs instructors this summer. I hope that's not too—"

"The art scene is amazing," I say quickly. "That would . . . I would love that." We look at each other and laugh.

"And I hear there are great restaurants." She squeezes my hand. "And really cute prep cooks at this one place."

I snort and run a hand through my hair. Jack was right about the job thing. As usual. We put together a sheet of extra character references and he made me schedule a *call*, not just email, with Gillian Andrus at Redwood House. Easier to turn down text on a screen than a real guy who made a mistake, I guess. I think the conversation surprised both of us with how easy and funny it was. She could hear my regret and my excitement and it felt like I would fit in. So she hired me over the phone.

It feels strange and not quite real yet. Still, the fear of going there in another month is less about how I'm going to *get* there now than what will happen—but it's good. A good fear, something to overcome, not shrink from. Rereading Andrus's books and looking at Redwood House's menu, I think it'll be a good place to grow, a hard but necessary step up. A bigger pond.

Olivia leans up to kiss me, tugging me back to this moment. I wrap her in my arms for a good solid kiss, letting my chest fill with our gold warmth, then rest my forehead against hers while her fingers close around my shirt.

"I would love it if you found your way there," I say softly, because I'm over hiding how I'm feeling from anyone, unless it's a feeling that needs space, like anger. If this is it, if this is all we have, I want her to know. "I don't really want to say goodbye," I murmur. "Not a lot of winter in San Francisco, though."

She laughs, burrowing her face in my chest, and sighs. "I know where to find winter when I want it."

It's a big question mark. Us. What it will be like to work at Redwood House. What it will be like to live somewhere else, do something new and big and challenging. But I feel bigger than I did this winter. Open, stronger, less hobbled by fear and anger, ready for something new.

My therapist says I might never get over my grief in the way I think, or my panic attacks, but that it's okay. That it's pretty normal, that acknowledging and facing all of it, and being vulnerable so people can help me, really takes tremendous strength. She said our grief doesn't really shrink, we just grow. Knowing Hunter and losing him will be part of who I am, and I wouldn't want to have *not* known him, just to avoid the pain. I can grow around the loss and it will be part of the shape of me.

Olivia kisses my cheek and I lean away.

"You want to do some painting?" I grin slowly, and she

matches it, squeezing my hand.

"That is exactly what I want to do."

I set the coffee outside the door and lead her into our new library.

If Hunter were here, I would tell him that he made me a better person. And as much as I hate it, and grieve, losing him made me better still. Kinder. More thoughtful, most of the time, more aware of everything I have. More aware of the people around me, and how even if we don't know how long any of us has, that doesn't mean we should live in fear.

All we can control is to do the best we can by each other, and make sure that no one goes into the woods alone.

"Your time may come. Do not be too sad, Sam. You cannot be always torn in two. You will have to be one and whole, for many years. You have so much to enjoy and to be, and to do."

— J.R.R. Tolkien,
The Return of the King

ACKNOWLEDGMENTS

I AM GRATEFUL TO BE PUTTING out another beautiful book with Page Street Publishing! A heartfelt thank you to my agent, Cortney Radocaj, for championing my stories and finding the perfect home for my debuts, as well as cheerleading All The Ideas and fielding my various fears and questions. Thank you again to my editor, Tamara Grasty for rolling the dice on me with two books, and for helping to steer this novel into the best version of itself. As always, I learn more with every book and you are a pleasure to work with.

A shout-out and deep thanks to the whole team at Page Street for their support, design prowess, enthusiasm, and care for every aspect of the books: Hayley Gundlach (senior managing editor), Alexandra Murphy (associate editor), Cassandra Jones (assistant managing editor), Lauren Knowles (senior editor), Meg Baskis (creative director), Laura Benton (senior designer), and Rosie Stewart (senior design manager).

To my ground support team of friends, family, and beta readers: Thank you. My parents for your love and enduring belief in me. My husband Dax for your undying devotion and your support in all arenas and for truly understanding how vital my "writing time" is. Thank you to my sister Jennifer Owen; I don't know what I would do without your tireless support, empathy, writing sprints, and kicks in the butt. My dear friend, Kate Millward—when you read a new story and say, "Wow, Jess," I know I've leveled up. Thank you for your decades of cheerleading, chats, and care. To my betas and writing buddies: R.A. Meenan, for all your comments and your support! I'm so grateful for our friendship and your perspective. Ally Marshall, thank you for your sharp eye, cheerleading, and observations. Hal Aetus, I appreciate your perspective and am grateful for key comments that plugged up some plot holes! Gary Washington, thank you for reading and for your observations and validation on scenes relating to PTSD, military, Warhammer, and general point-of-view.

This work truly takes a village to complete and I'm overwhelmed with all your support.

And if you've come this far, dear Reader, thank you, too.

ABOUT THE AUTHOR

JESSICA KARA is the author of *Don't Ask If I'm Okay* and *A Furry Faux Paw*, as well as an indie-published fantasy series. She volunteers with her local writing organization, Authors of the Flathead, and is a member of the Society for Children's Book Writers and Illustrators, and currently resides in northwest Montana.